THE GREAT HORSE RACE

G·K
Hall
&Co.

Also by Fred Grove
in Large Print:

Bitter Trumpet
The Buffalo Runners
Comanche Captives
Deception Trail
A Distance of Ground
Into the Far Mountains
Man on a Red Horse
Match Race
Phantom Warrior
Search for the Breed
Trail of Rogues

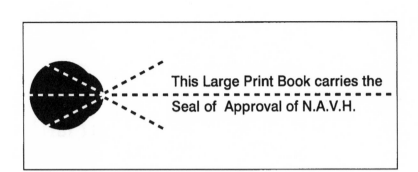

This Large Print Book carries the
Seal of Approval of N.A.V.H.

THE GREAT HORSE RACE

FRED GROVE

G.K. Hall & Co. • Thorndike, Maine

Published in 2000 by arrangement with Golden West Literary Agency.

G.K. Hall Large Print Western Series.

The text of this Large Print edition is unabridged.
Other aspects of the book may vary from the original edition.

Set in 16 pt. Plantin by Rick Gundberg.

Printed in the United States on permanent paper.

Library of Congress Cataloging-in-Publication Data

Grove, Fred.
  The great horse race / Fred Grove.
    p.   cm.
  ISBN 0-7838-9132-6 (lg. print : hc : alk. paper)
  1. Horse racing — Fiction. 2. Texas — Fiction. 3. Large type books. I. Title.
PS3557.R7 G74 2000
813′.54—dc21   00-033497

THE GREAT HORSE RACE

CHAPTER 1

Dude McQuinn rode craftily, yet in haste. Because he knew they were back there. Less than half an hour ago he had sighted them. A pack of strung-out riders, spurring and quirting jaded mounts.

Watching from a swell of prairie, he could not but feel a certain wry amusement. Corn-fed townsmen who fancied themselves members of the sportin' gentry. Not only poor losers, but abysmally ignorant of the pace required for successful pursuit. In a long chase such as this, you had to sit deep in the saddle, bent forward a bit, balanced, bearing part of your weight on the stirrups, and catch the rhythm of the horse. What was it the Good Book said that was so apropos? *The race is not to the swift, nor the battle to the strong.* . . . Pace was the thing. Pace. And, not forgetting to collect the bets immediately after the race.

Dude McQuinn scowled. What had happened should not have happened here in the primitive setting of Indian Territory. But for that smart-alecky lightning-rod salesman, the match race would have gone off without a hitch. Dude could still hear the jeering voices and see the anger darkening the faces of the cleaned-out townsmen:

"You say that dark bay horse is Cheyenne Bob? Why, I'd know that blaze face and four white feet anywhere. Seen him run many a time around San Antone. That's none other than the famous Judge Blair — fastest hunk o' horseflesh in south Texas. You boys have just been taken!"

But then, inasmuch as such a turn of the wheel of fortune had happened before, you learned to take advance precautions. After finishing eight lengths ahead of the local favorite, Coyote Walking had kept on riding, headed for Red River, to all appearances unable to control his runaway steed. When last seen, he was the picture of helplessness, tugging on the reins and waving and looking back with a pleading that brought groans of sympathy from the crowd, until the drummer spoke up.

Uncle Billy Lockhart had quietly departed earlier, driving the light camp wagon behind the fast-stepping sorrel team, the other short horse, Rebel, trotting behind.

Slipping through the crowd to the hotel, Dude McQuinn had hastened to the alley where his Kentucky saddler, Blue Grass, was tied, and ridden out of town. He was not greatly alarmed when, after some minutes, he spied the first dust of pursuit. Although lacking the speed of Judge Blair, the brown horse, rangy and durable, had a ground-eating running walk that he could main-

8

tain for hours. Horses of lesser quality soon fell behind, unable to match the killing iron in Kentucky blood.

By now, Dude figured, his pursuers had ridden out the bottom of their mounts, so he could rest his horse. He dismounted and loosened the cinch.

Somewhat sooner than he expected he spotted them again, more scattered than before. Dude McQuinn smiled: the pace was telling. For a briefness he was tempted, had he a saddlegun, to drop several bullets before the toiling riders and send them huddling back. But a wise itinerant horseman avoided violence whenever possible, reserving it as the last choice, for it was safer to run.

Well, this game had gone on long enough, and he dared not let them see him crossing Red River. He cinched up and mounted, waiting until he was positive that they had spotted him, which was soon evidenced by a flurry of distant popping sounds from their weapons. Swinging Blue Grass away to the north, he gave the long-legged gelding his head.

The hot wind began to whistle around Dude's ears. The bobbing shapes fell behind, shrank to mere dots, until lost in the late afternoon glare. He slipped from the saddle and led the way, then mounted and rode hard again. Afterward, he started a circling course toward the river.

Near dark found him at the river crossing, watering his horse. Fording the shallow stream,

he climbed the far bank into sheltering cottonwoods, treading the friendly soil of his native
Texas. Some two hundred yards on, hidden
from view on the Indian Territory side of the
river, burned the eye of a fire, close at hand to a
wagon and haltered horses. Coffee and bread
smells whetted the evening air. But he saw no
one.

"Pull up, you! Hands on the saddlehorn!"

Dude held up in disgust, recognizing the
grainy voice. "Is that a civil greeting?" he called.

Uncle Billy Lockhart and Coyote Walking
bulged out of the gloom from opposite sides, the
old man clutching a handgun, the Indian a
monstrous club.

"Could-a been anybody," Uncle Billy said.
"Took you long enough. What happened?"

"Some fool recognized the Judge. I had to take
to the tules, believe me. Then make a little circle."

"Some circle. More like plumb to Kansas."

"Didn't want to lead our friends straight to
the ford, though I don't think they'd invade the
sacred soil of Texas."

"You Alamo Texans! Well, did you have time
to collect the bets?"

"Don't I always? But it was close."

"Ah . . . that is sweet music to the ears of an
old man with thoughts of his place by the f'ar."
The handgun disappeared with incredible swiftness.

Dude noticed, as he had noticed before. That

10

swiftness of hand was one of many intriguing, and unanswered, aspects about Uncle Billy Lockhart, this puckish oldster who had the look of a saint: clear blue eyes set in a roundish face wreathed by white whiskers, and a bib beard of distinguished proportions. Though normally soft-spoken, his voice could take on the rasp of a jailhouse file, like just moments ago. And his hands, small and deft, like a woman's, could make a six-shooter appear as a gambler might flip a card. Despite that wonderful whiskery frontage of sanctity, and the frequent references to taking life easy by the f'ar, Dude sometimes sensed a different man out of a shadowy past.

Although Dude had been reared to respect another man's domain, he could not resist gently nosing into Uncle Billy's bygone days. Where was the fascinating old gent from? This man, both tetchy and likable, at times an old gentleman, at times just a salty old codger. His speech seemed interchangeable, as ingratiating as the demands of a trade or match race required. He could sound like a schoolmaster lecturing students, his language scholarly and impressive; he could be unlettered and rip out strings of cusswords rivaling a muleskinner's vocabulary. He could drawl like a Southwesterner, if need be, or go choppy and guttural, his hands cutting fluid sign talk, as he had in the Osage Nation the day Judge Blair outran the fastest horse of the Thorny Valley band and won a mound of blankets and beadwork.

11

About all Dude could make out for certain was that Uncle Billy didn't hail from Texas. That was obvious — when the old codger insisted on referring to the War Between the States as the "Great Rebellion"! That — and, when the occasion demanded, he could dye a horse so that its markings were identical to another's; that — and, administering the strong-smelling "potions" he mixed he could bring back an ailing horse in remarkably short time. When, however, Dude ventured a question that led into the past, he met either head-on bluntness or sly evasion, depending on Uncle Billy's mood and the extent of his aching arthritic joints at the moment.

What was his story? Was Lockhart his true name? Dude hadn't gone quite that far. The old man's age was another puzzle. His trackless face told very little. He could be younger than he looked, or he could be older. Perhaps it was like Grandfather Mr. Quinn used to say: "Here in Texas we don't care much what you call yourself. Most cowboys are known by nicknames, anyway. It's what you call others that decides the state of your health."

Unsaddling, Dude dipped oats into a *morral* for his horse, and, coming to the wagon, drew forth a wad of wrinkled greenbacks and a sack of silver from within his coat, sat on the wash bench, found pencil stub and memorandum book, thoughtfully dabbed the pencil point on the tip of his tongue, and made notations in the book.

"How much?" Uncle Billy inquired, gingerly lifting the lid of the Dutch oven to peek at the biscuits.

"Comes out forty-six dollars apiece, after deducting for expenses."

"Expenses? Seems there's always expenses just when a man's tryin' to lay a little by for his sundown years."

"Remember, we bought some supplies? Bought some and traded for some. Those Osage blankets and beadwork went pretty good. Wise notion, I say, to trade in a town before you match a race. Greases the hubs of commerce. Puts the town fathers in a receptive mood to wager on the local favorite." Dude, counting out the shares, stared at a worn bill. "Some nester squeezed this 'un a long, long time, looks like, 'fore he spent it in town."

"Just like white man," Coyote Walking said. "Always after money."

"Believe I know one Comanche that cottons to it, too." Dude, smiling, handed Coyote his share and the old man his. "What you aim to do with all that, Coyote?"

"Send it home."

"Tell you what I'm fixin' to do one of these days," Uncle Billy chimed in, digging inside his shirt for his money belt. "Gonna buy me a hotel. Gonna sit on the front porch an' watch folks go by. Gonna have my own place by the f'ar when the northers hit."

Coyote, bandy-legged and short, stout

through the chest, moved awkwardly to the other side of the fire and sat down. Afoot, Dude thought, a Commanche was graceless; mounted, he seemed transformed, nimble as a barn cat, hanging by a heel on the side, or under the horse, or sitting backward. Like a part of the horse itself. Like a feather in the breeze. Dude ran the last through his mind again, liking the phrasing. Sometimes he wondered if he wasn't cut out to be a poet, maybe.

Carefully, Coyote counted his share.

"Don't you trust me?" Dude asked, feigning hurt, and saw the even-toothed expression, more grimace than grin, more amused than not, cracking the broad face.

"I trust you," Coyote replied, looking down the long arch of his nose. His expression widened. "So far, white father."

"What he means," Uncle Billy put in, a little grin working at his mouth, "is that he trusts all white men as far as he can throw a bull by the tail against the wind. Can't say I blame him after what happened to the buffalo, and him stuck on that reservation at Fort Sill. He'd still be there, just a-molderin' away, if poor Hack hadn't got himself salivated over by that girl and we needed a jockey."

"Well," Dude said genially, "just as long as you don't dig up the tomahawk on us, Coyote. Remember, I never shot one single buffalo. Neither did Uncle Billy."

"Did I say that?" snapped the old man.

14

There he was again, buttoning up on his past. Son of a gun, he was tetchy at times. Dude dropped the subject.

After supper the wind hurried out of the southwest, hallooing through the tops of the cottonwoods, bringing the coolness of early spring. Dude rose and fed the fire, wanting to retain the snugness of this good camp. Above the wind he could hear the foxlike yappings of coyotes and the occasional *hoom-hoom* of a hoot owl. Unusual, he thought, how well the three of them got along, how they could guy each other and not take offense. Each so different. A cagey old horseman as smart as a bunkhouse rat. A sure-enough, full-blooded Comanche, educated to boot, who could spout poetry and whoop the last ounce of speed from a horse. And himself, the genial matchmaker and hand-shaking mixer, not averse to h'isting a glass now and then. Each sharing equally, lean or fat.

"You know," Dude said, "I believe even Rebel could've daylighted that local horse today. Eight lengths! Next time, Coyote, you might pull the Judge up just a little, so it won't look so one-sided."

"Whoa, now," Uncle Billy cautioned. "Anytime you check a horse when he's in the lead, you're gonna plant a bad habit. He'll get to where he starts lookin' back for company. Next thing you know the company catches up and your horse runs out of the money."

Coyote was holding a hand mirror, using bone

tweezers to pluck hair from his smooth face, even the eyebrows. He paused. "True, white father. Grandfather Billy is right."

"You dun right I'm right. Never get generous in a horse race, and don't call me grandfather."

Dude became thoughtful. "I been thinking we might drift on over into Texas for a little look-see. Match some races in the farming towns. Trouble is, Judge Blair is so well known we can't run him under his real name. The other side always backs off when they find out who he is."

Uncle Billy's eyes began to light up and acquire a conspiratorial anticipation. "You mean . . . ?"

"I mean," Dude answered, nodding, "there's more than one way to match a horse race."

Some of Coyote Walking's ease left him. He put aside the mirror and tweezers. His strong, brown hands, the hands of a horseman, cut abrupt signs as he spoke. "Comanche braves their ghosts there in Texas crying they are in Texas there," and made a sweeping westward motion.

"He's off again," Uncle Billy said, intrigued, cupping a hand to his ear, "talkin' that sing-song lingo. Tell us some more, Coyote."

"When Texas people this Comanche see mad they get like olden days their knives they take out off Coyote's scalp they take running he may be but save scalp this Comanche cannot his scalp come off it will you betcha."

"Don't forget, your ancestors lifted plenty of hair, too," Dude pointed out, shaking his head

16

consideringly, "including that of my Uncle Bert McQuinn, on the Salt Fork of the Brazos. However, from the stories I heard, if the Comanches hadn't got him the Rangers would."

"Why was that?" Uncle Billy asked.

"Seems other men's horses couldn't resist follerin' him home."

"Sad I am about your uncle," the Indian said.

"It had to come sooner or later."

"Sad I am also when I think we Comanches used to own all of Texas."

"Hold on! You learn that folderol in Carlisle School?"

"No folderol. My father told me before I went East to white man's school. Now, this Comanche his Texas when he comes to it goes is all gone. Gone like the buffalo. I am sad. Maybe this Comanche home better go now."

Of a sudden Dude could see his plans breaking apart. Usually, Coyote switched to the mixed-up gibberish only to entertain his new friends. But underneath his funning, Coyote was still an Indian, emotionally tied to the past and primitive superstitions. Just a young fellow, too, maybe twenty-three or so, though it was hard to figure an Indian's age, like the difference between twilight and dusk.

Dude donned his most cordial face. "My friend," he said, his voice carrying assurance, "they don't shoot Comanches on sight in Texas anymore. That's rubbed out. Gone. Times have changed."

Coyote Walking said nothing.

"You just keep on riding the way you have," Dude said even more earnestly, "and everything will be Jim dandy. You can go back to the reservation and live like a chief."

"My father is a chief and he is very poor. Many relatives camp with him and he must feed them as they would feed him."

"You won't go back rich, but neither will you go back as poor as you started."

Coyote Walking said nothing.

Another line of persuasion galvanized Dude. For a Comanche the most important concern in life was to be brave, always. And so he said, "You're the son of a chief. You must not show fear of Texas. Not you!"

"True, the blood of chiefs flows through my veins and my father is very brave. But I remember the old stories. I keep hearing Comanche braves their ghosts crying they are in Texas there." He placed both hands over his ears.

"Now lookee here, Coyote," said Dude, groping, "there ain't no Comanche ghosts in Texas. It's just your imagination."

Coyote Walking said nothing.

Dude turned to Uncle Billy for help and ran his fingers through his hair and around the neck of his collar. "Uncle Billy is saving up to buy him a hotel. You can save up for horses, blankets, rations. Heap glass beads and silver gewgaws."

That was a bad slip, that last about beads and gewgaws, Dude saw, seeing the Comanche's in-

18

stant disdain. Should have known an educated Indian didn't go for such baubles. While Dude searched for another approach, there came the soft rustle of wings overhead and a *hoom-hoom*.

Coyote Walking sprang to his feet and raised his arms. "Good sign," he said. "I will do as the owl person said."

"Do what?" Dude groaned, fearing the worst.

"Brave as I am, I still hear Comanche braves their ghosts there in Texas crying they are. But my father is poor and there are many relatives to feed." He beat his chest. "Let's that look-see take. This Comanche his Texas go he will."

CHAPTER 2

Rolling green hills sloping to well-kept fields. Timber sketching the course of a winding creek. Fat cattle grazing broad pastures. Neat farmhouses and portly barns painted red and white. Windmills standing like sentinels over such lush goodness and honest endeavor, the blades of their whirling wheels flashing in early afternoon sun. Beyond, on the flat, the sprawl and stir of a thriving little village.

"What settlement is that?" Uncle Billy called from the wagon seat.

Dude halted Blue Grass, unfolded the map, and ran a tracing forefinger south from Red River. "That's Cottonwood. Has to be. First place we've come to. Let's pull into the patch of woods down there off the road and get ready."

"What day is this?"

"Saturday. Can't you tell by all the dust being stirred up, it's folks come to trade?"

"Could as well be a hangin'."

They creaked on, Coyote Walking riding beside the old man, Judge Blair tied behind the covered wagon with Rebel and the three trade horses, a gray and a black and a strawberry roan bought that morning from a friendly farmer.

They drew up in the shade, and while Dude unharnessed the right-side sorrel of the team, Uncle Billy rummaged in the rear of the wagon for peroxide. It was like a traveling drugstore back there, pleasantly odorous of turpentine, white pine pitch, camphor, sassafras, Jamaica ginger, and other medicines, blending with the chuckbox smells. It was here that Uncle Billy mixed his horse "potions," as he called them, be it for colic or blind staggers, the heaves or fistula or whatever.

He found the bottle of peroxide and poured some on Judge Blair's neck, shoulders, back, and hindquarters, rubbing vigorously as he went along. Standing back, viewing his handiwork, he rubbed a place and nodded to himself. The peroxide made streaks on the dark bay hide, as if the Judge spent most of his time in harness. Next, Dude draped an oversize collar on the Judge and led the gelding forward and harnessed him to the wagon.

You could hitch him up and he'd pull like a workhorse, or use him as a saddle horse or a cow horse, and race him twice the same afternoon if money was scarce. He could tear five furlongs, running flat out; in these bush-track match races, however, a horse was seldom called on to go more than three hundred fifty yards, more likely one furlong or two fifty or three hundred. The quarter mile, which Dude thought of as the classic distance for a true short horse, was generally reserved for big match races on special occasions such as the Fourth of July or county fairs or the outgrowth of brags in a saloon.

A picture-book runnin' horse, the Judge. Head short, yet well developed, with alert fox ears; strong of jaw and the eyes large and spaced wide apart. Powerful front and hindquarters. Deep of girth. A short back and long underline. Legs straight and squarely set. Short cannons. A balanced horse, and that distinctive blaze coming to a point between his nostrils and those white-sock feet, hence the need at times for Uncle Billy's artistry. Yet, in harness, the Judge tended to droop his head and let his lip hang, which onlookers were always quick on to note and take for sluggishness; that and his drowsy manner, further deceiving, which wasn't lack of vigor but the outward sign of an even disposition.

A mystery horse, actually, of obscure breeding. Dude's knowledge was limited to what the cowman-owner, deep in his cups, had claimed the night of the poker game in San Antonio. Judge Blair's sire, the man swore, was none other than speedy Buck Shiloh, an outstanding son of the legendary Shiloh, a contemporary of the immortal Steel Dust. The main weakness of the claim was that Dude had never heard of Buck Shiloh. Judge Blair's dam, likewise lost in the haze of bourbon fumes that lucky night, was said to have been a Mexican sprinter named Lolita. No matter. Performance was what counted — that is, until you could no longer match an extra-fast horse and had to move on to other parts.

Hard times later at the Uvalde bush track: There was this dark bay gelding called Rebel running fifth in a five-horse stakes race of modest reward. And there was this keen-eyed little man, his beard reminiscent of your Grandfather McQuinn's, standing off to himself while he studied the horses one by one. He came over. "You know," he said, "that slow Rebel horse has almost the identical conformation of your horse. Why don't you buy him off that fella? He'd sell cheap, I figure, since Rebel is sure not payin' for his keep."

"Buy him?" Dude echoed. "Son of a gun, that horse ran last."

"He's dark bay, like your horse. Bet they'll weigh out within twenty-five pounds of each other. Each will top thirteen hundred pounds. Each fifteen hands or so. If it wasn't for your horse's white markings, they'd be spittin' images."

"Takes more than color to make a racehorse."

That smile, that puckish smile, which Dude was soon to recognize as portending surprise. "Though color can win a man some races," the old man said.

"Don't believe I savvy you."

"Haven't matched Judge Blair yet, have you?"

"Nope."

"You won't around here. Judge Blair is like

advertisin' P. T. Barnum is comin' to town."

"I still don't savvy you."

"In a way it's simple, in a way it's not. Takes a certain finesse. Have a drink with me and I'll tell you all about color and what a man can find at the end of the rainbow more times than not."

Now, as Dude went back where the horses were tied, the gray trade horse gave a short, peculiar cough. Uncle Billy wheeled that way, his diagnostician's eyes narrowing. The gray coughed again.

"Thunderation, he's got the heaves!" the old man erupted, and threw up his hands. Another moment, staring steadily at the gray, and slowly his disgust faded and he began shaking with laughter. "No wonder that farmer was so all-fired friendly. This horse has been doctored!" His laughter subsided. The puckish expression formed. "Just because we been slickered is no reason we have to stay that way. Believe I'll get into my medicine chest. Mix up a little potion."

He let down the wagon's tailgate and leaned inside, lips pursed. Glass rattled. He set aside a fruit jar and funnel, a strap and forked stick, smooth from use, and a measuring cup, muttering to himself as he poured: "Two ounces of Spanish brown . . . three of resin . . . two of gentian . . . two of lobelia . . . and eight of Jamaica ginger." He sloshed the mixture thoroughly in the jar and funneled it into an empty whiskey bottle. "Now, Coyote, take this strap and fasten it to the critter's upper jaw, and slip the fork of the stick under the strap, while Dude holds the halter rope." He paused, a significance to his movement, a sermonizing tone to his voice. "The old practice of drawing the head of a horse by the halter over a beam or pole to administer medicine is as cruel as it is absurd. Neither man nor beast can drink unless the lower jaw is free to move." A trickling smile: "Believe Dude will testify to that."

Motioning Coyote to raise the stick higher, Uncle Billy emptied the bottle down the gray's throat. "This will bring only temporary relief," he said, "but is good to trade on."

"Works, does it?" Dude asked.

"More times than not. Some horses need a double dose."

"Worked back in Illinois, maybe? Or Ohio?" Dude persisted, trying to draw him out.

Uncle Billy set the whiskey bottle on the tailgate and removed the strap from the horse's upper jaw before he answered. "Now, Dude, boy *where* it worked is not important. What counts is *how* it works and under what circumstances." He was evading again. He turned judging eyes to the sun, his tetchiness fading in anticipation of the day's prospects. "Pull in now will be just about right. Early afternoon. About now a man's on the lookout to trade or run his horse at somebody he figures he can outslick. But first let's curry and brush the gray. Slick him up good."

Dude nodded to that. After Uncle Billy had put away his bottles and tools, Dude climbed in-

25

side and opened his leather-covered trunk and took out a pair of worn overalls, a straw hat, clodhopper shoes, and bootjack. Seeing a buggy passing on the road to town he stepped behind the wagon and exchanged his planter's hat, checkered vest, string tie, boots, and pantaloons for the farmer's attire. Uncle Billy and the Comanche were likewise dressed when he came back.

They plodded on into Cottonwood, Dude riding beside the wagon, drawing the curious stares that strangers always do. Buggies and wagons crowded the broad street. Dude caught the hum of trade, the ring of metal on metal at the busy blacksmith shop, and observed the steady flow of people in and out of the stores. Two church steeples reached for the sky. One lone saloon stood in meek propriety at the end of the street; now and then a man darted a swift look around and slipped quickly inside.

Uncle Billy, chirruping to the team, drove past the stores and pulled up under a tree not far from the wagonyard.

They waited and waited; nothing happened.

Uncle Billy and Coyote began to doze on the wagon seat. Judge Blair hung his head like a harness horse. Usually, when a trader's covered wagon stopped like this, trailing a string of horses or mules, folks would soon stroll over and nod and speak and stare at the stock, sizing up prospects for a trade or match race. First of all, a trader's coming meant entertainment, a release from the unremitting drudgery of plow and hoe and tending stock. A trader was expected to be both genial and sharp, and without exception he was the last, if not the first. He was expected to carry a racehorse or two, certainly a short horse, maybe a long horse, horses of unknown speed and endurance, which added to the zest of the game; for it was a game, and you took your losses with a wry shake of your head, and whooped and hollered and tossed your hat into the air when your horse won.

It seemed that today, however, was an exception. Nobody showed up.

Hearing shouts and hoof clatter, Dude turned to look. In the wagonyard, a horse reared and pulled back while a farmer hung on to a rope tied to the animal's neck. A saddle horse, Dude judged, divining that somebody had made a trade he couldn't handle and take home. A score or so of farmers watched. Some shouted amused advice.

Uncle Billy craned his neck around the hood of the wagon. "What's the commotion, Dude?"

"Some plow chaser can't manage his saddle horse, looks like. What say we mosey over there, see what we can do?"

A reflective pause. Anticipation flecked the innocent blue eyes. "You mean . . . fetch my bridle?"

"And me my rope. Just might be the honey that draws the bees. Come on, Coyote."

The three ambled across, projecting an air of

obliging neighborliness as the crowd of chewers and whittlers turned their heads. Uncle Billy held a length of stout cord, a slip noose in one end. By now the sodbuster and the wall-eyed horse were going around and around, while the spectators shouted:

"Try a little sugar, Con!"

"Soft talk 'im, Con!"

"Blow in his ear, Con!"

"Tickle 'im under the chin, Con!"

"Shorten up on 'im, Con! Ear 'im down!"

Con showed them his young man's red-faced exasperation. "Can't! I'm all give out. Why'n't you smart-alecks help?"

As if acknowledging that the fun had gone on long enough, two men got on the rope. Even so, the horse, a well-muscled chestnut gelding, continued to pull back. It was still a deadlock, Dude saw.

He and Uncle Billy swapped looks. Dude shook out his rope and built a small loop and circled in behind, twirling the loop. He tossed for one of the gelding's thudding feet. He missed. Retrieving fast, he fashioned another loop, twirled and tossed again. The loop caught the right hind foot. Yanking in the slack, he held the kicking leg fast, without jerking the gelding down. Coyote joined him on the rope.

At the moment of the catch, Uncle Billy eased along the taut neck rope to the chestnut's jerking head, speaking softly as he approached. He slipped the noose around the straining neck, his hands moving gradually. He seemed to draw the cord through the mouth before the gelding knew it; working faster, he took the cord over the head, just behind the ears, and under and through the mouth again, and tied.

Suddenly he was holding looped reins. The chestnut started to rear. Uncle Billy pulled on the reins, a gradual restraint, no jerking or fighting. The horse checked, and Uncle Billy, motioning to the three men to give slack, removed the neck rope and called over his shoulder:

"You — Con! — saddle him now!"

Young Con hesitated, in disbelief, and at the old man's urgent motion ran for blanket and saddle and slapped them on and cinched up.

"Ease up, Dude!" Uncle Billy signaled. "Let him walk out of the catch." When the horse was free: "Mount up, Con. He's all yours."

With no little trepidation, young Con climbed into the saddle. Uncle Billy passed him the reins, saying, "Just keep a firm rein. If he starts to throw a fit and bog his head, pull him up. Don't worry. He'll behave."

"Giddup," Con said uncertainly, and the gelding took steps and humped its back, ready to buck.

"Pull up!" Uncle Billy yelled.

Con tugged on the reins and the chestnut's head came up and he settled down to an unwilling walk. They made a circle, and another, Con bumping up and down in the saddle. When the gelding tensed to act up again, Con hauled back and again there was peace. The gelding moved into a running walk. "I swapped for this horse this morning," Con called, out of breath. "But the stranger I got him off of don't seem to be around."

"All that horse needs is some schooling," Uncle Billy assured him.

Con took his horse through another circling running walk and dismounted. "What kind of contraption is that?" He stared, impressed, at the intricate weavings of the bridle.

Uncle Billy delayed until the onlookers had gathered around. "This," he said distinctly, "is Professor Gleason's Eureka Bridle. Used widely in the East by leading Thoroughbred trainers and veterinarians and just now reaching our Western borders. If you gentlemen will accompany me to our wagon, I'll demonstrate exactly how to use it."

They followed to the man, chattering and winking. At the wagon, Uncle Billy cut a length of cord from a coil and tied a slip noose and walked up to the gray, talking conversationally. "It's best to start with a gentle horse, such as this fine animal here. Being experienced stockmen and horsemen, you no doubt have already noticed his well-sculptured head. The ears small and pointed and wide between. The eyes large and full, likewise wide apart, which denotes superior intelligence. A horse kind and quiet to ride and drive, yet possessing a full degree of pride and spirit. Treated gently, but without pampering, a horse that can be a favorite of young and old alike . . . Note also the neck, long and tapering, with stout, heavy muscles on the top and thin through the middle. . . . As you know, a good horse must always have a short back, and broad and long hips, close-jointed, like this horse. The withers should be exactly midway between his ears and the coupling of the hip, which this horse demonstrates so capably. . . . From the point of the withers to the shoulder should be just as long as the coupling over the kidneys to the point of the hip by the tail, which this horse shows to perfection. . . . A good traveler, like this horse, must be wide across the chest and, for strength and durability, have the considerable width across the hips that you see here."

He audience began to shuffle, a hint of boredom, which Uncle Billy sensed at once. He raised high the length of cord and shook it, as if it had some magical qualities. "This is the most successful bridle ever devised for the management of horses made vicious by the inhumanity and ignorance of man, or for the purpose of doctoring the eyes or performing surgical operations. . . . You slip the noose around the neck like this, pass the cord through the mouth over the tongue from the off side, like so; then through the noose on the near side and pull forward firmly. Then over the head behind the ears from the near side. Then under the lip, above the upper jaw from the off side, then pass through the second cord and fasten firmly. There! This bridle will hold any horse under any circumstances."

"Will it work on mules?" a man asked, drawing nearer.

"Yeah, Otha, ask him," a voice urged.

"It will work on a bull elephant, provided you can get the noose around his neck."

There was a ripple of chuckles and much elbow nudging. The show was now in full swing, Dude saw.

"Who's this 'fessor Gleason?" another man asked. "Never heard tell of him."

"An old and trusted friend, now passed on to his final reward. Free at last of man's cruelty to his fellow creatures."

"Smart, was he?" Otha persisted, breathing sarcasm.

"Was he smart? If he were here today, demonstrating his genius, and he talked baby talk, you couldn't carry on a conversation with him."

"That bridle there — how much is it?" Otha asked. He leaned in, the better to see, his elongated neck remindful of a curious turkey cock.

Uncle Billy gazed skyward and pulled on his beard, eyes half shuttered in thought. "About a penny a foot at the store, I figure. Depends on how long you want the reins."

"You're not peddlin' bridles?" Astonishment and disappointment, for the speaker had expected the usual "catch."

"Nooo-noooo," Uncle Billy responded, feigning offense. "I remember the professor's last words to me: 'Go forth into the harsh world and spread the good news. Demonstrate how my Eureka Bridle . . . developed after many years of trial and error . . . is tied. Do it for the prevention of cruelty to horses and for the safety of mankind."

"So that's the story?" Otha said, still dubious.

"It is," said Uncle Billy, untying the bridle and, with ceremony, presenting it to the man, who studied it for a moment and asked, "Would you trade that gray?" Otha had a wheedling, eager voice.

"Maybe. You have a good horse?"

"He's right over there."

"What age?"

"Six."

"Let's see your horse."

Otha turned and the watchers parted for him. From the wagonyard he led a rangy brown gelding that moved lightly.

Uncle Billy opened the brown's mouth and peered long at his teeth. He said, "I don't quite tally with you about this horse's age."

"Some folks claim they can tell a horse's age when they can't," Otha countered, and nudged a neighbor.

The old man shot him a straight-on look. "A horse," he said, clipped and formal, "has forty teeth: twenty-four grinders, twelve front teeth, and four tusks. A mare has thirty-six teeth: twenty-four grinders, twelve front teeth . . .

33

sometimes tusks, but not often." He paused, alert to put down any scoffer. No one differed and he continued, "Teeth grow in length as the horse advances in years. At the same time, the teeth are worn away about one twelfth of an inch every year, so that the black cavities of the center nippers below disappear in the sixth year, those of the next pair in the seventh year. In the eighth year, the cavities of the corner teeth are gone, and the outer corner teeth of both upper and lower jaws just meet. . . . This horse is not six years old, my friend. He's eight. No younger, no older."

Otha blinked, impressed. A snicker here and there. He seemed to back off from the clear blue gaze. He gave a sheepish grin and shrugged.

Uncle Billy's manner said that he was not one to take both hair and hide in a trade. He smiled his understanding as from one trader to another and set about examining the gelding's eyes and neck, the withers and back, the knees and feet, and led the brown out and back. "He lifts his feet well and his eyes are full and clear," he said, nodding approval, and glanced at Dude for the first time. It was the signal to close the trade on this simpleton farmer.

Dude said genially, "Whatever Dr. Lockhart says goes with me. A mighty nice saddle animal. All things considered, though, we'll need some boot."

"Some boot?" Otha shook his head. "Why, this horse's got Steel Dust blood on his daddy's side."

34

Dude almost laughed outright at the mossy boast, but managed a straight face. It was like a stale joke, heard over and over when a trader or cowboy was trying to peddle a worn-out nag to some gullible greenhorn. Steel Dust was a short-horse sire of legendary fame, foaled in Kentucky and brought to Texas before the Civil War. If all such claims to his blood were true, the whole Lone Star State couldn't hold his offspring.

"Maybe so," Dude conceded, "but the gray's a little smoother, in my opinion. Look at him. Note his deep barrel and powerful muscular development." Long ago he'd learned that if a man said such things, a prospect would begin to think he saw features he had missed, when he hadn't. Yet Dude expected the man to parry some; often a prospect would inspect the horse's mouth, then argue. Instead, he saw Otha merely give the horse a long look. "Have to think about that," he said.

A sudden discernment swept Dude: Otha couldn't read a horse's mouth. Many men, including farmers, couldn't. Not like Uncle Billy. Which provided another opening. The gray was nine if he was a day. Dude said, "Likewise, the gray is three years younger than your horse and comes straight down the ladder from Domino on his mammy's side."

"Domino?"

"Lordy, man, you never heard of Domino? One of the great foundation sires of American Thoroughbreds! This horse comes from quality

35

folks, I tell you."

Otha appeared bewildered, also eager. "How much boot?" he dickered.

"He's fight at his peak. Also a good buggy horse. An easy keeper and as responsive to the reins as a body could ask. Almost any little gray-haired lady can handle him. . . . I figure twenty dollars is fair enough."

That excited a whistle of denial. "You're a notch or so high."

Dude studied awhile. "Oh, I'll be neighborly. Let's say eighteen."

Otha fidgeted. An eagerness skittered across his sunburned face. "Make it fifteen and I'll swap you."

"Mister, you just got yourself a fine, young horse!" While Dude was untying the gray, Otha, so eager his hands trembled, unsnapped his leather purse.

After Dude had added the brown gelding to the string of horses tied behind the wagon, he mingled and joshed with the chewers and whittlers while they looked at the horses and voiced further opinions regarding the Eureka Bridle. Trouble was, they said, remembering how to wrap and tie it. To accommodate them, Uncle Billy obligingly went through the steps once more, one by one.

"Keep in mind," he said, waggling an instructive forefinger, "that leverage is the key — leverage against the upper lip. Held constant, and provided you keep the critter's head up, it will subdue the wildest of mustangs."

Trouble still was, they agreed, he made it look easy when it wasn't. It was complicated. Just the same, they would try it when they got home, and they were sure much obliged to him and that Professor Gleason, who had invented the contraption.

Meanwhile, Dude noticed that Otha and the gray had vanished.

Before many minutes had passed a newcomer walked up to the group and stood around, eyeing all the horses. Although he wore a granger's suspenders and rumpled trousers and gingham shirt and a hat shaped like a chimney pot, there was a difference about him. It was his cutting eyes, Dude decided, and the intent way he observed the horses. One or two others nodded to him — that and no more, which told Dude that likely he drove his dealings down to the quick.

The man said to him, "You carry a racehorse, sir?" the words coming out with a rushing, businesslike effect.

At last! Dude had begun to think otherwise today. He looked casually back, and then along the street, and then again at the man, neither confirming nor denying. "Well . . ." he drawled.

"Last trader through here had a racehorse."

"Guess you matched him?"

"I did, sir."

"How'd you make out?"

"Sir, my Pepper Boy won it." His jaws worked on a walnut-sized wad of tobacco. He spat neatly, with deliberation, with satisfaction. A banty-rooster man, tending to heaviness, he conveyed the impact of restless energy and constant questing for prospects, none too small, none too large. A reddish beard fringed his aggressive chin and the slopes of his jutting jaws. As he talked, he laced his hands on the pillow of his stomach and rocked back and forth on his boot heels, as if keeping time with the rapid turnings and calculations of his agile mind.

"Well . . ." Dude said again.

"I was hoping you might be interested in a match race."

"Depends," Dude said doubtfully, looking off. It never paid to act too eager around these bush-track horseman. They'd shy off if they figured you carried a scorpion.

"You might think about it, sir."

That *sir* talk was beginning to irritate. "We've come a long way today."

"My horse is just down the street."

"Well, Mr. . . . ?"

"Sim Truesdale's the name, sir. I farm south of here . . . cotton and corn . . . and raise blooded horses."

"Mighty pleased to make your acquaintance, Mr. Truesdale. I'm Dude McQuinn." They shook hands formally. "That is Dr. William T. Lockhart, our trainer, late of Lexington, Kentucky, and that is our jockey, Mr. Coyote Walking, late of Indian Territory, whose father is a chief." Everybody nodded. Uncle Billy was fooling with Rebel's halter, and Coyote was currying the newly acquired trade horse.

"We just traded for that brown gelding there," Dude explained, as if putting off.

"I'd say you made a right keen trade, sir." His eyes slid back to Dude, who caught the tail end of an obscure expression.

"Like I said, Mr. Truesdale, we've come a long way today."

"Afternoon's still young."

"So it is," said Dude, his tone changing. "You know, I might take a look at your horse after all. I just might."

"I'll have him fetched up for you, sir." Truesdale quick-stepped to the street and waved, and immediately a boy rode up on a blue roan stud. When the boy slipped to the ground, Truesdale led the horse forward. Dude circled the racehorse for a look-see, something you always did, whether your mind was made up or not, because it was part of the ritual. Pepper Boy was short-coupled and chunky, and a mite nervous at being in town and around other horses.

"Well," Dude said after a bit, "I believe that ol' blaze-faced horse hitched yonder to the wagon can contest him."

Truesdale, whose attention had shifted to Rebel as the likely runner, whipped about and stared in surprise. His restless step lengthened to strides. As he went to the head of the wagon, Uncle Billy sidled up to Dude and muttered low, "Match him for as long as you can. That blocky

39

stud looks like a one-furlong bat out of hell to me. Notice how short-muscled he is?"

Nodding, Dude followed Truesdale to the wagon. Judge Blair seemed to doze in the traces while he tail-switched flies. His head drooped and the oversize collar slid halfway down his neck. His dark bay hide showed the toil of harness.

"This," queried Truesdale, his cat's grin leaking, "is your racehorse?"

"He tries, even when he's tard."

"How is he known?"

"His name is Red River Dan."

"The name is not familiar to me, sir, and I've match raced over a good deal of east Texas, into Arkansas, and down into Louisiana."

"Oh, we've matched him some downriver, when he's not in harness. Haven't owned him long. Got him off an old farmer that was sellin' out, moving to town."

"So he's won some?"

"I'll put it this way: He's won some, he's lost some. Just an ol' harness horse."

"Think he can outrun my Pepper Boy?"

"I never make predictions. But I'll put it this way: He'll do better than a one-legged man at a cowboy dance."

Laughter broke among the idlers, running from man to man. Truesdale jerked them a look, his mouth a thin line. The laughter died. He faced back. "What's his best distance, sir?"

Now that was sly. "Sometimes he goes far,"

Dude parried, "sometimes he goes short. All depends if he's on his feed that day."

"If he is today, would you like to run him at my Pepper Boy?"

Dude held a doubtful look on Uncle Billy. "What do you think, Doctor? I'd hate to be embarrassed."

"He seemed to take to his oats right good this morning."

"That settles it. We'll chance it. Mr. Truesdale, what do you say to four hundred yards for thirty-five dollars?"

"I wouldn't put a halter on my Pepper Boy for thirty-five dollars," Truesdale snorted, head high. He bit off a chew, journeyed it around like a piece of peppermint candy, and set his jaws, inflexible.

"Would you for fifty dollars?"

"I'll talk on that, but not that distance."

Dude reflected how the *sirs* ceased once you got past the bowing and scraping. "What distance would you run?" he asked, cordial about it.

"One eighth. That's as far as we run most races around here."

Dude folded his arms and drummed his fingers on his chin. Truesdale, as any horseman would, was angling to match his horse at his best distance. Dude said, "I see. However, our ol' horse has come a long way in harness today, like I said. He needs time to pick up his feet. I'll raise to seventy-five dollars if you'll raise the distance

. . . say to three fifty. How's that jibe with you?"

Truesdale rubbed at his mouth with the knuckle of his forefinger. He sized up the droop-headed horse again, and he sized up Dude again. "I'll run you three hundred yards for a hundred dollars."

"That's neighborly." Dude pursed his lips. "That is." Smiling, he held out his hand. They shook and Dude said, "Now about the starter."

"Ed Murphy starts most races around here. All lap-and-tap. No chutes."

"I don't like chutes, either. A horse can get hurt thataway if he's rambunctious to go." The frowns did it — the frowns that Dude read on the faces behind Truesdale. Tucking in his lips, Dude said politely, "Who is Ed Murphy?"

"A merchant. Well respected in the community."

"Would you flip for it? Say one of the gentlemen here or Murphy?"

Truesdale opened and closed his mouth like a trap. "Agreed," he said, yet with reluctance, and took out a silver dollar. "You call it in the air, sir." He was being formal again, and a wariness tapped Dude as he called, "Heads." Truesdale caught the spinning coin and slapped it on the back of his left hand and looked down. "Tails it is," he pronounced, and Dude, seeing, forced a smile.

"Our track," Truesdale said, assuming an official air, "which we call Cottonwood Downs, lies two miles west of town. It's customary hereabouts for each party to designate one finish

42

judge, and for a third to be chosen by mutual agreement."

Dude nodded. "Dr. Lockhart will represent us."

"Mr. Toode Yates is our man."

"An interesting name. May I ask what he does in Cottonwood?"

A wave of chuckles beat Truesdale's stiff reply. "Mr. Yates is the proprietor of the Lone Star Saloon. A leading citizen. A generous contributor to the church. I hope you have no objections, sir?"

"None at all . . . unless Dr. Lockhart has?"

"Is there a finish judge more capable than a judge of good whiskey?" Uncle Billy retorted, triggering appreciative snickers.

"For the third judge," Dude said, pointing to a rotund individual, "I nominate that gentleman there."

"I see you have a keen eye for character, sir. That's Mr. Dow Riddle, from out north of town. Fine with me, if he's agreeable."

"Let Big Whelan do it," Riddle said. "He's in town today. He knows racehorses."

Dude was all ears. "Who's Big Whelan?"

"A Texas Ranger," Truesdale said.

Dude could hardly refuse. "I can think of no higher credentials."

"Shall we go to the post, then, sir, within the hour?"

"Within the hour, sir," Dude agreed. Son of a gun, that Truesdale had him saying it now.

CHAPTER 3

"Something about this I don't like," Uncle Billy confided to Dude as Truesdale led his horse away and the idlers broke ranks, and a youngster ran up the street, yelling, "Horse race! Horse race!"

"You mean the Ranger? If somebody recognizes the Judge and tattles to Truesdale, he can always withdraw. There's nothing illegal in running a horse under another name. Same as a man's alias."

"Law or not, you could be run out of town. I mean that Truesdale — him so oily proper an' all. Sir this, sir that. He must figure he's got the edge somewhere."

"It can't be the judges. He didn't suggest Big Whelan."

"Then it's the break, and the break is everything in short racing."

Long before they reached the track, long-haired boys, farmers, and townspeople, afoot, on horseback, in wagons, buckboards, and buggies, were steaming ahead and alongside and behind the traders' wagon. Dust rose like a brown fog. By the time Uncle Billy pulled up the team, a crowd of a hundred or more had collected and more were coming.

Dude had to smile to himself. Although horse racing was associated with gambling and brawling and whiskey drinking, and suffered a regular Sunday pounding from the pulpit, here were Cottonwood's leading citizens and their ladies of unquestioned status. You could tell that by the way they sniffed at the noisy element, heads elevated, veils over their comely features, or held dainty handkerchiefs, likely rosewater scented, to delicate nostrils when the plebeian dust clouded about them.

With the wagon parked and Judge Blair unharnessed and Coyote leading the gelding around, Dude rode forward to look at the track.

"Cottonwood Downs" was no more than the familiar small-town bush track, a straightaway of two broad, parallel paths laid out on virgin prairie to three eighths of a mile. Stakes marked the finish line at every common distance up to four hundred forty yards. The turf was grassy, apparently little used of late. No grandstand. None was needed. Spectators lining the flanks of the course could see the start and the finish.

Riding back to the wagon, Dude saw that the curious had gathered to view the challenger of Pepper Boy, the local favorite. Uncle Billy, aware of his audience, was telling Coyote, "Give the old fella a little sip of water. And rub him down some more. Work on those trace-chain marks on his side and the collar marks on his shoulders. Don't want folks to think he spends all his time in harness."

A cocky young townsman, sporting candy-striped shirt and highwater britches and high-buttoned yellow shoes shined to the gloss of a billiard ball, raised a bantering voice. "You say that's Red River Dan? Where'd you get him? Outa some cotton patch?" And then he guffawed at his own jest.

So they were commencing to rib the old horse-man, scoffing grins on their rube faces, not knowing that they had a tiger by the tail. Dude checked reins to listen:

"That's a secret," Uncle Billy replied, looking mysterious.

"A secret, all right. Sure never heard tell of him around here."

"That tells me you haven't been far from home," Uncle Billy told him, rubbing on just the right suggestion of ridicule to make a body fume.

"I've been plumb to New Or-leans," the sport claimed.

"What's that again, youngster?" Uncle Billy antagonized, and held hand to ear as if to catch the words.

"I said *New Or-leans.* You deef? Or maybe you never heard tell of it way back there where you come from?"

"That's what I thought you said — *New Or-leans.* Is that that little dab of a place where they ride mules to church and race stick-horses on Sunday afternoon?"

"You talk big, mister!" The young man reddened as the wind of amusement shifted in his direction.

"Could be," Uncle Billy sneered, "you even picked up a little o' that French lingo down there? Could be you even learned to say *aw river,* though I believe the French" — unfurling his lower lip just so — "prefer to say *oh re-vwar.*"

"Keep talkin', old man!"

"I don't just talk," came the taunting reply. "I put something on the barrelhead. An' I don't mean Confederate money found in an attic trunk."

"Hold on! You belittlin' our Pepper Boy? He's never lost a match race."

"You mean just hereabouts . . . just around Cottonwood?"

"Listen! I mean around here and way off, too. Mr. Truesdale was on the lookout for fresh money last fall when he took Pepper Boy over into Arkansas. Pepper Boy just about cleaned out the western part of the state. Won three match races!"

"You don't say."

Dude felt a spark of sympathy for the sport. Once he set about it, Uncle Billy had the bent of provoking a greenhorn and leading him down impulsive paths.

"In record time, too!" the young man was shouting.

A hooting whistle. "You expect me to believe that folderol?"

"Well, at Fort Smith he run the quarter mile

in twenty-three flat."

"Must've been a regular windstorm at his back if he did."

"Keep talkin', old man!" The fuming sport was edging closer, commencing to dig for his pocket.

Dude scented the coup de grace as Uncle Billy summoned even further contempt. "Why, if Pepper Boy passed a terrapin, he met it — he sure didn't overtake it."

"Tell you what, old man! I'll lay you two to one — no, three to one, by grab! — that Pepper Boy daylights your horse!"

Ruffled local pride must be upheld, Dude discerned.

"Sonny boy," said Uncle Billy, blue eyes aglitter, "let me see the shine of your coin."

Nostrils flaring, jaw outthrust, the sport dug for his money. Dude dismounted and tied Blue Grass to the wagon. More partisans crowded in to bet. Dow Riddle was chosen to hold the stakes.

Quite abruptly, the hubbub tailed off the bettors, with uneasy glances, melted away, lost in the crowd flowing toward the track.

Dude glanced up, wondering.

An offical-looking man was approaching. A great bulk of a man. Big hat. Big head. Big shoulders. Big chest. Big hands. Big middle lapping over his broad belt. Big six-shooter wobbling on his hip. Big feet.

Needlessly, he said, "I'm Ranger Whelan . . .

also called Big Whelan," and his monotone matched the man.

"I can see why," Dude said, and held out his hand and volunteered his name.

"Understand I've been elected one of the finish judges," Whelan said, revealing the thinnest of smiles. "Thought I'd take a look at your horse."

"There he is — Red River Dan. Just took him out of harness."

Whelan started the usual scrutinizing walk around, his manner methodical and thoughtful. He had a mouth like a buildog's, a brow like a rock ledge, and eyes like granite chips. "Red River Dan? He's new to me, and I know every short horse from here to the river and up and down the river a far piece."

"He's not well known. Not like Pepper Boy. We've traded around and raced him some up in Indian Territory and on into Missouri."

"Pretty fast?"

"I'll put it this way: If he wins, it's generally by a nose. If he loses, it's by daylight."

"You're not one to brag, I see."

"I figure it's brag enough when I put up my money, such as it is," Dude said, smiling broadly.

Going on to the other horses. Whelan eyed the brands on the left shoulder. Seeing him study the black's brand a second time and spread its outline with his fingers, Dude, anticipating, said, "We bought that black off a farmer on Red

River a few days ago."

"Got the bill of sale?"

Son of a gun, Big Whelan was not only suspicious by profession, but by nature as well. "Got it right here," Dude said.

Whelan scanned the bill of sale, his heavy lips moving soundlessly over each word. "Says here you bought a gray horse, too."

"We did. Swapped him off in town a while ago for that brown gelding."

"All right," Whelan said, satisfied, handing back the bill of sale. "Just like for things to be on the up and up." He started off. No more than a step or two and he turned and stared again at Judge Blair. "If it wasn't for those harness and trace-chain marks, I'd say Red River Dan reminds me of a horse I saw run one time down in south Texas. Markings look the same."

"That's interesting," said Dude, catching Uncle Billy's warning glance.

"It is. Reason I remember is because that horse set a record in the quarter mile that day. Ran it in twenty-two flat. Into the wind, too. That is flyin'."

"A real scorpion," Dude had to agree.

"I'd say. You don't forget a race like that. Something you see maybe only once in a lifetime."

Dude nodded politely.

"Some rancher owned him. I believe . . . I believe the name of that horse was Judge Blair. Yes, that was it."

Big Whelan was pacing off for the track when Uncle Billy sighed and said, "Got a hunch we'd best not let the grass grow under us after the race is over."

Racetime.

Uncle Billy, spritely and dignified, stepped downtrack to the finish line.

Admirers of Pepper Boy watched while Truesdale fussed with the bridle, the cinch, the blanket, the saddle. Now and then he snapped advice to the slip of a boy who would ride the favorite.

Dude saw an unsmiling individual in a brown suit, his walk an officious quick-step, leave the crowd and come to the starting-line stake. So that was Ed Murphy, the other side's handpicked starter. Catching Truesdale's eye, Murphy waved to Dude to bring his horse to the track.

Dude decided to let Truesdale sweat some. Taking his time, Dude bridled his horse and carefully laid on blanket and light racing saddle, after which Coyote Walking, naked above the waist, his only covering breechcloth and long-fringed moccasins, grasped Judge Blair's mane and vaulted to the saddle. Coyote's blue-black hair hung full length, cropped at his neck. His complexion was copper-bright, his lips thin and even, his aquiline nose curved like an eagle's beak. Dude, admiring him, liking him, thought of a warrior ready to ride.

Murphy waved again, a peremptory wave. Truesdale, mounted on a white horse, waited at the starting line. He kept pulling on the nervous

51

Pepper Boy's lead rope and advising the boy.

"Truesdale's so edgy himself, yanking on the rope that way," Dude observed to Coyote, "he's making his horse jump around. More Pepper Boy acts up, the less energy he'll have to run."

"That stud looks fast to me, white father."

Dude mounted Blue Grass, took the lead rope, and they walked the horses to the starting line.

"It's the custom here," a huffy Murphy informed Dude, "to bring your horse to the track when the starter signals you."

"Guess I was waiting for the bugle call," Dude said, and smiled from the teeth.

"We also parade the horses past the crowd."

"Understand they do that at all the big tracks," Dude replied sweetly. "Go ahead, Truesdale. My ol' harness horse will trail along behind."

"I'm obliged to you, sir."

Truesdale moved off, hauling on the lead rope. When Pepper Boy swerved from side to side, Truesdale yelled at the boy, and the boy, in frustration, answered, "I'm doin' the best I can, Mr. Truesdale. Pepper Boy's just all het up to go."

The boy didn't look fryin' size, Dude saw. Yet, that meant that Judge Blair was carrying some twenty-five or more pounds than Pepper Boy. That's how it was in these bush-track races. You used your jockey and the other fellow used his. Like the storied featherweight Negro jockey who rode outlaw Sam Bass's famous sprinter, the Denton mare in the 1870s. Instead of a saddle, he smeared molasses on her back to help him stick on, and never lost a race, so the legend ran. Dude wished now that he had jawed with Truesdale about evening up the weights. Sometimes a man with the top horse was so eager to race that he overlooked an essential.

Applause began to mount as Truesdale led the blue roan Pepper Boy toward the finish line, marked by a white flag. There was a break in the clapping when Dude took his horse past the jostling, noisy crowd. As he neared the finish line, a young voice blurted, "That's an Injun! Bet he's a mean cuss!" At which Coyote glared and showed his teeth, making an overerocious face, climaxed with a scalp-lifting gesture. The boy, startled at first, began to grin. Coyote grinned, then, and waved to him.

That broke the silence. Somebody clapped. Others joined in, though by no means comparable to Pepper Boy's ovation. A short distance and Dude freed the lead rope so that Coyote could trot ahead.

Riding to the starting line, Dude reined to one side and sat his horse, watching, his mind now on Murphy. The start would be the usual lap-and-tap, with the horses walking slowly up to the line. If they were in motion, closely lapped, heads together, or nearly so, the starter would "tap" them off by dropping his hat or flag or his raised hand. In these short races the break often meant the difference between winning and losing. When a good horse broke on top, a real speed demon was required to catch him. Judge Blair was a fast breaker; a few jumps and he was tearing full stride. So far, Coyote had managed to get him out in front every time.

It followed that each jockey would try to maneuver his horse for the advantage at the last split second. If his position was not favorable, he could pull up so that the horses would not be lapped, and the starter would walk them through again. The danger today — and this worried Dude — was that if Coyote pulled up and still the starter signaled "Go!" Judge Blair would be left flat-footed.

They were approaching the line now, Pepper Boy acting up but under control. His jockey might be a mere boy, but he hadn't learned that finesse on Shetlands. Judge Blair, his disposition calm and unruffled, appeared almost unconcerned. Yet, the instant the signal came and Coyote urged him out, the Comanche's bandy legs flailing, Judge Blair would become a different horse.

Downtrack, Dude was aware of the rural crowd, hushed, waiting.

The horses were within a yard or so of the line when Dude saw the boy suddenly send Pepper Boy ahead by a neck. By all fairness, the starter ought to call them to walk through again. Instead, he dropped his hat and hollered "Go!" and Pepper Boy broke on top, the boy crouched like a leech. Only a neck's edge, but nevertheless an edge.

Dude's anger burst. He saw his horse leaping late, that shade behind, and tearing alongside the blue roan. Coyote had him flying full out.

At one hundred yards Dude could see no change. Pepper Boy still led. At two hundred yards Dude couldn't tell. Another hundred yet to go. Pepper Boy was a sprinter, indeed!

Coyote's whoop reached Dude dimly. At last he could see his horse moving up. Through the dusty haze the two sprinters seemed to blend, running stride for stride, like a perfectly trained team. . . . Of a sudden Dude glimpsed the boy going for the bat. Three times he hit the stud. Pepper Boy appeared to pick up. . . . Coyote whooped again, his cry more shrill than before. Judge Blair responded visibly, running lower and faster. The crowd was shouting.

It was over in the blink of an eye.

Dude's spirits rose. He thought . . . no, he couldn't tell from here. It had to be close, and the worst place to watch a race was from the rear.

With a glare for the starter, he dug heels into Blue Grass and galloped downtrack. The horses were easing off. The crowd was milling onto the track, watching after the horses, a rather quiet crowd, it seemed.

Dude had to hold up. Spying Uncle Billy, he saw the old man wave his hat and yell. Whooping, Dude swung down and led his horse through. Dow Riddle was there, handing over the stakes.

"Dude!" Uncle Billy called. "The Ju—" he slipped and hastily amended, loudly, "We won it by half a length, going away!"

At a touch on his arm, Dude met Truesdale's bitter eyes. "Just an ol' harness horse, eh?"

"Murphy gave your stud the break and he still lost," Dude answered, getting hot all over. "I'll run you any distance if you want another shot at us — but it won't be with Murphy starting."

Truesdale turned away.

Dude heard a voice, a monotone, distinctive and heavy: "Don't recollect seeing a horse run like that since Judge Blair broke the quarter-mile record at San Antone."

"He was kinda feelin' his oats, all right," Dude said, all modesty, hanging his head a little as he looked up a Big Whelan, which was the only way you could look at Big Whelan. "Red River Dan has his good days."

"Considerable more than good today."

Coyote came jogging up and Dude said, "Mighty fine ride, Coyote. Murphy gave the other horse the break and you still won it. Believe me, there'd-a been no payoff we'd lost."

Whelan continued to eyeball the horse, but he said no more.

That night, after traveling later than usual at Uncle Billy's insistence, they camped in a copse of oaks some miles beyond Cottonwood. A moon the muted lemon yellow of buckskin climbed the starry sky, and a friendly wind rustled the leaves, and the coals of the cooking fire burned cherry red. Supper over, the three sat around and talked.

"Truesdale made the mistake of matching Pepper Boy a shade over his best distance," Uncle Billy ruminated. "At that, we beat a pretty good horse." His face lost its conversational mien. "Dude, I got a bone to pick with you."

"Over what?"

"You told Truesdale I was from Kentucky. Where'd you get that?"

"Just jumped to my mind. Figured it sounded impressive. They do raise a few good horses in Kentucky, you know."

"Well, let me tell you —"

A short, peculiar cough intruded. Everyone grew still. The old man's widening eyes cut away to the horses. The cough sounded again and breathing quicker than natural. "Thunderation," he exploded, and snapped erect. "It's that brown trade horse! That simpleton Otha doctored his horse, too!"

Chapter 4

In front of them another settlement — more town than village this time, its breadth impressive to the wanderer's lonely eye, its array of church steeples posted like guardians — beckoned across the greening distance. And, in the very center of town, overlooking all, like a gruff old watchdog, rose a three-story courthouse of brown stone.

"That's Flat Rock," Dude informed his friends. "Don't believe I've ever laid eyes on prettier country."

"My Texas," Coyote brooded. "Gone my Texas."

"I don't hear any Comanche ghosts, crying they are," Dude gently mocked him.

"Because you don't listen, white father. They are here, all around us, everywhere. Crying they are, just the same. Their voices faint are they, but hear them I on the prairie crying are they."

"All I can hear is the wind it is."

"White man listens to different wind."

"Maybe so. What you ought to do, Coyote, is buy back part of Texas. Get a farm. Be civilized. Plant some crops."

Coyote folded his arms, a gesture of defiance.

his conformation and the proud manner in which he stands, and you need a fast saddler. . . . Offer a little boot with that smooth-looking spavined gelding, who won't limp till late this evening, when my treatment of mercury and lard wears off."

One pint of whiskey (sour mash) and three tablespoonfuls (not heaping) of gunpowder (common), the dose repeated within the hour, followed by a pint of linseed oil (raw), and before long Dude McQuinn had a first-class saddle horse.

Blue Grass was picking up his feet at the moment, and perking his fox ears, and arching his proud neck; when he rounded the corner to parade past the idlers again, traveling as straight as a ruler, Dude eased him into the fox trot. Now the fox trot is a fancy gait, between trot and walk, and pretty to watch, and as Blue Grass, like the show-off he was, arched his brown neck even more and planted each foot even more precisely, the judging heads on the benches nodded in approving unison as he dusted by.

Around the square again. Then, as they came to the idlers' corner, Dude shifted his horse into the rapid single-foot, each hoof striking the ground separately, which is the true single-foot. They swept past, Dude as easy in the saddle as if it were a rocking chair, his right hand holding the reins ever so lightly.

Instead of circling the square again, however, he single-footed on to the end of Main Street, wheeled, and brought Blue Grass back at a smart canter. Nearing the benches, he dismounted and pretended to fiddle with the cinch.

Presently, an elderly citizen wearing a floppy Panama hat got up and drifted over, tapping with his cane. His courteous voice conveyed the soft tones of a native-born east-Texan. "That is one considerable saddle hoss you have theah, sah. Just about th' truest single-footer Ah've witnessed in yeahs."

"Thank you, sir," said Dude, on his manners.

"May Ah inquire as to his breedin', sah?"

"Why, yes. He's Kentucky bred. Sired by Aladdin, out of Maryland Belle," Dude supplied genially, reeling off the first fictional antecedents he could call to mind that sounded of royalty.

"Uh-huh. With all due respects, sah, th' sire and th' dam do not strike a familiar chord in my memory. No matter. Judgin' by this gelding's gaits, he comes from quality blood." He paused. "Happens my son-in-law is on th' lookout for a fine saddler; should you so desire to sell yo' hoss?"

"Be like parting with a member of my family," Dude said, while looping the reins through an iron hitching ring. "I'm obliged to you just the same, sir. As a matter of fact, I'm just passing through. My little outfit is camped outside of town. We carry a few trade horses and one ol' runnin' horse." A smile gullied his face. "That is, he runs when he feels like it. At the moment he's in need of more conditioning."

"A runnin' hoss? Thorough[b]red or short hoss?"

"Short horse."

"You've come to th' righ[t] place, thanks to Providence. Flat Rock has a t[...] ble tally of fast hosses, long and short. Race [...] ich Saturday, spring through summer, up int[...] Racin' is an institution heahabouts, carried [...] from our fo'fathers. Perhaps you took no[...] ur track?"

"You bet I did, as we came [...] right nice layout, worthy of a growing comr [...] ity like Flat Rock."

"Thank you, sah. Allow me to [...] ent m'self. Ah'm Colonel C. Travis Bushrod."

"I'm Dude McQuinn, sir. It's [...] honor to make your acquaintance, Colonel. [...] uite formally, they shook hands. Dude sai[...] io more, waiting him out. Colonel Bushrod pr [...] cted the image of the old-time Southern g [...] tleman: courtly and as straight as a rake handl[...] 'ean to gauntness, his white-goateed face fine [...] oned, dignified, and justly proud. His rich eyes were a shade of brown that laid a dark cast o[...] r his cheeks. His cagey eyes were openly gar [...] Dude, yet without discourtesy. But the strong impression Dude had was of a military erectne[...] stemming from bygone days of flaring banners and the roll and smoke of cannon and musketry.

When the colonel turned to return to his bench, Dude ventured a guess. "Would I be wrong in assuming that you served in the War Between the States, Colonel?"

"You have a discernin' eye, young man. Ah

served from beginnin' to end." Facing about, pleased, the colonel appeared to grow more erect. His eyes flashed.

"Maybe with General Hood?"

"With *General John B. Hood*, sah, an' others. In th' A'my of Tennessee."

"Well! So did my grandfather McQuinn. He was in the Battle of Franklin, Tennessee."

"As Ah was, young sah. Franklin was th' Gettysbu'g of th' West, an' more. Ah can say that without fear of contradiction, sah. Thirteen assaults against th' Yankee breastwuks, while Gen'ral Pickett cha'ged once, followin' a two-hour bomba'dment at Gettysbu'g. We had no advance preparation. None a-tall. Hood wouldn't wait fo' our guns to come up. We cha'ged across two miles of open ground. Pickett's boys went about a mile, though Ah am takin' nothin' a-tall from them, mind you. . . . Pickett, they say, lost some thirteen hundred men. Hood lost six thousand, Ah know. An' next day Ah saw five of Hood's gen'rals laid out on th' back gallery of th' McGavock House."

"Would you do me the honor of having a drink with me, sir?"

Colonel Bushrod inclined his head. "Ah would, young sah, Ah would."

"And your friends here as well?"

Before the colonel could reply, the squad of idlers rose as if on one command and stepped forward in unison, and with Dude and the colonel leading off, they all crossed the dusty street, whereupon Dude, looking about, asked, "Shall we repair yonder to the Tremont House, Colonel, sir?"

"Indeed. Indeed. You have chosen Flat Rock's finest establishment, sah. Th' most commodious. Th' finest food and drink. Th' main gatherin' place of hossmen. Ah might add that, in addition to hoss breedin' and hoss racin', religion is sometimes preached theah, an' politics discussed, th' latter offsettin' th' former, Ah fear."

They entered the Tremont House, a two-story structure, its broad porch teeming with rocking chairs, its barn-like lobby abounding with black leather settees and chairs and polished brass spittoons placed at strategic locations. In the coolness of the saloon, at the long, polished bar, Dude said to all, "Name your pleasure, gentlemen." Noticing that the colonel did not speak up at once, Dude turned to him. "What would you like, sir?"

"Yo' choice is mine, Mistah McQuinn."

"Would Old Green River be to your liking?"

"Indeed. Indeed. Jason, heah, serves that with great regula'ity."

His drink before him, the colonel took a tentative sip as Dude raised his own glass. A moment's hesitation, and the colonel threw back his head and downed the contents at a single dash. The whiskey was hot, very hot. Dude winced expecting his elderly guest to hump over and cough or gag.

The merest flush rose to Colonel Bushrod's cheeks, no more. And then, standing like a stone wall and in a voice as clear and steady as if he had just drunk from a sweet-water spring, he said approvingly, "You are a judge of good whiskey, sah. Mark of a true gentleman. Ah congratulate you. Ah do."

"You honor me, Colonel. Won't you have another drink?"

"Oh th' one condition that you join me."

"That I will, Colonel."

Early in the game Dude McQuinn had perceived that the roundabout approach was the key when seeking to match race your horse in a strange neck of the woods. It was not only wise, it was protocol, almost ritual, like a carefully conducted ceremony observed by generations of bush-track horsemen: the back-and-forth talk, the sizing up of the horses, the step-by-step palavering over distance and wager, the starter, the judges, the condition of the track and maybe angling for the side of the track you wanted for your horse, and sometimes the question of weight carried by each horse.

And so, after some time, and more Old Green Rivers, and as the idlers departed one by one, he found the colonel and himself alone at the bar.

"Colonel," he said, voicing respect that he sincerely felt, "if you don't mind . . . I wish you would tell me more about the Battle of Franklin. Sometimes Grandpa McQuinn would talk about it. Sometimes he wouldn't. He was bitter about the terrible loss of life there."

Although the colonel did not respond immediately, he stood a little straighter.

"If I have offended you, Colonel . . . if I have caused you to recall unpleasant memories of the Lost Cause . . . such was not my intention."

"Not a-tall, my boy. Not a-tall."

"Would you have another Old Green River?"

"With you, young sah. With you."

"My pleasure, Colonel."

They had another Old Green River, downed at a single instant. Dude forced himself to steady a bit, whereas the colonel, so far as he could tell, stood no less erect, unchanged save for the somewhat brighter flush tinting his lean cheeks.

"What you must understand about th' Battle of Franklin," Colonel Bushrod began, "is that it should nevah have been fought a-tall."

"Now that is interesting to know."

"It is. It is. Theah's a secret that's nevah been told."

"I'd like to hear it."

There was a lengthy silence, which Dude did not invade.

"Heah's th' picture," the colonel said finally, as if having overcome painful memories. "Allow me to sketch it fo' you from th' very beginnin'." His voice, at last, sounded just a bit thick.

"Please do, Colonel."

"Wal, th' Yankee Gen'ral Schofield is across Duck Rivah behind his breastwuks at Columbia. Gen'ral Hood comes up on th' prod, but he does not attack th' Yankee in his wuks. No, sah. Theah, young sah, Hood executes one of th' mos' beautiful moves evah seen on th' chessboa'd of wah . . . akin to our immortal Jackson."

Dude nodded, still thrilling to it, though he had heard the story times before.

"Wal, sah, Hood demonstrates befo' th' wuks with all his awtillery. Meanwhile, his engineers have laid pontoon bridges at a fo'd five miles above Columbia, where a tol'able good road leads to Spring Hill." Of a sudden Colonel Bushrod slapped the bar a resounding whack. "Even befo' th' bridges are ready, Nathan Bedfo'd Forrest's riders are fust across. Hood follows, unopposed."

"I'll venture to say that you rode with General Forrest?"

"Ah did, sah. Ah did. Mounted on a brown Kentucky saddler, much like yo' hoss. Why he caught m' eye out yonder on th' street. Kinder took me back."

"I can understand. Grandpa McQuinn rode with General Forrest, too."

"McQuinn . . . McQuinn? Somehow th' name does strike a kinder familiar chord, but Ah cain't quite place it." He studied on that until Dude broke the silence:

"That's easy to understand, sir. There were thousands of men, and Grandpa was only a private."

"So was —" The colonel gave the impression of catching himself, yet his pause was so brief

68

that Dude couldn't be certain. In another moment he was fixing Dude a significant glance. He leaned in. He tapped Dude on the chest. He said, "Hood had th' Yankee Schofield outflanked. At that point jus' one brigade posted across th' Columbia pike at Spring Hill 'ud cut th' Yankees' escape to th' no'th. Hood had th' Yankees all but bagged."

Colonel Bushrod paused, which was the signal for another Old Green River, which they downed somewhat more slowly, but still at a single thrust. Dude's head was spinning. He gripped the edge of the bar for support, trying to appear casual. On such an occasion as this nothing mattered more than "holding your whiskey like a man," as indeed the colonel was. Other than a further softening of his accent, and his deepening flush, he seemed as before.

"Did Hood give the order to cut off the Yankees?"

"He did, sah. He did."

"But why . . . ?"

"It was nevah carried out. Some folks say it was nevah written. Some say it was written an' sent. Some say a lack of ammunition prevented th' attack." The colonel's voice thickened. He drummed that emphatic forefinger against Dude's chest. "But Ah do know that night . . . while th' Yankees came stragglin' up from Columbia . . . their wagon trains passin' within sight of our campfahs . . . some high Confed'rate officahs . . . instead o' hurryin' on to Spring Hill . . . went

69

visitin' th' ladies. That, young sah, is why th' needless Battle o' Franklin was fought. That's th' secret that's nevah been told."

Dude was convinced. This was one version he hadn't heard. "Grandpa McQuinn said one story was that Hood was drunk," he mused.

"A grave cha'ge, sah. A grave cha'ge. Which cain't be proved or disproved."

"Grandpa said if a body ever had reason to take a nip now and then, it was General Hood. Him with one bad arm and a poorly healed stump of a leg, shot off in Virginia."

"True, sah. True." The colonel, with a wave of his veined hand, dismissed the past. A wry smile puckered his face. "No mattah how many times Ah tell that story, th' outcome nevah changes. Th' battle is always fought an' lost, or stalemated, as some folks claim. . . . that reminds me of th' noble animal Ah once rode. Would you sell him fo' a fair profit?"

"Just can't let him go, Colonel."

Colonel Bushrod shrugged in resignation. "So Ah feared. So Ah feared. Then about that runnin' hoss you spoke of. Would you consider matchin' him?"

Finally, Dude saw, they had come full circle, feeling their way through the bourbon fumes and the meandering reminiscing, and the match up was at hand. "I might," he said, careful not to sound too eager. "What've you got in mind, Colonel?"

"Wal, m' son-in-law, Mistah Cassius Pyle —

he runs th' Tremont House, heah — has a tol'able stable o' sprinters, includin' a fair-to-middlin' filly named Texas Rose. He might listen to a match race. He might."

"Is Mr. Pyle at hand?"

"Happens he's out in th' country today, lookin' about his holdin's. But should you wish to make his acquaintance, he will be at th' track in th' mawnin'."

"What time do you suggest I be there?"

"About eight o'clock — aftah he's had time to observe th' schoolin' of his hosses."

"Mighty fine. My outfit will be there. You understand, Colonel, that any bet we make will have to be of a modest nature? My horse is not quite up to snuff yet. Whether we run or not is up to my trainer, Dr. Lockhart."

"Of co'se, sah. Of co'se. We're just o'dinary dirt fa'mers an' hoss folks heahabouts. Ah'm indeed obliged to you, Mistah McQuinn. Good day, sah." Colonel Bushrod bowed and took his dignified departure, his step unwavering, his cane held as a boy might hold a stick, unneeded.

Ordinary in a pig's eye, Dude thought, a caution coming upon him. He paid the bartender.

CHAPTER 5

"Already eight o'clock," Dude groaned, and held a hand to his roaring head. Just the mere thought of Old Green River sickened him.

"Never let on you're in a big rush to match your horse," Uncle Billy said instructively, his tone reminding Dude that he spoke from the lofty eminence of experience. His usual early-morning grouchiness was receding before the give and take of the jousting before them. "Other fella might back off, figure you've got the edge somewhere."

"The colonel said eight o'clock."

"We'll be there soon enough. If you match this race, keep in mind that Rebel looks best up to one eighth. He's neither too fast to scare anybody, nor so slow they think he's sorry horse. We don't want to overmatch him by too much. You know how he is."

They rode side by side, the old horseman astride the brown trade gelding, now cured of the heaves, and Coyote Walking on the smooth-looking Rebel.

"Do you have to remind me?" Dude answered, and grinned despite his thundering head. "Though I'll never forget when Rebel beat that good Springfield mare by a neck. Sure crossed us up. Couldn't match him after that and set things up for the Judge. The local boys figured ol' Rebel was a scorpion."

"That was a fluke. Still, it backs up what I've observed time and again — that every runnin' horse has one good race in him, same as every buckin' horse has one explosion in him. So he's run his one race."

"Even though we found out later the mare had bucked shins."

"Give Rebel credit. He won, didn't he?"

Approaching the track, Dude saw a lone sorrel being breezed out fast on the far side of the oval. Two railbirds watched intently. One the colonel, the brim of his white Panama hat flapping like gull wings as he talked and pointed with his cane, the other a younger man holding a stopwatch. When the jockey brought his charge around and eased up, the watch holder waved him on to the barn.

Uncle Billy said to Coyote Walking, "Take Rebel past them at an easy trot. Go on around. Nothing faster than a lope. We want this to look strictly conditioning. Second time around, on the far side, breeze him out one eighth. Not hard. Easy all the way."

"Look at this track," Coyote said. "It's even been graded. Maybe Rebel like it he will and run faster."

"He had his one miracle at Springfield. Get on out there."

Coyote took Rebel through an open gate and out onto the track, trotting smartly past immediately interested railbirds, on around, and past the watchers again, loping. What a shame it was, Dude thought, that handsome Rebel's heart just wasn't in racing. Like a pretty girl who couldn't make biscuits. Which proved anew Uncle Billy's axiom that conformation alone wasn't enough, that only performance counted. Watching, Dude saw Coyote reach the straightaway on the other side a second time and urge Rebel out for one eighth. Nothing, Dude knew, to cause a railbird to glance at his stopwatch.

The colonel waved and he and the younger man were walking over when Coyote trotted his horse by. "He acts like he wants to run today," Coyote called, loud enough for the approaching two to hear.

"That's a little better," Dude said. "Walk him down and back. Cool him off carefully."

"Good mawnin', sah," the colonel greeted, as friendly as could be. He pumped Dude's hand. "Want you-all to make th' acquaintance of my son-in-law, Cassius Pyle. This is th' gentleman I was tellin' you about, Cassius — Mistah Dude McQuinn. And this, Ah presume, is Dr. Lockhart, th' trainer?"

"It is," said Uncle Billy, stepping forward. As the two old men met, it seemed to Dude that they eyed each other like antagonists.

Cassius Pyle shook hands vigorously, briefly. Dude was prepared for an obsequious inn-

74

keeper, bowing and fawning. To the contrary, Pyle's manner was brusque, bordering on impatience. He had a large head and a round, heavy face. His scrutinizing black eyes bore a bold inquiry. There was something of the dandy about him even at this early hour: white duck trousers and white coat and white shirt, wine-colored cravat tied just so, and straw hat, the crown flat, planter's style, and black Wellington boots that glistened. His thick, brown mustache, sweeping down past the tight corners of his mouth, would have done credit to Jason, the bartender at the Tremont House. He was, Dude judged, a well-rounded forty, more or less, accustomed to dining high on the hog.

"Daddy-in-law tells me you might like to run at us," Pyle opened. His tone was brisk, and when he wasn't rubbing his hands he was flecking dust off his white ducks.

"Depends on Dr. Lockhart's sayso," Dude said, and turned to Uncle Billy, who said, "We've been on the road of late, trading mostly. No time for match races. Our Rebel horse needs hardening up. I figure he's about a week or so away from bein' ready. Maybe so, and maybe not."

"Wal," said the colonel, "he seemed to take to th' track right nicely. He did, he did."

They all turned as Coyote walked Rebel back. Without delay, the Comanche unsaddled and started rubbing down the gelding, beginning at the forequarters and working back. Uncle Billy watched in frowning concern. "Work on him good, Coyote. Don't want him to sore up too much."

Colonel Bushrod, moving in for a closer view, murmured, "So you call this hoss Rebel? A highly likely name fo' this noble animal, Ah say, Ah say." He circled the dark bay, nodding as he went. "Excellent confo'mation, gentlemen. Excellent." He looked across. "Son-in-law, we might be bitin' off mo' than we can comfo'tably chew."

Now Cassius Pyle rounded the gelding, his careful eyes not missing a hair, it seemed. He stopped and planted his feet wide. He folded his arms. "Daddy-in-law," he said, after further deliberation, "you could be right . . . if Texas Rose still has fever and is off her feed."

"She seemed sprightly this mawnin' when we breezed 'er out."

"Off her feed?" Uncle Billy asked, curious, and when Pyle nodded the old man took the floor. "Have you tried Professor Gleason's Original Conditioner?"

"Professor Gleason?" Pyle was dubious. He had no sense of humor, no horseman's repartee. That was plain, Dude decided right there.

"An old cure — simple and easy to acquire," Uncle Billy assured him. "Take pulverized caraway seed and bruised raisin, four ounces each; of ginger and palm oil, two ounces each. Always twice as much of the first as the last, in whatever quantity you wish to make it. Give a small ball once a day until the appetite is restored. Use mashes at the same time. . . . Or you can add a pint of raw linseed meal to her feed. Linseed acts as a digester, is excellent to open the pores, hence a good spring tonic."

Pyle looked blank, but the colonel jogged his head in appreciation. "Thank you, sah. It's good to know that."

Once in his element, Uncle Billy was loath to let go. "And there's Professor Gleason's Original Sure-Shot Conditioner, a stronger preparation. Take the tincture of asafetida, one ounce; tincture of Spanish fly, one ounce; oil of anise, one ounce; oil of cloves, one ounce; oil of cinnamon, one ounce; antimony, two ounces; fenugreek, one ounce . . . and one-half gallon of brandy. Mix well and let stand ten days, then give ten drops daily in a gallon of water. I guarantee you that will make an old horse get up an' howl!"

"Believe Ah know some ol' hosses of a different breed that could use some of that," Colonel Bushrod drawled behind a half smile.

Son-in-law was beginning to fidget again, and seeing that Uncle Billy was about to launch into the components of another "cure," Dude said, "Let's take a look at that filly," thinking that if both sides didn't quit apologizing for their horses, they'd never get this race matched.

They left Coyote still rubbing down Rebel and took the long walk to the huddle of barns, Pyle assertively in the lead. He went to a stall and led out a straight-legged palomino filly of speedy proportions.

After a circling size-up, Uncle Billy ran his hand along her withers and neck and rubbed her nose and murmured nonsense to her. He examined her eyes and teeth, and turned his head to listen to her breathing. He took out his watch and felt under her jaws for her pulse. After a minute or so, he said, "Believe this pony's all right."

"She sure looks like she can bend the breeze," Dude praised.

"She can sometimes," son-in-law said, still downplaying his filly.

Dude said to him, "How'd you like to match her for fifty dollars?"

"That's chicken feed around Flat Rock," Pyle said in a stiffening voice.

"Not in our little outfit."

"I won't take this filly out on the track for that."

"What would you take her out for?"

"Two hundred dollars."

Dude wheeled abruptly away, whistling "Dixie."

Cassius Pyle, tossing the colonel a look, said, "I'll come down to a hundred and fifty."

"I'll go up to seventy-five," Dude fenced, strolling back.

"A hundred twenty-five," Pyle dickered, planting his feet wide again.

"You ain't feedin' a bunch of hungry stock, Mr. Pyle, and tryin' to match one ol' horse. I'll go a hundred even." Saying that, he rationalized that sometimes in this game you had to lose money, more than you wanted to, before you made money.

"You're on!" Son-in-law slapped his hands together, cordial for the first time. "How far you want to run?"

"Two hundred yards."

"That's short for us. This filly has Thorough-bred blood and prefers the longer routes."

"Happens my ol' Rebel horse is not Thor-oughbred and likes to go short."

"An' Texas Rose, here, has been off her feed." Son-in-law studied the tip of one shiny boot. "Why don't we just call it one eighth?"

"All right. When would you like to run?"

"Well, we race here every Saturday afternoon. Next Saturday suit you?"

"That's rushin' us some. But Rebel might be ready at that. We'll just see."

By now they were almost falling over each other to be agreeable. Dude stuck out his hand. They shook.

A reminding voice came between them. "Al-though this is a gentleman's agreement, Ah be-lieve it is customary fo' both sides to put up a little fo'feit money. What do you think would be suitable, Mistah McQuinn?"

"Whatever you say, Colonel."

"Fifty dollahs?"

"Fifty it is."

"Spoken like a true hossman."

79

"I'll place mine with Jason at the Tremont House bar. I guess he's reliable?"

"Oh, Jason is, sah, he is. Grew up heah in Flat Rock. I knew his daddy."

On the way to their mounts, Uncle Billy said, "That forfeit move was just to see if we had any money. That old man's as wise as a treeful of owls. He knows you generally don't put up unless it's a big match race and a lot bet. And that was just a come-on about that filly bein' off her feed."

"I gathered as much."

"When a horse has fever, the pulse will run from fifty to seventy-five per minute. Hers was beating thirty-six to forty — just right for a healthy critter."

As evening wore on after supper, the old horseman saddled up. "Believe I'll mosey on into town an' listen around. What's the name of that place again where you got your snoot wet?"

"The Tremont House. Cassius Pyle runs it. Owns it, I guess."

"That's exactly where I'm headed, then."

"While you're there, place the forfeit money with Jason the bartender."

Long past midnight, it must have been, when Dude, sleeping under the wagon, heard a horse walk up and stop, and bootsteps proceeding unsteadily to the water barrel and a tin cup rattling against the barrel and water splashing and someone slurping and sputtering.

"That you, Uncle Billy?"

More splashing, more spluttering. A pause. "Who'd you think it was — Paul Revere?"

Dude got up and pulled on his boots and lit the lantern and went to the water barrel. Uncle Billy was mopping his face with a bandanna while he clutched the wagon's sideboard for support. His eyes were closed. When he opened them against the light, he blinked and closed them again and heaved out a groan. Bourbon fumes laid a stain on the damp night air.

"Uncle Billy, you're roostered!"

"Sure as hell am, but I came home with all the dope. Tha's what counts. Dude, boy, we're up against some sure-'nough cagey horsemen this time. Slicker than a one-eyed gambler."

"How's that?"

"One thing, this Texas Rose . . . just a comin' three-year-old . . . has won all 'er races. She'll make Rebel eat dust."

"Well —"

"Was hopin' it might be more respectable. I knew she could run the instant I laid eyes on her. It's down the line I'm worried about, though." He weaved to the wagon tongue and slouched down. "They've got a blue-streak sorrel gelding called Diamond Dick, an' a dun stud called Night Owl that runs like the heel flies are after him. You won't see either o' these horses next Saturday."

"Why not?"

"They've beat ever'thing in this part of Texas.

Nobody will match 'em anymore, even with odds."

"That's what they said about Pepper Boy. You can understand that."

"I could — if it was just a matter of speed."

"What're you gettin' at?"

"They *always* win. *Always.* Fella from Sherman brought a top Peter McCue colt in here early this spring. A sure-'nough scorpion called Johnny McCue. Big an' rugged. Well, Night Owl daylighted him. Heap of money bet, too. Big crowd came over from Sherman. Went home broke."

"You mean somebody fixed Johnny McCue?"

"Something was wrong. That horse didn't run right. Johnny McCue's owner swore he'd never come back. But couldn't prove anything. Had hot words with Cassius Pyle. City marshal had to break it up. No . . . that horse didn't run right. Like he wasn't himself."

"A horse can have an off day."

"I said that horse didn't run right. Didn't act right, either."

"Who told you all this?"

"Jason Carter, the Tremont House bartender, after he closed up the place tonight. That is, we closed it up together, me an' him. Had us a few toddies."

"A few?"

"That's what I said."

"Oh, all right. But whoa, now. This Carter's on the other side of the fence."

"That's what you think. Jason was in line to be manager when the old one passed on. . . . You see, it's the colonel and his sister, Miss Lucinda, that own Tremont House. . . . About that time this Cassius Pyle fella shows up. He's a whiskey drummer outa Kansas City and no dumbbell. He knows a bird nest on the ground when he sees one. He sweet-talks the colonel's daughter, Miss Sally, into marryin' him. The colonel proceeds to set Cassius up — a farm, for one. Even gives him half interest in the horses, though the colonel still calls all the shots. You can give odds on that! Around strangers, however, the old gent pretends that son-in-law does. . . . Colonel also makes him manager of Tremont House over Jason. All this goes to son-in-law's head, which is already barn size. Now he treats Jason like a field hand."

"Did Jason say what to look for?"

"Just be on the lookout, he said."

"That could mean anything. You know what Shakespeare said: 'All's fair in love and war.' "

"— And horse racin'. He must of meant that, too."

"Why'n't you two white men bed down?" Coyote Walking called from the other end of the wagon. "Besides, it was Cervantes who wrote that, and he didn't phrase it that way. He said, 'Love and war are the same thing, and stratagems and policy are as allowable in the one as in the other.' "

"— And horse racin'!" the old man shot back

83

stubbornly. He swayed to his feet. "Deliver me from an educated Injun. Be that as it may, this Comanche's headin' for his bedroll. I don' feel so good right now."

In his blankets, listening to the wind purring off the prairie, thinking of what Uncle Billy had told him, Dude had an arousing thought. It strengthened in him. He sat up and said, "We forgot something. We can't work the Judge out at the track. But we can on the road." He quit speaking. Uncle Billy was snoring, chuffing like a steam engine. Well, it could wait till tomorrow.

Dude woke to the aroma of coffee and over him what resembled a white-bearded gnome, growling tetchily, "Figured I'd be late rollin' out, didn't you? Come an' get it or I'll throw it out to the coyotes."

It was yet early when Dude took Uncle Billy down the road to a long level stretch. Here, he said, they could work Judge Blair about day-break, beyond sight of the track and barns.

Dude waited. Nothing was said, until, bit by bit, the usual early-morning scowl quit the whiskery face and Uncle Billy nodded. Every other day was the conditioning schedule the old man prescribed "to harden a horse up." Warm him up walking, trotting, loping, galloping for half a mile or more, then "breeze him out" over the distance he would run in the race, preferably in competition against another horse. In the Judge's case at this early stage of the game in Flat Rock, distance had to be a guess, but likely no farther than three hundred fifty yards. Rebel, of course, would take his turns at the track as he prepared to meet Texas Rose, scaring nobody with eye-blinking breezes, and likewise resting every other day. The alternate rest day, Uncle Billy opined, kept a horse from resenting hard work and made running fun.

Before nine o'clock the morning of race day, farmers and stockmen and their families were raising dust past the camp on the road into Flat Rock, for it was also trade day — Saturday.

The morning passed quietly, settling into the familiar race-day routine, yet lacking the tenseness when Judge Blair was running: Dude playing a game of sol on the wash bench, Uncle Billy puttering in his odorous medicine chest, Coyote, as usual, immersed in a book.

Dude looked up. "What are you reading?"

"The poet Hamlin Garland, white father."

"I've heard of him," Dude said vaguely.

"He writes of wind and grass. I think he would understand why gone my Texas."

"I keep tellin' you, Coyote, the only way you can get back any of your Texas is to buy it. Stop mooning and make some folding money. Just keep on ridin'."

By noon Dude observed a steady procession trailing out from town and filing into the grounds bordering the track, although the first race wasn't scheduled until two o'clock. Rebel ran in the third outing.

85

"No need going over early," Uncle Billy said. "Don't want to excite Rebel."

"Little excitement might be good for him."

"And have happen what did at Springfield?"

Dude didn't answer. Sometimes he felt acutely sorry for Rebel and his many humiliations.

By and by, setting out for the track, they had turned off the main road, heading toward the area of the barns, when a buggy dashed past, bringing a slithering rush of wheels and rapid hoofbeats. Dude recognized the high-stepping chestnut and the little white-haired lady he had seen in town that first day. He touched hand to hatbrim. She smiled back, a favoring, motherly smile.

Uncle Billy pinned him a look. "Who's that?"

"Don't know."

"She seems to know you."

"Aw, she just smiled. Ever see a sweeter, more kindly smile?"

"I tell you one thing. She can handle the reins. Look at her drive! That little lady knows horses."

They drew up on a grassy expanse adjacent to the barns, amid a confusion of horsemen's wagons and buckboards and buggies, and runnin' horses haltered and groomed, and others being walked back and forth as carefully as though they were children.

Coyote uncinched and rubbed down the gentle Rebel, tenderly, yet deeply, as if imparting speed, and spread a light blanket over the gelding's short back.

Before many minutes, Cassius Pyle and Colonel Bushrod, each conspicuous among the overalled horse gentry in their white ducks and white hats, came ambling along the line of stalls. Catching sight of Dude's outfit, they waved and hastened across and, with the colonel taking the lead, vigorously pumped hands all around.

"Getting ready to start the first race," Pyle said. "We're still scheduled to run third. You're welcome to stall your horse, if you like. No charge. Daddy-in-law will see to that." He winked at Dude. "He owns the track."

"Glad to, sah," the colonel seconded. "Glad to."

Dude had never experienced such hospitality among competitive horsemen. He thanked them and declined, unprepared for this new and accommodating Pyle, a striking contrast to the curt man the day they had matched the race.

On that, the two went to a stall where the golden head of Texas Rose could be seen. She looked like a queen. Two burly men stood guard.

"Just like white man," Coyote commented after them, his headshake rejecting. "Always shaking hands. Always grabbing hold of you, like you're a mean mule and might run away. Just like white man."

"I suppose," Dude said, guying him, "it takes a Comanche to shake hands right?"

"We don't grab people and crack their knuckles. We learned long time ago when white seizes

87

your hand and holds you fast that white man's heart is not always true. We Comanches learned that when we signed white man's talking paper and gave my Texas away. This Comanche those two white men like does not."

A foghorn-voiced man astride a fat gray horse was riding slowly past the packed stands, calling the first race, a three-hundred-yard go. He rode to the paddocklike area near the barns and repeated the call. Promptly, there was a stir of activity and two mounted horsemen led forth their prancing runners, a bay and a black, the jockeys aboard, and paraded onto the track and past the stands to the head of the straightaway where the official starter waited.

In moments, while Dude watched, the chattering crowd hushed and the jockeys rode their mounts toward the starting line. Suddenly the starter dropped his hand and shouted and they were off, closely lapped. It was the bay all the way, by daylight the last fifty yards. Afterward, the victorious jockey rode to the winner's circle. A short wait and the second race was announced.

"Time to saddle up," Uncle Billy said.

Dude nodded, feeling reluctance. "If Rebel was a mudder I'd pray for rain, bless his heart."

When the third race was announced, Dude mounted Blue Grass and led Rebel away, which wasn't really necessary with so docile a horse, just part of the ceremony. He said to Coyote, "Pull his head up a little. Make him prance when we parade past the stands."

Coyote did and Rebel pranced, tossing his handsome head. The crowd murmured approval: "What a pretty horse! Bet he's lightning-fast!"

Dude's conscience turned over. If they only knew!

Now Texas Rose was parading. Dude could tell by the noise from the stands behind him, the ahs, the cheers, the sudden burst of applause for a local favorite. He glanced over his shoulder. Pyle was on the lead horse, as puffed up as a white knight. But, son of a gun, if that palomino filly wasn't a walking picture.

An energetic elder, his long-tailed frock coat and erect figure combining to give him the dignified air of a judge, introduced himself as Will Sawyer, the starter. He said, "I'll shout *Go!* when the horses are well lapped — just so there's no daylight."

Rebel was ready now, as ready as he could possibly be. Dude cautioned Coyote, "Stay lapped up tight — this looks like a quick break," and got out of the way.

Texas Rose pranced up, as light and quick on her feet as a March foal. Her jockey hardly looked old enough to be in the fourth grade, nor heavier than a wet gunny sack.

Sawyer waved the horses forward. Together they advanced.

Dude held his breath.

The horses were lapped. Good ol' Coyote had Rebel up there.

"Go!" And, simultaneously, the downward slash of the starter's hand.

They broke. A clean break, no bumping. Still, quick Texas Rose got the jump by a neck.

Dude heard a voice roaring encouragement. It was his own. He was punching the air with his right fist, fighting for his horse.

During the first seventy-five yards Rebel stayed with Texas Rose. At that point Dude let out a moan. Rebel was losing ground, like always. Coyote whooped and rapped him with the bat. Rebel hung on, as if against his will. Dude had to avert his eyes.

When he dared look again, Texas Rose was streaking across the finish line and poor Rebel was eating two lengths of daylight.

Pyle flung Dude his triumph and galloped his horse down the track, the white tails of his coat flying like victory banners.

As soon as Texas Rose had taken her turn in the winner's circle and Pyle and the colonel had led her to her stall, Dude hustled straight over there and paid his bet.

"My," he said, admiring the palomino, "how this little lady can ripple the breeze. Pretty as a picture, too. Congratulations, Colonel. You too, Mr. Pyle. "

"You are a true gentleman, sah," Colonel Bushrod replied, gracious in victory. "You are, indeed."

"No excuses, though I was hoping Rebel would make it much closer," Dude said, looking down.

"Ah know how you feel, Mistah McQuinn, havin' quaffed th' dregs of defeat m'self many, many times."

"I knew Rebel wasn't in top form . . . yet —" Dude looked down again. "He's done better, and he will do better before long. Just needs more conditioning. You saw how he faded the last half of the race." He shrugged. "Not much time to train a horse when you're carryin' a bunch of trade stock."

A tiny flame of interest began to dance within the colonel's eyes. "Think you might like to match yo' hoss again?"

"I know he can beat what he did today."

"Always like to give a man a second chance who has pride in his hoss."

"That's neighborly, Colonel."

Bushrod and Pyle shuffled considerate glances. They looked at each other for a longer spell without speaking, until the son-in-law remarked thoughtfully, "Although Diamond Dick is coming along, he is far from his peak of last season."

"Ah thought he was over that sore stifle joint?" The colonel's tone was one of surprise.

"He is Daddy-in-law. Only he's somewhat slow coming along, is all."

"No trouble keepin' a shoe on that right front foot?"

"No, sir. It's just about grown back where he got it stepped on early in March."

"Ah'm greatly relieved to hear that. Ah am, indeed. In that case, Mistah McQuinn, we might

91

treaty with you, should you so desire, to run against Diamond Dick. Of c'ose, Ah cain't give you a definite answer until Ah've examined him personally m'self and am convinced of his soundness fo' th' track."

Dude, keeping his face smoothly noncommittal, said, "I understand, sir. By the same token, I hope my ol' Rebel horse quickens up the way I know he can. Meanwhile, we'll await your examination and reply."

CHAPTER 6

On the Monday after the Saturday race, the three rode at a slow jog through the predawn darkness. First light was yet minutes away, the promise of the good day yet waiting to be born, the good land yet in the grip of night silence, the damp air redolent of the sweet scent of prairie grass.

Inspired, Dude said rememberingly, "This reminds me of what Grandpa McQuinn used to say it was like when he was in the War Between the States, ridin' with Nathan Bedford Forrest's boys, and they'd be out on early-morning scout lookin' for Yankees."

"War Between the States? Thunderation, you mean the Great Rebellion!" Uncle Billy whanged at him.

"I mean," Dude started to retort, and let it go unsaid, as he had before, for most times the salty old codger was likable enough. Once he had his black coffee and got his arthritic joints limbered up, and had gone out to look over each horse, which invariably he did, and the sun had risen — he was first-rate company. Anyway, it was too early for sociable conversation.

Jogging on in silence, Dude let his thoughts

wander. Was Lockhart really Uncle Billy's name? Could he be the much-quoted and mysterious Professor Gleason?

Sight of the dark bulk of the race stands and the linear lines of the track's railing, spectral in the muddy gloom, cut short his musing. Fawn-colored light began to glow in the eastern sky.

It was Coyote Walking who pulled up first. "Hear that?" he called warningly.

Dude caught it. The rapid beat of a horse rounding the turn nearest the barns, traveling faster on the far straightaway. Now he made out the horse against the breaking light, running quite fast, running stopwatch time. The jockey kept his mount coming hard around the turn and onto the straightaway leading past the stands. The horse vanished like a blur past dim figures standing by the rail.

"What's going on?" Uncle Billy pondered. "Why're they on the track earlier than usual?"

"I'll give odds that's Diamond Dick," Dude said. "My guess is they don't want us to see him breeze."

"Makes sense. That horse ran flat out for over half a mile."

"Let's wait awhile. They don't know we saw their horse. Let 'em think so. Not that it'll make any difference when Rebel takes on that Diamond Dick."

After some minutes, they rode noisily up to the track, talking as they went, and Coyote took Rebel trotting down the stretch. On around,

94

loping now, Coyote worked the gelding. Second time around, on the far stretch, he breezed Rebel slowly for one eighth before letting up, an unimpressive workout by any judgment. When he clattered up, Uncle Billy told him, "Keep going until somebody shows up. Slow and easy."

Coyote was halfway around when from down the track Dude saw a white-hatted figure looming through the dissolving murk.

"You gentlemen are early birds this mawnin'," the colonel called. His voice seemed to touch a higher key above his normal greeting. He strode over.

"Nobody else on the track and Rebel likes the early coolness," Dude said. "Gonna be a scorcher today."

Coyote brought Rebel up at a cooling-down walk, and Uncle Billy said, "That's enough. Let's go."

"How's Rebel lookin'?" Colonel Bushrod queried, giving the horse a long scrutiny.

"Believe he's quickening up a little," Dude answered. And as if doubtful: "Didn't clock him. I was hoping we might see Diamond Dick."

"Ah'm restin' him today. Want to take another look at that stifle joint. Came out this mawnin' to watch a neighbor's hoss work. Good day, gentlemen."

That afternoon, while Uncle Billy did some horse tradin' around the square, Dude entered the Tremont Bar, deserted at this hour.

"How's my friend, Uncle Billy Lockhart?" Jason Carter asked, busy polishing glasses.

"Fit as a filly ready for her maiden race."

"Such a fine old fellow, even if he is a Yankee. Tells a good story, too. Speaks ill of no man. So understanding. Such a kindly face. Why — why — he looks like a saint!"

"That's Uncle Billy, all right."

Except for his size and his eyes, Jason Carter squared with the typical bartender's appearance: a giant of a man growing soft and heavy around his middle; slicked-down brown hair parted exactly in the middle, his face the indoor shade of the putty-colored polishing towel in his hands, an abundant mustache that swept downward in an oxbow, and string tie, white shirt, and a silver watch chain looping across his loose-fitting vest. His soft brown eyes wore the weariness of a tired bird dog. Dude thought: A sleeping giant, capable of deeds beyond his experience or belief, if ever aroused. Without further adieu, Jason Carter reached for a bottle of Old Green River.

"I see you remember," Dude said, his tone appreciative.

"I remember. I remember a lot of things." Here, his voice betrayed, was a lonely man, cast aside and unnoticed.

"Uncle Billy told me to buy you a drink."

Carter looked pleased, yet he hesitated. "It's against the rules of the house."

"New rules?"

"Yeah, new rules."

"Wasn't anybody at the desk when I came through the lobby."

"Believe I will. Thank you, Mr. McQuinn."

"The name is Dude." Raising his glass: "Here's to better times, Jason."

Jason Carter took his fast, eyes on the doorway.

"Ever get out to the races, Jason?" Dude poured another for Carter, then himself.

"The big ones, sometimes."

"Happen to see Night Owl daylight Johnny McCue?"

"I was there. Sort of sneaked off from here."

"I hear the McCue colt didn't run up to his notice."

"He was snorting like a wild stallion. Like he couldn't get his wind. His eyes bulged."

"Sick, maybe? The heaves?"

"Would those Sherman folks a-put him on the track if he had the heaves?"

"I wouldn't my horse."

"Johnny McCue," Carter said, watching the doorway, "just wasn't himself."

"Was he fixed?"

An idler strolled in and called for whiskey, had it and left, and Carter plodded back to where Dude leaned. Monotony and disappointment and the nature of his work had left the print of controlled impassiveness on his strong-boned face, a face that suggested a hidden liveliness and warmth waiting for the trigger of release. He said, "I can't rightly tell you because I don't know."

Dude toyed with his glass, thinking Carter would tell him if he knew, that he would have told Uncle Billy had he known more than barroom talk. "I believe you would," Dude said. He looked up to meet Carter's eyes boring hard into his and Carter saying in his soft-spoken way:

"I appreciate good horses. To me, they represent freedom and beauty. I keep a good saddler. Take him out every Sunday afternoon." He took a long breath. "If I had a fast horse and somebody fixed him, I'd fix that man's lamp, believe me." Gradually, a forthright smile overspread his face, chasing its remoteness. "If you had the favorite, I'd say beware. But being as your horse is Rebel, I don't figure you'll have to worry about that."

"He's better than he showed against Texas Rose," Dude vowed. "I'll match him again if Diamond Dick's sore stifle joint comes around."

"Sore stifle joint?" For exclamation, Carter hammered home the cork of the Old Green River bottle with the heel of his hand. "Why, that horse has never been in anything but top condition. He was brought along careful-like. Never ran till he was three."

"Or," Dude continued, still fishing, "if they can keep a shoe on the foot he got stepped on last March."

"Stepped on last March? Diamond Dick ran at Denton two weeks ago. Won going away. He's never been hurt. Somebody's trying to —" Carter checked himself all at once, his locked lips forming a straight line of impassivity. His eyes sought the door; wearily, he said, "Here comes the afternoon cavalry charge from the courthouse square." As Dude turned to leave, Carter's urgent and low-pitched voice drew him about: "I just remembered. They say Johnny McCue seemed all right till minutes before the race. Since the owner had big forfeit money up, he decided to run his horse anyway."

"You're all right, Jason. Thanks."

"Tell Uncle Billy howdy for me."

"Will do."

Dude was passing through the lobby when Colonel Bushrod bustled in off the street. He wagged his cane importantly. "How fo'tunate! You, young sah, bein' just th' gentleman Ah'm on th' lookout fo'."

"What can I do for you, Colonel?"

"Ah'm pleased to repo't that Ah've examined Diamond Dick an' found him in tol'able condition to run, so we're ready to treaty with you, Cassius and I."

"You are considerate, Colonel. How much you want to bet?"

"You name it, sah."

"Same as last time?"

"Agreed. Agreed. If you'll lengthen th' distance."

"Just don't make it too far. My Rebel's no Thoroughbred, you know."

"How does three hundred fifty ya'ds strike you?"

In match racing you did not appear too eager
— never. After a considering pause, Dude said,
"As encouraged as I am by the way Rebel is
rounding into form, three fifty is still too yonder
for him."

"Three hundred, sah?"

Dude chewed his lower lip.

"Two hundred fifty, sah?"

"I've got to go for that, Colonel. You are fair."

Now in a tone that said no man could be more
courteous than Colonel C. Travis Bushrod:
"About when shall we contest these hosses?"

Like a ripe apple, which best not be left too
long on the tree, the running of a match race
ought not be left hanging more than a few days
when you are traveling about, tradin' and racin',
lest the fickle wheel of fortune take an unfortu-
itous turn. Dude shrugged and said, "Saturday
afternoon?"

"You have pride in yo' hoss. Ah see that. Next
race day it shall be."

They shook on it, like gentlemen, and had a
drink of Old Green River.

On Wednesday, just before dawn, they took
Rebel through the cool darkness to the track. A
dead stillness prevailed. Before, Diamond Dick
was working at about this time of morning. That
set Dude to wondering. "Hold up," he said.
"I'm going downtrack for a little look-see."

He dismounted and followed the outside railing for some distance. He halted, sighting no

100

movement as first pink light streaked the eastern sky; going on, he neared the stands and paused again, watching there and on toward the dimness of the barns. He heard nothing, he saw nothing move. He waited.

He was ready to turn back when a solitary figure materialized in the stands and seemed to be peering toward the upper end of the straightaway. Dude froze against the railing. After a time, the watcher sat down. Around the barns the silence and absence of activity held unchanged. Diamond Dick would not work out until later, if at all.

Dude, bending low, went back. "Let's not work Rebel here this morning," he told Uncle Billy and Coyote. "Somebody's down there in the stands. I figure it's Cassius Pyle. I don't want him clocking Rebel's slow breezes."

"What difference it make? We're already matched."

"Point is, Uncle Billy," Dude replied patiently, "Pyle and daddy-in-law must be led to think that Rebel's on the improve. Else why would we match a slow horse?"

"Reckon I'm not awake yet," the old man fretted. "Rebel runs slow Saturday, what then? He still looks slow."

"We still say he hasn't reached his peak, see? And maybe, just maybe, we can make Rebel look a dab more respectable against Diamond Dick."

"There's no substitute for speed."

"You said yourself the other day he might

learn to break faster, even if he can't run faster."

"So I did."

"We haven't worked him much on the break," Dude persisted.

"Come to think of it, we haven't." The old man's tone softened, his codger's crabbedness retreating, growing fainter, and Dude's mind opened afresh on a perception made stronger by time and observation: Uncle Billy's interior world, his whole being, was inextricably tied to love of horses, of working with them, of curing and caring for them, of making them perform up to their potential as runners or making them behave. When one challenged, he responded with his knowledge. It was, to him, an irresistible game without end, as varied and fascinating as the horses themselves and the conditions affecting them. He said, "I've got an idy about the break. We can school Rebel on the road near camp and breeze him out there as well. Let daddy-in-law and big-britches son-in-law wonder why we don't work our horse at the track. . . . Y'know, Dude, boy, once in a great while you Alamo Texans come up with a notion that holds water. Only don't get me wrong. I said *once in a great while.*"

Until now, Dude thought as they rode off, it hadn't mattered whether Rebel ran faster or not. Now it was important, evolving out of necessity, if they were to outslick Pyle and the Colonel, or get outslicked in turn. A stir of guilt troubled him. Poor Rebel!

"The key," Uncle Billy explained as they reined up on the road adjacent to camp, "is to turn your horse a little just before he breaks."

"How does that help him?" Dude was skeptical. This was something new.

"Gives your horse momentum, if you stop and think about it. He pushes off and sorta swings into his getaway. First, a short step to pull on — for impetus, see? — then a leap, and he's long gone! Most fellas figure if their horse is set straight ahead and his feet are well under him, that's the best possible position. It's good, better than being off balance, but not the best. I'll beat 'em out every time if my horse knows how to start sideways. I don't care if it's lap-and-tap or out of a chute, I'll break on top."

Still skeptical, Dude asked, "Why haven't we schooled the Judge on this?" aware that he was hearing the lecturing tone of the Cottonwood wagonyard, before the audience of rib-nudging loafers and mule-and-horse swappers and skinners.

"As you know," Uncle Billy continued, "Judge Blair is an exceptional horse. That he was gelded is another testimonial to man's ignorance and carelessness toward *Equis caballus*. In my opinion, which I do not hold lightly, he might have been another Steel Dust or Shiloh or Peter McCue. Sired by Lightning out of Thunderstorm, some poet fella might pen. Him being so nimble and quick, he hasn't needed the sideways or swinging break. He's a natural fast breaker; Rebel is not. Be that as it may, you never know when you'll be matched against another scorpion, like Jason says this Night Owl stud is. So it might be wise to school the Judge on this, too."

"Say, wouldn't it be funny if Rebel takes the break and beats Diamond Dick?"

"Miracles don't happen twice, Dude, boy."

"I suppose," Dude said, quirking his mouth, "that Professor Gleason developed this sideways break after years of trial and error?"

"You really want to know? Well, he did not. First and only time I ever saw it a country fella had this little bitty bay mare, and he started her sideways and outbroke a big, strong horse over a length. She had it won right there! You see, while your horse is taking that first small step and pushing off, swinging into his break, the other horse is in his long step."

"Where was this?" Dude posed the question subtly, unable to resist the favorable opening.

"Why," said Uncle Billy, for once showing no offense at the delving, "that was so long ago I can't rightly remember, except it was in the country somewhere on a bush track. Why?"

"Just wondered, is all."

Ignoring Dude: "Try it again, Coyote. Don't turn him quite so much. . . . That's about right. You've got it. Ready? Now, Go!"

Come Saturday, watching from the finish line behind the three judges, hearing the chattering crowd in the stands, Dude saw Uncle Billy go to the starter and, with many gestures, explain how his horse would break. Dude still entertained doubts. Would the swinging break work?

Moments afterwards the jockeys were waved in and Uncle Billy spoke final instructions to Coyote Walking, and Coyote had Rebel moving up, lapped on the sorrel Diamond Dick, that pint-sized kid in the irons. *Good, Coyote! You've got Rebel turned just right.*

Ready. *Go!*

Son of a gun, Rebel outbroke that sorrel a full length! Dude couldn't believe it. Rebel was off and running like his tail was on fire.

Dude was shouting and waving his arms, making a spectacle of himself. To hell with setting up Pyle and the colonel. Come on, Rebel!

At fifty yards it was Rebel by daylight. At seventy-five Diamond Dick was closing. At one hundred yards he was lapped on Rebel. For half a dozen strides more the horses ran head to head.

Dude bit his lip. It was happening again. Poor Rebel!

Diamond Dick stuck his head out front, and then his neck, and then he was half a length out. Rebel was running as fast as he could, or wanted to. Coyote let go his most curdling screech, a frightening sound through the drumfire of hooves. That always seemed to spur Rebel. It did this time, as Dude saw him come on a stride or two faster. For a hopeful moment Dude thought

Rebel was going to close on the sorrel.

Rebel did not; he could not. Coyote took to the bat. Still, Rebel could not, and Coyote, as if sensing that that was useless, didn't hit him again.

Dude's shout died in his throat. Wave after wave of hurt pride for his horse rolled through him. Dully, he watched Diamond Dick, flying faster with each long stride, whip over the finish line, sporting a length of daylight.

Dude turned on his heel and walked down the track toward the barns, conscious of self-reproach. He was waiting when Coyote rode up, shaking his head.

"Cool him down extra nice, Coyote. The ol' boy ran as hard as he could. Leastwise, you two won the break. You did all you could."

"First time he ever did. Bet that scared those hand-shakin' white men."

"Well, there's another day coming on this track — and I hope it's soon."

Colonel Bushrod, flanked by the cocky Cassius Pyle, was as merciful as ever in victory and showed a courtly graciousness as he took Dude's money and Dude said, "Had us a hot little set-to there the first hundred yards or so, didn't we? Have to hand it to you folks the way you've brought Diamond Dick around." He let a half grin surface. "I'd say he's fully recovered from that sore stifle joint and that foot he got stepped on last March. Mighty fortunate."

"Indeed, thank you, Mistah McQuinn. Indeed. Must give yo' Rebel hoss credit, too. He flat took th' break away from Diamond Dick. Nevah happened befo'."

"I told you Rebel's improving. Texas Rose daylighted him two lengths. Diamond Dick just one length."

"Tol'able improvement, yes."

Now. Now was the right time to spring it. "Enough, sir, to bring me to the point of foolhardiness, you might think." Dude crossed his arms and gazed down, and dug the toe of one boot into the dirt and kicked at a loose clod, and when he squared his shoulders and looked up he seemed to be summoning the last ounce of his mettle. "I'll put it this way, Colonel: I don't like to get beat. After what Rebel showed me today, I'll match you again."

Colonel Bushrod gave a start and straightened, eyes glinting astonishment. "You are audacious, young sah. Or should I say reckless?" He shook his head and expelled a snort of disdain. "Ah'd almost hate to take yo' money again, I would."

"Don't feel that way, Colonel. I'd take yours with delight."

The colonel stood silent, still taken back, assessing this unexpected challenge. A crowd of followers had collected. Among them the colonel's two burly track employees. Dude had them pegged: collectors — at hand had he refused to pay or had taken to the tules.

"However," Dude said, his tone one of back-

107

ing off, apprehensive that he had seemed too eager, "I'd have to have some odds."

"Odds? That is a hoss of another shade, sah."

"Two-to-one odds would seem fair to me, since you've outrun my horse twice. Daylighted him both times."

Colonel Bushrod wasn't accustomed to being on the defensive. Dude divined that when the colonel slanted his inquiry at his son-in-law, who said after a moment, "You've lost twice, yet you want to run us again?"

"That's right. I'll run at any horse you'll put up." Dude shrugged genially, hoping for Diamond Dick, thinking there was scant difference between the gelding and the filly Texas Rose. "All I want is a chance to get my money back — or part of it." Something in Pyle's cocksure face prompted him to fling out: "Of course, if you're afraid to match me again . . . ?"

"Not for another measly hundred dollars will we match you!" Pyle's face was pinking. He came in a contentious step.

Dude grinned. "Did I say a hundred? I'll bet you five hundred, if you'll give me two-to-one odds."

Pyle couldn't quite carry it off. The crowd stirred, waiting. Pyle turned his head, and the colonel, no doubt aware of what the crowd expected of him, said coolly, "Ha'dly see how we could decline such a challenge, son-in-law, even at two to one." He regarded Dude at length. His eyebrows lifted. A suggestion of mockery. Then:

"Believe you said *any hoss*, Mistah McQuinn. Very well . . . we'll run Night Owl against you."

Night Owl? Dude beat down his surprise and managed to keep a fairly fixed expression, thinking that sometimes you pushed your brag too far.

"You may decline if you wish, Mistah McQuinn."

Now that he had taken the first jolt of surprise, Dude said, "You're matched, Colonel," only wishing it were Diamond Dick or Texas Rose. In Night Owl they had drawn the top scorpion; somehow he had miscalculated, yet he should have known.

"Not over the distance we ran today," Pyle was saying.

"You know my ol' horse can't go a full quarter."

"Four hundred yards?"

"Come, Mr. Pyle."

Son-in-law glanced about, pretending to seek the crowd's opinion. "Three fifty?" he said, condescending.

"Three hundred," Dude jockeyed.

With a patronizing air: "It makes no difference to Night Owl, one furlong up to five eighths. Three hundred yards will be a good breeze. Next race day soon enough?"

"I need two weeks to get ready for Night Owl." *Two weeks to get our money bet around town.*

Pyle shrugged indifferently, nodded agreement, and started to strut away, when Dude, tiring of the other's arrogance, raised his voice. "Let's not forget the forfeit money between gentlemen. Say, two hundred dollars?"

Pyle tossed him a careless nod.

CHAPTER 7

While traveling through the country and jockeying around to the build-up of a big match race, you learned to take certain safeguards.

On Monday after race day, Uncle Billy and Coyote Walking drove the wagon into Flat Rock and by late morning had sold all the trade horses, which left the fast-stepping team of sorrels, both of which could be ridden, and Rebel and the Judge, and Dude's Blue Grass.

And that afternoon the outfit made the light wagon ready, greasing axles and tightening wheel rims, in the event that another sudden departure became prudent, such as had happened last in Indian Territory.

Meantime, you resumed working your slow horse on the track at earliest light, ostensibly to further an air of secrecy as to his condition and improving speed, while, on alternate mornings, you breezed your fast horse in some distant pasture or, in this instance, on a little-used road.

And, to the railbirds frequenting the courthouse square and the Tremont House bar, Dude played the hopeful horseman of an itinerant shirt-tail outfit, letting it be known that his horse was "coming along" or "starting to hit his stride," but shying away, always genially, from revealing any clockings. And when somebody said flat out that you were a fool to run at Night Owl, and thereupon dug for odds money, and another for daylight money at two hundred yards, you grinned and said, "Difference of opinions is what makes a horse race." And, whereupon, you pointed out how Rebel outbroke the speedy Diamond Dick, and you didn't see how you could pass up those odds and the daylight money, too, so let Jason Carter hold the stakes.

In addition, it was helpful to have a friendly townsman such as Carter placing bets for the outfit, always getting odds, never even money.

On Wednesday, Dude came to town for that purpose and tied up in front of the Tremont House, choosing an hour prior to the regular afternoon sally from the courthouse square, when the bar was generally empty of patrons. So it was today.

"Tell me about this Night Owl stud," Dude began.

Jason Carter ran a towel inside a glass and out, rubbing, polishing, and hung the towel over his thick arm. The look in his eyes projected pure sympathy and not a little puzzlement. "You're sure you want to know, Mr. McQuinn?"

"It's Dude — remember?"

"Mean you don't know?"

"All I know is that Night Owl is said to be very fast."

"That — and unbeaten. That includes unofficial outings against Texas Rose and Diamond Dick."

"Fast company there."

Carter resumed his polishing.

"Go on. Tell me more. I can take it."

"He stands sixteen hands, weighs over fourteen hundred pounds."

Dude blinked. *Bigger than the Judge.* He said, "Bigger than Rebel, all right."

"And faster."

"Oh, we'll see."

"Night Owl's favorite lick is the half mile, which he runs consistently in or under forty-eight seconds."

"But we're going three hundred."

"He's burned that in sixteen flat."

Dude stared hard at his glass. "What you know about his breeding?"

"Top blood on both sides. The colonel bought him as a yearling in Louisiana. They say it took a wad big enough to choke a Missouri mule, and the colonel is not one to get reckless with money. Night Owl is by Night Runner and his dam is Miss Blue Owl. Guess you've heard of 'em?"

Nodding: "Speed, speed, speed."

"Why'd you take on Night Owl, Mr. McQuinn? You don't have a chance." There was that puzzled look again.

"Our horse will be at his peak, come post time. You saw him take the break from Diamond

Dick? The colonel says that's the only time it's ever happened."

"I saw the race. I saw your horse fade badly the last hundred yards, too."

"We're working on that." Sometimes it was difficult to sound convincing when the man was honest, like this Jason. Dude leaned in. "Wonder if you'd place a few bets for us, old friend?"

"If you insist on losing your money."

"I want odds."

"No trouble there. The courthouse-square bunch is still looking for fresh money." A great embarrassment came over him. "I hate to tell you this, but nobody — nobody — is betting on Rebel."

Handing over the money, Dude spoke softly, almost inaudibly. "Thanks, Jason . . . and if you feel like gambling, you might put a little *dinero* on Rebel, yourself." Then he walked out, his mind closing on the sobering fact of Night Owl's vaunted speed. Anytime you challenged the top horse, you could only hope that yours was feelin' his oats that particular day.

He mounted Blue Grass and swung away, the saddler striking his rocking-chair walk. Dude waved as he passed the idlers on the benches. They waved. Were those cat-ate-the-mouse grins he saw? He grinned back.

An oncoming sight cut short his thinking. A high-stepping chestnut drawing a spick-and-span buggy and, by now, the familiar white-haired lady at the reins. Dude tipped his hat and smiled broadly. She beamed.

Who? he wondered again. Whoever, she was a mighty sweet little ol' lady. Made a man think of home and light in the window, of chicken and dumplings and hot apple pie.

Next Sunday they were heading for camp after galloping Rebel at the track, when the realization jumped to Dude's mind. He turned to the others, the words leaping: "Has it occurred to you-all that we haven't yet seen Night Owl? When do they work him?"

"You're always worryin', Dude," the old man said. "Could be they take him to the track after we're gone. Maybe they don't want us to clock him."

"I didn't catch any sign of activity around the barns," Dude recalled.

No more was said then.

In camp, Uncle Billy fell to rummaging through his medicine chest, and Dude to tallying the outfit's funds, shrinking by the day as he rode in with more money for Jason to bet. Fretting, he drew out his memorandum book and the pencil stub, sharpened it with his pocketknife, and while he figured this way and that, Coyote Walking took his parfleche from under the wagon seat and disappeared behind the wagon. The parfleche was a rectangular-shaped box of stiff-dressed rawhide, painted various bright colors, mostly blue, in which the Comanche kept his belongings.

Dude closed his eyes for some moments, wrestling the figures over and over in his head.

Boy, if they didn't win this race they'd be down to grub money. Hearing footsteps, he opened his eyes and sat up abruptly.

A different Coyote Walking stood before him, a boyish-looking Coyote that Dude hadn't seen before. Stuffed into an archaic dark suit, much wrinkled and too small for him, the trousers hanging high water at his ankles above box-toed shoes. A choking black tie and tight gray flannel shirt and broad-brimmed hat, rounded at the crown like a chimney pot, completed the getup.

"Son of a gun, what's this?" Dude made as if to shrink back and raised his hands before his eyes.

Coyote swiped awkwardly at his blue-black hair, cropped at his neck. "My Carlisle School clothes, white father. The hat is mine which I bought. The shoes, which I did not buy, hurt my feet."

"Well you're not goin' back to school, I hope? Thought you said you graduated?"

"I did, with honors. Have you forgotten today is Sunday? This Comanche look-see take he will at one of the white man's medicine houses. I will go there and shake the white man's hand, I will, and white man will shake mine, which I dread, and I will listen, and maybe this Comanche find out he will where those two white men the Night Owl stud are hiding and why, and then another look-see take we all will."

"Coyote, you took the thought right out of my head. Good!"

116

He rode off on a wagon horse to the distant pealing of church bells. The day promised heat.

When he returned, the afternoon was spent and he had the coat slung across his saddle. Not speaking, he hurried out of his schoolday trousers and the box-toed shoes, tore off the choking tie and shirt, and slipped into his worn linsey-woolsey pants and moccasins.

"Well — ?" Uncle Billy spoke up.

Although Coyote Walking was an educated Indian, he was no less on ceremony. For moments he appeared to gather his thoughts, and then, formally, he said, "The white medicine man, the one you call the preacher man, grabbed my hand and shook it again and again until I hurt, and there were other white men there and they too shook my hand and held me like a mean mule and pounded me on the back, saying how glad they were I was saved from my heathen ways." He paused to massage his right hand and flex his fingers. "The medicine man read from his black medicine book and talked so long everybody nodded, like this, and then the medicine man waved his arms and made much loud talk and everybody stood up and the white men and their squaws sang and wailed like coyotes on hill. How strange, to sing when they had no drummers! . . . I wanted to tell them how we Comanches tried the Sun Dance once, long ago, and it didn't work, but might for them — but I did not. We Comanches have manners. We do not interrupt when another person is talking or sing-

ing. And I wanted to tell them how we Comanches seek *puha,* which is power, and go way off
on hill, taking only one buffalo robe, one bone
pipe, and some tobacco, staying alone four days
and four nights, which does work — but I did
not, for the medicine man was talking when the
other whites weren't singing and clapping their
hands, like this." He ceased clapping to rub his
right hand once more.

"Get to the point, Coyote," Uncle Billy said.
"What did you find out about Night Owl?"

A ceremonious pause. Dude, although as impatient as Uncle Billy, had learned from Coyote
that you can't hurry an Indian any more than
you can the sun. And so he waited, and Coyote
said:

"Some white men can be generous. They
shook my hand again these white men, every
one, even harder than before, and invited me to
big feast. Then they rushed to their wagons and
buggies and the medicine man insisted that I
ride beside his buggy, which I did. . . . Now there
are many things I do not understand about the
white man's ways. Their medicine man drove a
poor horse and his buggy was held together with
much rawhide, and he was as lean as a winter
wolf. That man was hungry, that medicine man,
he was, because he kept talking about fried
chicken, which made me feel sick; for fowl is
tabu among us Comanches, who as you know
are all very brave. Man who eats fowl will become cowardly and run from his enemies just as

118

the fowl flees from those who pursue him."

He paused again. "On the way to the feast we rode by a place you white men call farm, a place where you tear up Grandmother Earth with iron thing you call plow, and there was race track there and road leading up to some white man's lodge. It was so big, this lodge, I felt small when I rode past it."

"Uh-oh," Dude said. "That track — you're gettin' warm, Coyote."

"As a matter of fact — as you would say, white father — I was very hot in my white man's clothes. These white people went into some big woods not far from that white man's lodge and had their big feast there where it was cool."

"Did you sample that fried chicken?" Dude asked, listening with a smile.

Coyote turned disdainful eyes on him. "I did not. This Comanche devil in belly does not want nor coward be. I ate bread and potatoes. . . . After the white people had eaten everything, and while everybody was singing and wailing again and clapping their hands, like this, I walked through the woods and came to that track. There I saw nice red barn and corral. . . . you know how white men always keep their horses close to their lodges so their horses can't graze on the prairie and be free like Comanche horses? . . . In this corral I saw one big horse. A very big horse. A mouse-colored horse." He looked to Uncle Billy for help. "Grandfather, what is it you white men call this color of horse?"

"*Grulla*. From the Spanish, meaning 'crane.' They're a kind of bluish gray. A mouse dun. You get that color from a mix of liver chestnut, mahogany bay, and some black horses. It's right handsome. And don't call me grandfather."

"Two men guarded this big horse. Pretty soon I saw one man dressed all in white leave the lodge and come to the barn and talk to these guards. That man was the man the colonel calls son-in-law and Cassius Pyle." Coyote Walking folded his arms, a sign that he was finished. "That is all I know."

"That's plenty," Dude said. "Mighty good work, Coyote. Proves it pays to go to church." He pursed his lips and frowned, focusing his eyes on Uncle Billy. "Why don't they use that nice track near town, where they stall Texas Rose and Diamond Dick? Why hide anything, if they are hiding something? We know Night Owl's never been headed."

The old man grinned cynically and Dude saw the competitive glitter light up his trackless face. "It's an old play, wrinkles all over it. They want us to sweat. Else they're hiding something about that stud. Some peculiarity he has. I told you this is a slick bunch, Dude, boy. . . . At first light tomorrow morning let's be posted in that picnic grove, primed for an eyeball look-see at fast Mr. Night Owl. I want to see 'im break, and I want to see 'im run."

Long before daylight they were on the road,

Coyote Walking taking them roundabout through the grass-scented murk as the windless night hung on. They tied up in the timber, well away from the house and barn, and moved to the edge of the woods by the track and waited.

After about an hour, Dude saw a cone of light in the big house and another light fix the location of a smaller house behind the big one. Soon he caught the pleasant smell of woodsmoke. Down by the barn, lanternlight glowed. A wedge of pink flushed the sky.

As if on that signal, a white figure left the big house. Another figure departed the smaller house and joined the other man and they walked to the barn. There Dude lost sight of them.

Very shortly, a smaller man led a horse out onto the track. Forthwith, a second horse appeared, followed by the figure in white. A voice began bellowing orders. It seemed to belong to the man in white. That, Dude figured, would be Cassius Pyle.

The horses started around, walking, their jockeys riding high. At the turn they began trotting, working side by side, coming along briskly. Reaching the straightaway on this side, they galloped. Suddenly the morning blushed.

"There's your mouse dun on the outside," Uncle Billy told them. "They're bein' mighty careful with that horse. He sure looks big and stout."

Before Dude's eyes, the oval track shaped as a copy of the Flat Rock course, minus railing, the far straightaway covering three eighths of a mile.

The horses galloped on around to Pyle, standing on the track. He motioned the jockeys toward the head of the stretch and followed them a way and stopped, taking the position of starter. As the horses turned and walked up, lapped, he shouted and dropped his hand and the horses broke.

A short distance and the jockeys wheeled their mounts and rode back, and Pyle, his bellowing voice raucous and demanding, started them again. Strong daylight bathed the track.

Without warning, Uncle Billy stood up. "I've got it!"

Dude yanked him down. "They'll see you!"

"I've got it!" he chuckled, kneeling between Dude and Coyote, eyes glued on the horses.

The horses were walking up again. This time when they broke, they kept on running. The mouse-colored horse shot ahead and lengthened his lead, steadily picking up daylight, his strides long and powerful. At three hundred yards the jockeys eased up. Both horses were being walked to the barn before Uncle Billy spoke again:

"Night Owl's not extra quick on his getaway — that's what they're schooling him on against that other horse, after what Rebel did to Diamond Dick — and he's got one bad habit. He veers to his right every time. Notice how they put the other horse on the left, so they won't bump. But, boy, can he run! Dude, we're gonna flip for sides Saturday. Better pray we don't get the right side, or Mr. Big might plow right over our horse."

"It's fixin' to get full daylight," Dude said. "Let's go!"

Dawn, Friday morning before the race:

The outfit scouted up and down the road for passersby before taking Judge Blair out. For the next ten minutes or so they walked and trotted him, and, last, galloped him three hundred yards, the distance he would run. No breezing this late.

Watching the workout, Dude did not spy the oncoming shape of the vehicle coming from town until late. Buggy, buckboard, or wagon? He couldn't tell at this distance. "Coyote," he hissed, "get the Judge off the road behind the wagon."

Coyote was already reining away into the woods.

The vehicle became rapidly visible through the dingy light. It was a one-horse buggy. A high-stepping horse. A chestnut. A white head loomed in the driver's seat.

Dude relaxed, and when the elderly lady pulled up, he tipped his hat and said, "Good morning, ma'am. Aren't you out a little early?"

"Not fo' me." She was a tiny little slip of a thing, and her somewhat high voice, so kind and motherly reached him like a sweetly sung hymn. "Ah'm an early riser, and Ah promised an old friend out in th' country to help at her quiltin' bee today."

"I hope you have a pleasant day."

"Oh, Ah shall, Ah shall. Every day is about what we mere mortals make it. Early mornin' birdsong is m' greatest delight. My, how sound carries this time of day. In fact, drivin' up, Ah'd swear Ah heard a hoss gallopin' somewhere."

"You certainly did, ma'am. We just finished working our horse here on the road."

"Oh, a racehoss!" Her voice trilled pure delight. "Ah love hosses, especially racehosses."

"That's a mighty fine buggy horse you have there."

"Thank you, young man. You appreciate fine hossflesh, that is evident." She turned, glancing casually toward camp. Across the dimness, only Rebel and Coyote and the team were visible. Coyote, bless him, was going through the motions of giving Rebel a thorough rubdown. "Ah do believe Ah recognize that dark bay yonder. Ah know! You are the gentlemen who've matched Night Owl."

"We are. That's our horse Rebel there."

A flurry of haste seemed to come over her, just when Dude thought to introduce Uncle Billy. "Ah must not keep you gentlemen from yo' chores. Good luck tomorrow, even though Night Owl is our local champion."

"Thank you, ma'am. You are very kind."

She favored him with her sweet smile and, chirruping to the eager chestnut, shook the reins and drove on, soon traveling at a lively clip.

Uncle Billy, his eyes following the buggy, said,

124

"A quilting bee? I don't believe it."

"You say I'm always worrying. Well, I say you're always suspicious."

"You bet I am before a horse race."

"For your information, a quilting bee starts early and lasts all day. It's a social gathering, where the old ladies exchange news."

"News? You mean gossip." He gazed after the buggy again. "I still don't like it, Dude. An old lady — alone in her buggy on a country road at five-thirty in the morning — drives up just when a man *happens* to be workin' his horse."

"A coincidence," Dude said.

"Tell you one thing. Tonight I aim to keep my gun handy and we'd better hold the horses in close to the wagon."

CHAPTER 8

Twice during the long night, Dude, in his bedroll,
under the wagon, heard the old man scout out to
the road and come back. Again he heard him, circling the wagon, and sensed more than heard him
go into the woods behind the horses and stay
there a long time. Around midnight he felt a
touch on his forehead, at which Dude pulled on
boots and took his turn on watch. If at a track,
they would be sleeping in Judge Blair's stall, in
case somebody tried to slip in and fix him. There
were many ways: pounding on cannon bones to
buck his shins so he'd resent running tomorrow;
jabbing the powerful forearm muscles with a
knife-blade; chloroform or laudanum on a cloth
held to the wide nostrils. It took very little to
throw a horse off.

There were no sounds that should not have
been. Only the wind bothered Dude. He could
feel it changing, beginning to fret and whip out
of the west, bringing a patter of rain. He groaned
aloud, thinking of that dire complication. But
when the hour came to wake up Coyote Walking, the wind and the rain had stopped.

Race day dawned. The windless sky was overcast and a bank of dark clouds lurked off there to the west, threatening, not moving. It might rain, it might not.

Uncle Billy studied the sky without comment and went to see about the horses. Returning, he dipped a sparing ration of oats into Judge Blair's *morral*. Rebel and the other horses would get their full feedings. The old horseman had drawn into his usual shell of taciturnity before a big race, turning over in his mind, Dude knew, every possible occurrence as he set about his chores. Rain would be the worst turn, and rain or not they had to run or forfeit.

After breakfast, Coyote Walking examined the racing bridle and reins inch by inch, and likewise the girth on the light racing saddle. That done, he sewed a tear in his moccasins. Come post time, he would be stripped to breechcloth and moccasins, a primeval sight that invariably seemed to bother the other side, as if an Indian might possess some savage advantage gained through harmony with nature. More truth than not, Dude thought, something that Coyote himself could not explain, for he seemed to flow with the motion of a horse, to be an extension of the horse.

While Coyote sewed, Uncle Billy dug into the depths of the medicine chest, carefully pouring and measuring and mixing special ingredients that, unlike his cures, he had not revealed even to Coyote and Dude, reserved for today's special circumstances. Putting bottles away, Uncle Billy led Judge Blair and Rebel into the woods behind the wagon and, coming back, took two jars and a long paint brush much like an artist's and returned to the horses.

Dude got out his memorandum book and pencil, thinking of Jason Carter and that this final morning should find the Tremont House buzzing with local fans eager to place odds on Night Owl. Now and then a wagon or buggy rattled by on the dusty road. His thoughts kept tracking back to the weather and its importance, and what had happened in that little southeastern Kansas town when rain began to fall just as the race ended. Luckily, Dude had the winnings in hand, and the outfit's wagon, camp gear packed and the team hitched, was close by. They'd better do that today. . . .

Hearing Uncle Billy leading the horses back, he stood up and stared at the blaze-faced, white-socked horse the old man led around in front of the wagon. "Figured you'd be finished by now," Dude said, wondering at the delay.

"I am."

"But this is the Judge."

"Better look again." The clear blue eyes, quite bright and relishing, hurled a secret amusement.

"It's Rebel!" Dude said, after another moment. "He looks just like Judge Blair."

"You finally figured that out. So the job will stand inspection. Reckon I've still got my old touch; been a while, you know. . . . Another thing. You never know. Just in case. Believe

128

we'd better pack up and take the wagon to the track. Have everything ready if we have to hit for the tules."

"Been thinking the same thing."

In moments the old man led the second horse around. "What do you fellas think?" he asked, touching Judge Blair's forehead, now a dark bay. "This stuff's not dry yet."

"He's the spittin' image of Rebel," Dude pronounced, rounding the gelding to look for any telltale white. Judge Blair's generous markings made the changeover all the more difficult. The white socks extended from the cornet halfway to the knee on the forelegs and halfway to the hock on the back legs. Dude could see no variation in color where Uncle Billy had dyed the white. And if there was any unlikeness in conformation between the two horses, it was Judge Blair's front. A difference, Uncle Billy had once remarked, that only a mother's eye might notice.

After taking his own look-see, Coyote said, "Grandfather Billy, I hereby bestow a new name on you. A Comanche name. Your new name is going to be He Paints the Horses."

Caught off guard, the old man was surprised and gratified, for only a moment, however. Behind a covering gruffness, he said, "That beats callin' me grandfather," and critically examined his handiwork on Judge Blair. "Takes a damned sight longer to dry than it does to come off when wet. Just hope the weather holds."

They began packing the wagon.

Noon.

More farm families passed on the road to town.

The three of them stood at the edge of the woods and observed the unchanging sky, dark and threatening. "Wish our race wasn't the last one," the old man said, "but maybe this will hold off." They came back and waited, idling around camp.

At two o'clock Dude mounted Blue Grass and the other two climbed to the wagon seat, the blaze-faced Rebel and the bay-faced Judge Blair tied behind. As the outfit swung out on the road, a distant clap of thunder sounded. And as the track and the stands and the barns shaped before them, Dude picked up the unbroken hum of the people milling there, as of bees swarming, and his own excitement, subdued until now, began to awaken. A roar went up when a race finished and the voices fell away like a receding wave. Sunday racing was considered sinful, but Saturday racing, like today, was community enjoyment, with the betting ignored.

Dude led the outfit behind the stands and crossed the road that ran on to skirt Flat Rock before striking westward, the road they had decided as the quickest route to take immediately after the race. Their plan was simple and irrevocable: If a hard rain fell minutes before the race and the dye started running, Uncle Billy and Coyote would quietly pull out with the horses, while Dude informed the other side of the forfeit, claiming a lame horse. But if rain wasn't falling at post time, but near, the race was on; and if rain began falling when the race started, Coyote was to continue on as if he couldn't control his spirited runner. Uncle Billy would follow with the team and wagon, while Dude collected the bets.

A calamitous possibility fell upon Dude. What if Judge Blair lost? It happened to the best of horses. But the Judge was consistent, and wasn't he the fastest horse in south Texas? That reminder was always a comfort. Only performance counted.

Circling around, they pulled up on the grassy paddock area close to the barns among horsemen's wagons. Here and there country owners and trainers and jockeys watched over their nervous mounts, quieting them, or walked them back and forth, cooling them down, or saddled with extreme care.

Uncle Billy had scarcely stepped down from the wagon when Jason Carter walked over. In slouch hat and sack coat and yellowish-brown trousers, he seemed a new man. Gone, Dude perceived, was the bartender's mien of impassive weariness. Jason Carter was actually enjoying himself today.

He said, "Two more match races before yours. They're trying to hurry along before it rains. Will Sawyer is starting your race. He starts all the races."

"Is he fair?" Dude worried. The first two races hadn't mattered, inasmuch as they knew Rebel couldn't win. Today everything might hang on the break.

Carter shrugged. "All I can tell you is that Night Owl has yet to lose a race here." He rubbed the underside of his nose. "Say, I'm out of money. You gentlemen want me to place some more? I can get you three to one. Took some of that, myself. Couldn't pass it up."

"Let it ride," Dude told him, thinking of how much was out. And why had he insisted on that much forfeit money? If not for that, and it rained, they could plead a sick or lame horse without loss. He looked up at the sky. It was turning darker and the air felt thick and damp. He couldn't remember when he'd been so worried before a race and when so much rode on the outcome.

"Another thing," Carter obliged. "The right lane is badly cupped. See you later."

"Look over there," Uncle Billy murmured to Dude, a note of caution underlying his voice. "That must be the town marshal."

Dude looked. Across the way three men were conversing: Colonel Bushrod, son-in-law Pyle, and a heavyset individual on whose vest hung a star as big as a tin cup. The two muscular collectors flanked Night Owl's stall.

"They're coming over," Dude said.

"Good. We're gonna flip for sides — or else!"

Smiling and affable, the colonel shook hands

132

all around. "Gentlemen, this heah is Marshal Sug Vance. He's watchin' the barns. Marshal, meet Dr. Lockhart and Mistah McQuinn." Vance's handshake had the clamminess of a damp dishrag, and his bulging eyes, set close together in a blank face, made Dude think of a dead fish. Vance grunted a greeting.

"Would you gentlemen," the colonel went on, "like to discuss conditions of th' race at th' track office?"

"It's just a formality," explained Pyle, equally affable. "So there'll be no misunderstanding."

Such formality, it cut through Dude's mind, hadn't come up when they ran at Texas Rose and Diamond Dick. He said, "We'll be glad to talk about the race. We don't want Will Sawyer to call the break unless the horses are head to head or close to it, and we figure it's only fair and square to flip for sides."

"Agreeable with us," the colonel drawled. "Son-in-law, you go fetch Will."

At the office beneath the stands, which, if it was an office, Dude had not seen its likes before — no more than a shed, no desk or chairs, not even the inevitable spittoon — they began to go over the details. The distance of three hundred yards. The bets to be paid immediately after the race.

Agreed — until Dude broached the break.

Will Sawyer, pulling at the front of his long-tailed frock coat, momentarily lost his dignified air. "Are you lodgin' an official complaint as

133

to how I've started your horse and Colonel Bushrod's . . . and, uh, Mr. Pyle's horses?" he demanded, tactfully adding the last, the point of his goateed chin tilting at Dude.

"Not a-tall," Dude replied, buttering him up. "We didn't lose at the break, it was down the stretch. Just so the horses' heads are about even. That's all we want, Mr. Sawyer."

"I'm not in the habit of callin' the break if the horses aren't well lapped," Sawyer replied testily.

"That raises another point," Pyle put in, aggressively rolling his white-duck shoulders. "Do you intend to turn your horse again at the break?"

So they had caught that. "How can I say, Mr. Pyle? It's up to ol' Rebel. How he feels. What his mood is. You never can tell. Sometimes he breaks straight, as he did against Texas Rose. Sometimes he turns a little, as he did against Diamond Dick."

"And all the time I thought it was the jockey who controlled the horse," Pyle said, his voice dry.

Dude shrugged. "All we ask is a close head-to-head start."

Uncle Billy was hacking his head up and down, short, jerky motions that told Dude to go on, to stand firm, that this wasn't the time to join the local benevolent society.

"A head-to-head start or call the horses back," Dude insisted.

"What are we arguing about?" Pyle asked, genial for him. "That's all we want, too."

"And that is exactly what both horses will get," Sawyer stated. His reddening face was taut.

A feeling took Dude. Will Sawyer was fair and square. Well, maybe.

"Theah'll be no fuss from us about th' break," Colonel Bushrod said, his judicial tone final. "Now, Mistah McQuinn, you said you desired to flip fo' sides. So do we. Let's git to it." He took a coin from his pocket, a half dollar.

"Mind if I take a look?" Dude asked, neighborly about it.

Bushrod drew back, his affable expression retreating, now forming again. He held out the coin.

Dude turned it over. A genuine half dollar, it was. Not like the trick coins he'd run across now and then, just when the other side was set to call the toss. He handed it back, smiling. "Thank you, Colonel. Just so everybody's satisfied."

Colonel Bushrod, exhibiting tolerance, passed the coin to Sawyer and said courteously, "Ah should like fo' Mistah McQuinn to call th' toss if he so desires."

"Very well. You call it in the air, Mr. McQuinn," Sawyer said, and flipped.

As the spinning coin reached its zenith, Dude called, "Heads. "

Sawyer caught the coin in his open palm. Everyone leaned in, staring.

"Tails it is, gentlemen," Sawyer announced. "You've won the toss, Colonel Bushrod. You may take your choice of sides."

"We choose th' left side," the colonel said, his manner once again gracious, bowing first to Sawyer, then to Dude and Uncle Billy.

"Fair enough," Dude said, swallowing and bowing in turn, and, with Uncle Billy, went outside.

"Means we have to break on top," the old man said.

Dude, nodding, studied the threatening sky. Those dark clouds, hanging like hammers across the western sky, were moving ever nearer. He compressed his lips and tried to estimate the time left before the storm hit, which it was surely going to do.

At that moment, above the noise of the restless crowd, Dude heard shouts and a clattering down by the barns. It lasted briefly, muffled by the throaty roar from the stands as a race started, and the rapidfire of hooves, and, in moments, the crescendo of the finish, and the dying away of the shouting tumult. Dude thought, One more race before ours.

Moving through the jam of people at the lower end of the stands, and on to the barns, Dude and Uncle Billy reached the wagon. The discussion at the office had consumed some minutes, longer than Dude liked to be away from his horse before a race.

The old man, eagle eyes only for Judge Blair, drew the racing bridle over the dark bay nose and head, slipped home the snaffle bit, brushed the stout back and draped on the blanket, which he smoothed carefully, and laid on the light saddle and cinched up. Turning to Coyote Walking:

"Lead him around."

While Dude and Uncle Billy watched, Coyote led the gelding away from the barns and out onto the level stretch of grass. Judge Blair's calm disposition was never more evident than amid the coming and going prior to a race and during the tense moments leading up to the break. An odd alarm sounded in Dude's mind. Today his horse acted nervous. He kept shaking his head. Dude attributed it to the boom of thunder he was hearing regularly and the threat of the rising wind.

Jason Carter joined them. "There's enough Night Owl money around here today to start a bank."

"We've placed about all we can," Dude said, as the weather and the horse crowded his mind.

"May be in your favor if it rains. They say Night Owl's never run in the mud."

Dude gave him a pained look. "Don't believe rain would exactly favor us either."

Turning away, he saw Coyote pause and stare inquiringly at the horse, go on and pause again and stare, bewildered. All at once Coyote led the gelding back. "Something's wrong," he told them. His dark eyes, again on the horse, now held mounting dismay.

"What!" Uncle Billy rushed to the horse, Dude behind him.

"He's not right," the Comanche said. "He acts

funny. Like something strange bothers him."

Uncle Billy opened the gelding's mouth and peered. When Judge Blair shook his head, the old man examined the fox ears and, painstakingly, the snaffle bit and the nose-band and the cheek straps, the front strap across the forehead, the headstall, and the throatlatch. He stepped back, his face clouding. "Coyote," he said, worried, "did you leave him while we were gone?"

"Just . . . just for a little bit, grandfather."

"What!"

"There was this runaway. Old white woman in buggy. Her horse spooked. She came right by here, yelling for help. I ran out and caught that horse by the bridle — stopped him. Old woman she looked faint. I held her horse till she came to. She thanked me and drove away, that old woman did."

"Old woman in buggy?" Dude repeated, a revel of suspicion threading up through him.

"Yes — that little white-haired woman who drives fancy chestnut. You know, the one who came by camp early yesterday morning."

"There's only one little white-haired lady around Flat Rock that drives a fancy chestnut," Carter broke in. "That's Aunt Lucinda — the colonel's sister."

"Coyote," Uncle Billy said, not ungently, as he might speak to an erring boy, "did you see anybody around our horse?"

"Some men from the barns rushed out to help. I got to the buggy first. Those men were behind me — between me and our horse." He was being careful, even here, Dude saw, not to say Judge Blair's name in front of Jason Carter.

"That ties in," Uncle Billy said gravely. "I hate to admit it, boys, but somebody has fixed our horse. And, for the life of me, I can't figure out what they did." Shaken and furious, he stared helplessly at the head-shaking gelding.

Coyote was beside himself. "Grandfather, it's the way he breathes. It's not right. You didn't look up his nose."

With both hands holding up the gelding's head, the old man peered into the left nostril. For a sudden he wheeled to the wagon and flung open the medicine chest, pawing aside bottles and tinware. He whirled around, holding a small, pincerlike tool. His voice fell harsh and pressing:

"Get him behind the wagon. Don't want those crooks at the barns to see what we're doing." And when Coyote had led the horse there: "Hold his head up, Coyote, Dude. He's not gonna like these tweezers. There! Hold, 'im, now. Use some muscle — he's no colt. Bear up. Now! Hold 'im there!"

He inserted the tweezers solicitously, probing. His fingers closed. With great care, he withdrew the tweezers. Out came a spongy ball, fluffy and yellow, which he stuck down in his shirt pocket. Muttering, he shifted to the other nostril. "Damn it to hell, hold 'im! He's actin' like a pampered horse." He probed gently, closing the tweezers, and pulled out another yellow ball, exulting:

"Sponges! Thunderation, they tried to fix our horse with sponges so he couldn't get his wind! Been a coon's age since I've seen this cute little wrinkle." He whipped about. "Dude, bet all we've got left. Give it to Jason. Not a word to anybody, Jason. Let 'em think they've still got us fixed. Understand?"

Dude dug out the last of the outfit's bankroll and shoved it at Jason, who legged for the stands.

"Now," said Dude, recovering somewhat, "we know what that pow-wow in the so-called office was all about and why daddy-in-law and son-in-law were so friendly: to draw us away while sweet little Aunt Lucinda pulled runaway act on Coyote. Guess we know too what happened to that Johnny McCue colt."

Two horsemen hurriedly led their sprinters by for the next-to-last race. Dude smelled rain on the wind. Time seemed to hang endlessly while he watched the two horses parade past the stands, go to the other end of the straightaway, and turn, and dance toward the starting line. One horse was acting up. He broke too soon and the starter sent them back.

Dude squirmed at the precious moments lost.

The horses approached again, lapped this time. The starter dropped his hand. The horses tore away like angry demons, setting off the crowd's shouting. A drumming fleetness and the race was over, and the winner, requiring an excessive amount of time, it seemed, was led before the stands; and finally, to Dude's ease, he

140

saw the announcer coming on his fat gray horse, reining up and facing the stands, and calling the last race in his foghorn voice. A prolonged build-up of which Dude caught only fragments on the wind:

". . . Night Owl . . . owned and trained by Colonel C. Travis Bushrod . . . and Mr. Cassius Pyle . . . both of Flat Rock . . . running against Rebel . . ." The fitful, moist wind, gusting now and then, snatched the trailing words.

Dude, turning to mount Blue Grass, delayed at Uncle Billy's voice: "Wait. Let them go first. Let 'em sweat. I got a hunch they're as scared of the mud as we are of the rain."

Across, Dude saw Night Owl saddled and primed, and Pyle, mounted on the lead horse, heading the stud away, the gnat-sized jockey in the irons.

"All right," the old man said, once again the veteran horseman in his competitive element, making his studied moves. And after Dude and Coyote had mounted: "You know what to do, Coyote, if it rains, which it's sure gonna. Stay on the west road. Use your own judgment when to pull up. I'll follow soon as I can — me an' Dude. . . . Now remember to keep the Judge head to head up to the line. Remember that Night Owl always breaks to his right. You want to be long gone when that big stud busts over there. It's gonna be close, boys. The race will hang on the break. . . . Dude, if you have any trouble collecting from this bunch of crooks, I'll be right handy. All's fair in love and war an' horse racin' — that Cervantes fella be damned." He patted his belt where, unnoticed till now, Dude saw the handgun. The clear blue eyes sparkled. Catching that anticipatory gleam, Dude had the uncomfortable sensation that Uncle Billy would welcome trouble.

"No, you won't," Dude said. "Your job will be to get Rebel out of here and down the road. Can't have a blaze-faced horse turning dark bay." He didn't understand why, but in tight places like this he always felt protective toward the old man, despite his evident self-reliance.

They rode off to a swelling ovation for the local champion. Dude, leading Judge Blair, came to the stands, aware of the thick silence greeting his horse. Silence, save for a derisive voice hooting, "Slowpoke Rebel! Slowpoke Rebel!" whereupon Dude tipped his hat.

Just then the wind kicked up and Dude tensed as thunder bellowed west of the barns. Son of a gun, it was coming! He led off faster and moments later, nearing the starting line, when he took in the lead rope, he felt the first hiss of rain. Furthermore, Judge Blair's lane, the right-hand one, was more deeply cupped than he had thought likely.

Nearby, Cassius Pyle sat his lead horse like an impresario.

Will Sawyer, hurrying, motioned the jockeys to walk up for the start.

The jockeys headed the horses about. They

advanced together. At once the boy put Night Owl to the fore, too fast, challenging Coyote to close if he could. The distance was too much. Wisely, Coyote held up so that the horses were not lapped. They crossed the line like that, and Sawyer waved the riders back to try again.

Dude was sweating. The mouse dun was a big tall horse carrying a heap of muscle where it counted. He loomed over the Judge.

Side by side came the horses. *Stay with him this time, Coyote.* When the boy sent Night Owl ahead again, seeking the advantage, Coyote matched him, head to head now, sticking there. The horses looked even-Stephen. Coyote turned his horse a little.

Sawyer shouted *"Go!"* his hand falling at the same instant.

A fair start, the mouse-colored stud and the dark bay gelding leaping out, the Judge taking the break. Suddenly it was raining and the sky was firing salvos of thunder.

In wrenching alarm, Dude saw the Judge stumble and start down and Coyote jerking his head up, still going. The other horse was veering out, a mass of bluish-gray muscle. Dude's breath hung.

But Judge Blair wasn't there. He had his feet again. He was running like a scalded cat, those fox ears laid back, a low, dark bay blue slicing through the sheen of rain.

But the mouse-dun horse could run also, and he had heart. The boy straightened him. He was running flat out, taking great, ground-gulping strides. He reached Judge Blair's tail. He reached Coyote's stirrup. They ran like that for a hundred yards or more, locked in stride, while the rain slashed and the crowd screamed.

Dude's perspective became distorted, the horses just smears of violent motion. Was the mouse dun moving up?

And then Dude heard Coyote's unmistakable screech, a savage thing linking man and horse. A flash of time and Dude saw them rushing past the judges and was conscious of the din of the crowd suddenly tapering off, and he dared hope.

He sat his horse for another count, then plunged down the track, Pyle racing alongside him. Down the course the boy was pulling up the dun. Beyond, ahead, Coyote and Judge Blair still ran through the rain's green curtain. Coyote was flapping his arms and tugging at the apparent runaway's reins.

Dude pulled to a halt by the judges, huddled against the stands for cover. He called, "Didn't my horse win it?" though their faces told him.

One nodded, lamely. "But Night Owl was right on his tail, coming up. Another fifty yards he'd've caught your horse."

"Like hell!" Dude threw back and rode on whooping. *Sired by Lightning out of Thunderstorm.*

A vigilance began to temper Dude. He slowed his horse to a walk, searching. The wagon and Rebel were still there, seen dimly through the sheeting rain; but no Uncle Billy. Dude bunched

144

his lips. He spotted the colonel walking slowly for the barns, seemingly oblivious of the storm. Pyle was at his horse's stall, dismounted, and the jockey, shaking his head in disbelief, was riding up on Night Owl.

Riding slower, Dude saw the colonel walk up to Pyle and mutter something and he saw Pyle nod. Where were the two toughs? And that tin-star marshal, Sug Vance? At this time and place you controlled your hurry, but you also presented a firm front. When collecting after a race, Dude had never carried a handgun. Today, for the first time, he wished he did. That caution clung to him, building, as he dismounted and stepped under the stall's overhang.

"Well, Colonel . . ."

Before, after Rebel's two losses, Dude had paid immediately, without being "hit up" for the money, as they said around the bush tracks when a loser was slow in paying. Obviously, there would be no voluntary payoff today. Colonel Bushrod didn't speak. Neither did Pyle. Dude had the inkling that they were waiting. A knowing that sounded within him a moment later when he heard the crunch of boots behind him and, turning his head, saw the two collectors and the marshal.

Dude eased back two steps, a position that placed them on his right and the colonel and Pyle on his left. The boy jockey, no part of this, was unsaddling. Dude said distinctly:

"I came for my winnings, Colonel."

Bushrod said nothing, but his eyes were darting. He wet his lips. He drawled, "Theah's some question about th' race," without his customary politeness.

"Some question? I just saw the judges. They said my horse won. Nothing was wrong. I want that money, Colonel."

"You see, a foul was committed down th' stretch. Yo' hoss cut in on Night Owl when he tried to pass. That's a foul, sah."

"Foul?" Dude drove a ridiculing laugh at him. "Why," he roared, "your horse was at my horse's tail when they finished. My horse took the break, stumbled, and still was never headed."

"Just th' same, Cassius and I intend to file a protest with Marshal Vance, heah. He has jurisdiction, since th' track is on city land."

"Your son-in-law there told me you owned everything here."

"Not th' land."

He was, Dude realized, being drawn into a roundabout argument designed only to delay and circumvent the payoff. "Colonel," he said, "you're trying to welch on me. I want that money and I want it now. Pronto, as we say in Texas."

Other horsemen, drawn by the quarrelsome voices, began to drift over and watch.

Vance bellied forward, his voice as deadpan as his face: "You threatenin' the colonel? I'll have to take you into custody till this is settled all due and proper. Come on."

"Whoa, now, Marshal. You listen to me. I'm

making a charge. Somebody tried to fix our horse while the colonel and Pyle drew us away to talk about the race. I'm accusing them here and now!"

"We deny that," Pyle shouted, startled. "Where's your proof?"

"Right here. Everybody look at these sponges."

Dude wrenched around at the sound of Uncle Billy's cool voice. The old man, who apparently had stepped up with the other horsemen, had withheld his entrance until it counted most. He held out the two fluffy sponges for Vance's inspection. His handgun bulged at his belt under his shirt.

"Some railbird with a lot bet on the race did that," Pyle blustered, trying to swagger it off.

"Pay off," Dude told him, "or we'll spread this all over Flat Rock. We'll ruin you. I'll start at the courthouse square, from there across to the Tremont House bar. It was a clean race. Ask these men."

"It was," a man said.

The colonel laid his glance on the horsemen, then on Pyle. "Although we are innocent of this unfounded claim, I guess we have no recou'se. Pay him, son-in-law. Pay him."

Pyle rolled his shoulders, a gesture that spelled unwillingness. He was painfully slow about it as he dug for the money and paid. Dude counted the greenbacks swiftly. It was there, all of it. He said, "You are true gentlemen," and bowed to the colonel and Vance. *Never press your luck too far. Leave the other side some vestige of right, no matter how slick they tried to be, when you've gained the upper hand.* "Just a little misunderstanding," he added for the watchers' benefit, and, catching Uncle Billy's eagle eye, he said, "Let's go back to camp," and, facing into the driving rain, he stepped to the saddle.

By the time he turned Blue Grass, the old man was bounding for the wagon, nimbly on the seat and slapping the reins, Rebel trailing at the rear on a halter rope.

Dude's pulse jumped when he saw the horse. White dye was running down his face, rapidly returning him to dark bay. Dude reined Blue Grass alongside, between Rebel and the barns, and when Dude glanced over his shoulder, Pyle and the colonel were talking earnestly to the two collectors and Vance. Maybe it wasn't over yet!

New and sickening doubts struck home as Dude rounded the row of barns. Where was Jason Carter? He had hundreds of their money. Was he part and parcel of this, too? And why had the colonel and Pyle given in so readily unless they planned to get everything back?

Uncle Billy urged the sorrel team to a gallop. Dude saw no signs of pursuit yet. Neither, after covering some distance, did he see Coyote and the Judge ahead.

Little by little, Flat Rock's outer buildings emerged through the green mantle of rain. Onward, Dude saw they were coming to where the road turned westward from town.

In the fork of the road two horsemen waited,

their mounts' heads lowered against the down-pour. Dude recognized Coyote and Judge Blair, once more a blaze-faced horse. The other rider on the claybank he couldn't place — wide hat, slickered from neck to boots, saddle bags loaded, and bedroll tied behind the cantle. Smelling trouble, Dude dashed ahead of the wagon.

Across the slanting rain a face formed beneath the broad hat. A normally putty-colored face turned rosy by excitement. Jason Carter's voice propelled urgency and concern:

"Don't take the west road. They'll expect you to go that way!"

"But where?"

"Right through town, where they'd least look. Then take the north road. Come on!"

Dude saw no alternative. He waved Uncle Billy that way and they raced for town, slipping and slinging mud. When they reached Main Street and turned north, Carter pointed behind them, and, dimly, Dude saw a snarl of riders tearing onto the west-going road. Four riders, which tallied up to son-in-law, the two thugs, and Vance.

Well beyond Flat Rock, they paused to rest the horses.

"The county line is just a couple of miles on," Jason Carter informed them, gathered at the head of the wagon. "You'll be all right once you get there." He fished under his slicker and drew out a loaf-size roll of greenbacks and handed it to Dude. "That three-to-one money fattens up

149

fast. I cleaned up some, myself. Never saw a horse run so fast or change color so fast."

"When you match race horses," Uncle Billy opined, "you either smarten up fast or go back to milkin' cows."

"Or bartending."

They all laughed, after which an awkward silence set in, a depressing silence there in the cold rain. It was time to move on, but nobody stirred. Something of Jason Carter's Tremont House personality seemed to return to him, that mask of impassivity that covered the worth of a true and obliging man.

They were all waiting, Dude sensed, unable to put into words the bond each felt. "What about you, Jason?" he asked quietly. "You were seen riding through town with us. The colonel and Pyle will soon hear about that. You can't go back there."

"I know. I was through this morning, when Pyle found out I was taking bets on your horse. I quit before he could fire me. Just walked out. That made him madder than ever."

"Well, you're welcome to join us," Dude said, and looked at Uncle Billy and Coyote. They nodded.

"I was hoping you might say that," Jason said, his face lighting up.

"So what are we waiting on? Let's get across the county line."

Peace, Dude sighed as they went on, how wonderful it was. Rain or shine.

CHAPTER 9

Buffalo Draw.

That was the name of the little town off there clutched in the palm of the vast prairie world. Looking, Dude felt his hopes rise again. This time, maybe, they could run Judge Blair under his real name; or maybe nobody would even want to match a race. That would be the day! Dude had yet to see a village or town in Texas without its racehorse or two. Or, maybe, they could rest for a week in the shade of these cool live oaks.

Jason Carter, who seemed unable to do enough around camp or on the trail, volunteered to give the town an advance look-see, and Uncle Billy said go ahead, before they showed what horses they carried. The open air and eating Uncle Billy's grub had done wonders for Jason. Gone was his putty color and several inches of tallow around his middle. The sociable, soft-spoken big fellow was as strong as a draft horse. When the wagon overturned crossing a rocky gully, he had righted it alone, and then, a sheepish look overcoming him, excused himself for taking hold so fast. Dude shuddered at the consequences should Jason ever lose his temper. Mountains would move; the prairie would tremble. And he was so doggoned polite. Only this morning, after three days from Flat Rock, had he quit calling everybody *mister*.

He rode off on his claybank saddler and reported back late in the afternoon, as amiable as when he left, the drift of bourbon fumes trailing him, though as steady as a snubbing post.

"Buffalo Draw," he said, "is a town with the hair on. Everybody in the saloons was packing six-shooters and Bowie knives and the bank's all boarded up. Been robbed so many times the banker gave up and moved off to Fort Worth and took up storekeeping. But," he continued cheerfully, "the town boasts one big horse-and-mule barn, one well-equipped blacksmith shop, where the smithy also makes bridle bits and spurs; one saddle shop, one general store, one hotel, the Wranglers' Rest, and the undertaker doubles as the town barber. That saves him the trouble of fetching one all the way from Jacksboro when there's a buryin'."

"How many saloons?" Uncle Billy asked.

"Six."

"How many churches?"

Apology edged across his face. "Just one — and the preacher's left town. Starved out."

"Six saloons. That's the tipoff. A lively trade town always has more saloons than churches."

"Never heard that before," Dude said, to discourage him. "Always heard it was the other way around. The more churches, the better the trade town, and trade means horses and mules. Churches draw respectable people. Churches mean schools. Schools mean —"

"Don't preach! I mean a good horse town. Never saw it fail. Where you got saloons, you got horsemen."

"— And a rowdy element."

The old man stared at him, shocked. "Don't have Texas fever, do you, Dude?"

"I did hear a lot of horse talk," Jason interceded politely. "There's a long straightaway on the other side of town. Place called Parker's Prairie, named after an early settler. Somebody cleared off a five-furlong strip. After that you run into mesquite. These Buffalo Draw boys get around. They've heard tell of Judge Blair. Several said they saw him run in south Texas."

"There we go again," Uncle Billy reasoned, frowning. "They won't run at the Judge as such, and if they did they'd want odds and what we won wouldn't amount to a hill of beans. If somebody's eyeballed the Judge just once, they'd remember his markings, like that lightning-rod fella across the river in Indian Territory." It was forming again, Dude recognized, that gleam surfacing up through the mobile countenance, that expression that presaged action. Sure enough: "I've got a little idy that's worked before. Dude, boy, what say tomorrow morning we sashay into town and see what we can find again at the end of the rainbow."

"Aw," Dude protested, "let's just rest here and after a few days head on to some county seat that's tamer. I'm tard."

"We're all tard. But how am I gonna put away enough to buy me a hotel an' have my place by the f'ar, an' how's Coyote gonna send money home to his daddy the chief now and then to feed that herd of relatives, if we don't keep on matching us some races?" His glance shifted to Jason and his tone mellowed to a reminiscent longing. "I sure took a shine to that rambling Tremont House back yonder in Flat Rock, that long porch where you can rock an' watch the folks go by. About how much would a layout like that set a man back?"

Jason thought about it. "Two . . . three thousand. Depends how fancy you'd want to make it. Whether you put in horsehair settees in the lobby. Whether you stuffed the mattresses with corn husks or prairie hay or genteel cotton. How often you changed the beds, and how much you paid the help. When Cassius Pyle took over, things took a tight turn. He'd put four men in a bed and charge 'em the full rate and change the beds no oftener than once a month, only then if the customers complained about the bedbugs. He fired half the help, and them that was left got their wages cut. . . . And that wasn't genuine Old Green River I served, it was Old Scat, the hottest, meanest, cheapest bar whiskey there is." He looked down, striking a confessional attitude.

"There's no such thing as bad whiskey," Uncle Billy said. "Some's just better than others. Furthermore, I've got a sure-shot potion that's just the thing for bedbugs. Like reptiles, they can live years without food. I read of a German fella, a Dr. Goetz, that kept some in a bottle for six years without a particle of nourishment. . . . Best idy is to keep the bedding and bedstead perfectly clean. My remedy is to pour hot water into the crevices, then apply benzine to the different parts of the bedstead. Corrosive sublimate is a very good but a very poisonous cure, and can be fatal to the unaware sleeper." He grimaced. "Anyway, I'm still short my hotel money, even though we did right well in Flat Rock. We need two or three more big cleanups like that." Cocking a fond eye: "What do you say, Coyote? You with me, you Comanche?"

"With you, I am, grandfather. Hearing I am Comanche relatives way off crying they are hungry they are. More money this Comanche will need, else my father the chief honor will lose."

"You see, Dude, boy," the old man said, waxing enthusiastic, "we have no choice. Till we're sittin' pretty on Easy Street, let's count the coin with a horse that can move on down the track." He softened his voice and his face altered, a mixture of rogue and saint, compelling, persuasive, and the promise of adventure yonder. "We're pardners. Each of us depends on the others. Each shares equally. Coyote rides, I take care the horses, you set things up and spread the goodwill. Now Jason is with us to help out about any-where."

"Oh, all right." Dude gave in and threw up his hands in mock surrender. How could you say no to the likable old codger? Still, a suspicious fore-knowledge cautioned him. "Now just what is this new idy of yours?"

"You'll see in the morning. Want to study on it. You always need to vary a wrinkle if you can — in case some smart-aleck's seen the old one someplace."

During breakfast, Dude recognized the long-familiar signs as his old mentor looked forward to another horse race. No early tetchiness this morning; in lieu, he was as sociable as a traveling drummer in a new town. He moved spritely, he conversed and he listened; and Dude had the in-sight anew that horses and horse racing kept him going and provided him purpose in life.

Fond of voicing observations in his lecturing tone, he was sometimes chiding this morning, sometimes serious. When Jason liberally diluted his coffee with sugar: "Break some biscuit into that and you'll have puddin'." And as the talk shifted to buying and trading horses, Dude heard conclusions that he knew almost by heart now: "In a good horse the ears must be small and pointed and wide between. The eyes must be large and full and stand out prominently. An intelligent horse must have considerable width between the eyes. Judge Blair is a fine example . . . A horse with thick ears, small, flat, sunken eyes, with a thick, clumsy neck or a curved nose, is a horse liable to be vicious and clumsy or awkward, and never can be taught anything."

Jason leaned forward, absorbed. "What can you do with a horse like that?"

"Not much, if he's ruined. Feed him up. Groom him well. Brighten his eye and trade him off to the first stranger." Manifestly delighted to have a new listener: "I know some horses are mean. They'll bite a hunk out of you or kick you or run over you, if you turn your back. People have helped make them that way. Many times they've been traded around and handled by impatient, short-tempered men. . . . I have one iron-clad rule: Never hit a two-year-old. And never strike a horse in the head. A horse's strongest mental faculty is his memory. If he remembers ill treatment, he will remember gentleness and patience. Work with a horse every day. If man would give as much attention to his horse as he does to his dog, which is around him most of the time, consider how much easier the horse would be to handle and respond."

He got up and filled his cup from the blackened coffee pot and squatted beside the wagon. "Ran into an English fella once who was as smart as a forestful of owls about horses. He told me about steeplechasing. The English are great hands for those long races. They like what they call a 'stayer.' He said when a horse falls at a certain fence in the course of a race, he is liable to fall at the same place again. The horse has that in his memory, you see. A clever rider, the English fella said, would see that his mount doesn't take the jump at the same spot again."

The impressed Jason asked further, "How can you tell a broken-winded horse?"

"Easy. He pinches in his flanks, with a very slow motion, and drops them suddenly. And a horse with the heaves can be easily detected by observing the motion of the abdomen, and if you hear a short, peculiar cough. As for lameness, always have the horse travel by walk, trotting, and running before buying. . . . Any of us can be fooled. The trick is not to stay fooled. A country fella named Otha pulled a slick one back there in Cottonwood; in turn, we slicked him, even got some boot for a horse with the heaves. . . . Remember, Jason, he who buys a horse needs a thousand eyes."

He got up and threw out the coffee grounds in his cup and strode to the end of the wagon, and Dude heard him prowling through his medicine-chest plunder. In a moment he called for Coyote and the two went to Judge Blair, Uncle Billy holding a bottle and brush and a small brown sack. Coyote led the gelding behind the wagon.

Dude grinned at the stealth. The old man was childlike the way he maneuvered to surprise you, to withhold his artistry until the last possible moment. Playing the game, Dude winked at the puzzled Jason and revealed nothing.

When, shortly, Coyote led the Judge forth for inspection, and Uncle Billy stood back, thumbs hooked in belt, examining his work, Dude crossed over with Jason and said, "What have you two pulled now?"

Coyote showed him an even-toothed smile of silence.

Dude gawked. Judge Blair's blaze face was the same, but his white-sock feet were now dark bay and he looked unkempt and hard-used. Cockleburs clotted his usually handsome mane and proud long tail.

"Guess he looks enough like a sorry ol' cow pony," Uncle Billy said. "Put that wreck of a stock saddle on him, Coyote. And that old saddle blanket with the tattered ends." When that was done: "Now lead him over to the wagon and tie up. I want to see how he stands."

Coyote did that. And Judge Blair, as he did when in harness, hung his head and sagged, hip-shot, to all appearances deep in sluggish slumber.

"Well," Dude admitted, "he looks sorry, all right."

"Good. I say that's the sign of a smart horse. He knows what to do. Slap a flat saddle on him and take him to the track and he's all racehorse. Hang a set of harness on him with an oversize collar and he stands like a tard workhorse. Put a stock saddle on him and he acts like an ol' cow pony that's been goin' since way before daybreak. . . . That's fine, Coyote. Let him stand there. Now let's slick up Rebel."

While Coyote curried Rebel's mane and forelock and tail, Uncle Billy brushed the dark bay till he glistened.

"He looks so good we won't be able to match him," Dude worried.

"Oh, we'll match him. Wait till they see him work. Coyote, I understand you Comanches are supposed to know all about Mother Nature. The earth, the sun, the stars, the moon. That right?"

"Right, grandfather. Right."

"Thunderation, if you don't sound like that Colonel Bushrod when you repeat yourself like that. What I want to know is, will we be having rain today or within the next few days — say it takes that long to match these Buffalo Draw fellas?"

Coyote Walking turned his face to the cloud-less sky and folded his arms, intent for a time. "There will be no rain today," he pronounced solemnly. "Nor tomorrow, nor the next day. However, smart as we Comanches are, I cannot promise what will happen the fourth day."

"That's good enough. Just so you don't do a rain dance, meantime."

Afterward, to give the dye time to dry, they sat around and Jason filled them in on further details about Buffalo Draw. The Red Butte Saloon, he said, was the hub of the town and Mayor Horse Yoder owned it, and R. V. Sweeney was the proprietor of the horse-and-mule barn. Yoder, incidentally, was one who had seen Judge Blair run in south of Texas.

Around one o'clock the outfit pulled up across

from Sweeney's Horse & Mule Barn at the edge of town. Not one vehicle moved on the street. Not one person. The single church steeple reared like a lonely bastion above a sea of sin. Wind, whipping out of the southwest, sent dust devils skittering here and there. A can rolled hollowly. The neck of a broken whiskey bottle glinted in the dust outside the saddle shop. A loose board banged on the face of the violated bank, its name hidden in shame behind the weathered planking. And not one sound issued from the blacksmith shop. A scattering of horses occupied the saloons' hitching rails, most of them before the Red Butte.

Dude, riding Judge Blair, dismounted and tied up next to Rebel and sauntered over to the barn. One man sat in the gloom of the runway on a bale of hay, his face shadowed. He spoke no greeting, he nodded not.

"Afternoon," Dude opened, careful to exhibit his most genial manner. "Just passing through. Little short on feed. Reckon you have oats for sale?"

The man rose; still not speaking, he shuffled out to the doorway. Piece by piece, as he left the gloom, his features became visible: the great prow of reddish nose dominating the long face; the crimped mouth, hinting that he measured his words by the thimbleful; the ginger-colored whiskers, uncropped, that ran from ear to ear in a sweeping crescent; the trader's eyes banked under the shaggy outcropping of his sandy brows. Still, he did not speak, but his eyes were reading the outfit's horses.

"You have oats for sale?" Dude tried again.

"Have."

"How much?"

"Dollar bushel, unsacked. Sack's two-bits extra."

"That's reasonable," Dude said, knowing the sack was not.

"Is."

Dude gazed up the dusty, near-empty street. "Nice little town you have here. Sure is."

"Some like it, some don't."

"By the way, there happen to be a track hereabouts?"

"Is," the man said, and no more.

"Be all right if we sorta breeze our horse on it?"

"Air's free, so's track." The narrow face shifted, an alteration so slight Dude barely noticed. The man asked, "You carry a racehorse?"

"A short horse. That dark bay out there tied behind the wagon next to that ol' cow pony with the saddle on." Dude loitered and kicked at the dust, waiting. When the man failed to heed the prompting, Dude, indifferently, swung away, saying, "I'll have my uncle bring the wagon over. See how much we need." Looking back, he pulled on his chin. "Now where'd you say the track is?"

"Didn't. West of town — half mile."

"Sure much obliged to you, Mr. . . . ?"

"Sweeney, R. V."

"Pleased to meet you, Mr. Sweeney. My name's Dude McQuinn." He put out his hand and smiled.

Sweeney looked down and up and down again, as one might regard some suspicious foreign object, on his face that barely discernible hint of interest; and held out his hand, as impersonally as one might reach for a door latch. Dude had never felt flesh so limp.

"Where from, McQuinn?"

"Oh, around. Just travelin' through. We trade a little, we race a little. We win some, we lose some."

Once more Dude delayed his departure, expecting Sweeney to talk up a match race, and once more Sweeney was noncommittal.

Casting him a genial nod, Dude rejoined the outfit.

When the oats were purchased and loaded into the wagon, the outfit toiled along the street and out of town. As yet nothing stirred back there. Dude rode on a short way and looked again, in time to see Sweeney hotfooting up the street and into the Red Butte Saloon. Not many moments passed before two men came out and mounted and rode after the wagon.

"They're coming," he told Uncle Billy, driving the team.

Dude found Parker's Prairie a smooth racing strip, wide enough for six horses. The starting line showed scant service of late and one side of the track was as even as the other.

Pretending to fuss over Rebel, Uncle Billy saddled the dark bay and ostentatiously adjusted the throatlatch, and when Coyote was in the irons: "Don't use the swinging break. Breeze him out a couple hundred yards or so at his natural speed . . . you know. Give 'em a good look."

Coyote had Rebel warming up down the track and trotting back when the two riders arrived.

"That scar-faced bird is Horse Yoder," Jason whispered as Dude tied Judge Blair to the tailgate where he couldn't be missed. "Other one is Luke somebody. Hangs around the Red Butte. Bums tobacco. Tries to work up poker games for the house. Mainly, he's a bird dog for Yoder."

The riders, nodding greetings, slacked reins to watch the horse work.

At the last moment, Uncle Billy waved Coyote over and fussed with the blanket again and told Coyote to dismount while he uncinched and lifted the flat saddle, smoothed the blanket, and cinched up again. Standing clear, he motioned Coyote to the saddle and walked to the starting line.

Coyote heeled his horse forward, the old man dropped his hand and shouted "Go!" and Rebel broke. That is, he started. It was, Dude saw, his usual getaway, neither quite fast nor terribly slow; nothing to write the home folks about. A so-so takeoff. For the initial seventy-five yards he ran fairly well. There, like always, he began to fade. Coyote took him on for the one eighth and pulled him up.

Dude cut his eyes away. The sight imposed a feeling of regret and a stronger guilt. More and more he felt that whenever they used Rebel. *Someday, old boy, I'm gonna turn you out to pasture where there's live-oak shade and a sweet-water spring.* A voice encroached, a booming voice:

"Welcome to Buffalo Draw. I'm Horse Yoder — the mayor. But the boys all call me Horse. They don't cotton to fancy titles." And he vented a braying laugh, and Luke, beside him, took it up, braying even louder and jogging his head up and down all the while, and running his tongue in and out between the gap in his upper teeth.

Dude grinned and nodded. But, boy, if he'd ever seen hardcases, these two filled the bill!

Horse Yoder was rawboned, florid, and loose-lipped. A scar, beginning at his left cheekbone, ran jaggedly to the corner of his mustached mouth. When he smiled — and he was smiling now — the scar gave him a leer. He wore a six-shooter and a Bowie knife at his belt. He kept his left hand fisted on his hip, the elbow pointed straight out.

Luke seemed a poor imitation of Yoder, his handgun and knife worn in the same bold fashion, everything slung low. He sat his saddle like Yoder, head reared back, left arm akimbo. His murky brown eyes followed Yoder's every move, alert to Yoder's whims. Luke was dirtier than necessary, even in a land of infrequent baths, and he fancied his hair like an old-time buffalo hunter's, long and greasy.

"Wonder if you boys would hearken to a little match race?" Yoder called.

"Depends on our horse," said Dude, walking out to the riders. "He's been soring up lately and limping."

"Looks all right to me."

You mean he looks slow and you figure your horse can take him. Dude said, "Today he does. We might run at you if you don't insist on forfeit money. Can't chance that with an iffy horse."

"Never did believe in fortfeit money, myself," Yoder replied, all magnanimity. "It's the race that counts. Like to take a gander at my horse?"

"Nothing to lose," Dude said and shrugged.

"Awright. Luke, you ride down to the barn and tell R.V. to put a halter on Daylight."

The moment had come to observe bush-track courtesies, Dude was aware, and he introduced the outfit, and Yoder got down and pumped everybody's hand except Coyote Walking's.

"An Indian jockey?" Yoder questioned, his mouth hanging. "We don't cotton much to redskins around here. Too many raids in the early days. Folks don't forget."

Dude froze, his anger flashing through his surprise. This was unexpected and the first instance of leftover frontier bitterness since Coyote had joined them.

"Can he grunt a little American?" Yoder asked in a nasty voice.

Before Dude could retort, Coyote, surprisingly

and calmly, pounded his chest and pouched out his lips. "Old days gone. Me good Injun. Heap skookum Injun. Heap friend." And smiling devilishly: "The poet said: ' 'Tis the empty vessel makes the greatest sound.' I liken myself to the Neapolitan prince in *The Merchant of Venice* of whom Portia said, 'He doth nothing but talk of his horse.' Should you wish to read that sometime, Mr. Yoder, I believe you'll find it in act one, scene two, about line forty-three."

Yoder stood motionless, startled into silence. Without another word, he went to his horse. Dude, meeting Uncle Billy's eyes, made the sign for scalped.

They trailed Yoder to the barn, and Luke led out a short-coupled sorrel gelding. In the runway there they looked him over. At the rear of the barn another horse, obviously a stud, was making a challenging racket, kicking and snorting and pacing his stall. Dude couldn't tell much about Daylight. The gelding appeared to possess speed, but so did Rebel. He circled the gelding again, deliberately delaying.

"How about it, friend?" Yoder prodded.

Catching Uncle Billy's nod, Dude said, "We'll match you."

"Now you're talkin'. How much and how far?"

"We'll go three hundred yards for . . . say, two hundred dollars. How's that jibe with you?"

Yoder sneered. "Hell, friend, that's just a spoonful of mush in Buffalo Draw. Luke, you might as well take Daylight back." Luke obeyed at once, jogging his head vigorously and putting on an imitation of Yoder's sneer.

Dude allowed himself to reveal a grin at the old ploy. Shrugging, he countered by turning away, a movement that drew Uncle Billy and Coyote and Jason. He was near the entrance when Yoder wheeled front and asked in a leveling tone, "Would you hearken to three hundred bucks and four hundred yards?"

Dude, strolling back, saw Luke stop on that cue. Dude said, "It's not the money, it's the distance. Our ol' horse just breezed one eighth without any trouble. Question is, can he go four hundred yards? He could go lame on us. We can't match you at that distance. You can see why."

"That I can, friend, and I like to be fair." By now Luke was leading Daylight back. "You call the distance," Yoder said agreeably.

"Three hundred yards," Dude answered, firm about it.

"— And four hundred dollars?"

Dude lowered his head and chewed his lower lip, scratched the side of his nose, and kicked at the dusty litter. The stud was banging his stallboards again. Dude nodded. "It's a go — four hundred dollars — three hundred yards."

Yoder slapped his thigh in agreement, and Luke gave a gaptoothed grin, jogged his head, and slapped his own leg.

"When?" Yoder asked, smiling, as cordial as a country peddler.

168

"Day after tomorrow. Our horse does better if he works every other day. He'll sore up as it is."

"Whatever you say, friend Dude. Hope you don't mind if I call you by your first name?"

"Not a-tall. Sounds neighborly. Like back home." Dude had never met a rough customer who was so friendly.

"Two o'clock suit you?"

"Suits me fine."

Dude was ready to talk starter and judges when Sweeney, who had watched the back-and-forth jockeying in tight-lipped silence, said, "Mind if I get in on this? Winner take all?"

"You got a horse?" Dude asked.

"Back there."

Yoder flung Sweeney a belittling look. "You don't mean that big stud you bought off that Arkansas trader a while back?"

"That's the one — Bubba Red."

"Aw, he can't run. He's not a smooth horse."

"Never said he was. But he can run enough." The trader's eyes flared. "Been working him out in a pasture south of town. Didn't know that, did you? Was fixin' to match you when these boys hit town."

"Let's have a look-see at this Bubba Red," Dude said, figuring how Sweeney's entry would sweeten the purse.

Luke led Daylight away and Sweeney disappeared into the barn's rearward gloom. There followed the squeal of a stall door opening and a sudden clatter of hooves, and Sweeney and a horse fairly rushed down the runway, the livery-man hanging on to the halter rope with both hands. Everybody jumped out of the way. Sweeney brought the horse under control.

Bubba Red was a bright bay stallion, big and rough and high-strung, and he didn't seem to like the company Sweeney was keeping — or any company. The wild way he walled his eyes made Dude think he saw as much behind him as he did in front, and he was muscled up like a Turkish strongman.

"Won't tell you what I clocked him in at three hundred yards," Sweeney bragged to bait Yoder, and Yoder chuckled and said, "Man, how the wind blows out here," and laid back his head and hummed a few tuneless notes. "What'd you use, an hourglass?" He found immense pleasure at his own remark, and Luke, coming back just then, joined him in self-congratulatory laughter.

"Is my horse in — or are you birds afraid Bubba Red will run off with the money?"

Yoder, still enjoying his recent banter, said, "Luke, R.V. thinks he's got him a racehorse. Awright if we let 'im run at us?" Receiving an empty grin and a series of head-jiggling nods: "It's awright with me, R.V., if you hanker to give away your money. What's your notion, friend Dude?"

"A three-horse race is jake with me, friend Horse." While agreeing, he was ignoring his vague wariness. Everything was too sudden somehow, too spontaneous. Why had Sweeney waited till Yoder made the match?

Before he could have second thoughts, Sweeney took Bubba Red to his stall, and when he rejoined them they began discussing the starter and judges. To Dude's surprise, Yoder suggested one of the outfit and Jason became the starter. The judges would be one from the outfit and one of Yoder's choice and one of Sweeney's. You couldn't ask a fairer shake than that.

Yet Dude's uneasiness lingered that evening in camp outside of town. "It's odd to me that Yoder didn't know Sweeney was training a horse," Dude said.

"Strikes me the same way," Jason sided in. "In a town as small as Buffalo Draw everybody knows when you get up and when you blow out the lamp to turn in."

Uncle Billy said, "Sweeney could work that horse on the sly, couldn't he? Real early of a morning or in the evening? Sneak him out the rear of the barn and be off? Sure he could. Anyway, Sweeney's money fattens the pot."

"Why," Dude fretted, "did Sweeney hang back till Yoder matched us? Why didn't he get in when Yoder did?" And when the old man had no answer: "How do you size up their horses, Uncle?"

"Daylight sorta puts me in mind of Pepper Boy. He's a speed horse. Clean-legged. Good balance. Kinda wish we'd matched him at four hundred — farther the better. . . . If you want to get right down to it, there are some things I don't like about him, though. Head's too long. Eyes a trifle too close together. Ears a mite too lank. An' come to think of it, he's a little short in the shoulder. . . . Now, Bubba Red is all muscle and big bone. Awkward but powerful. Bet my hat he's part Percheron. But you can't tell a winner by the way he looks. I'd have to see him work before I passed judgment." He tucked in his lips and half shuttered his eyes, a sure sign that he was backtracking. He jerked. "There is one thing about that horse. Comes to me now." He paused to assemble his thoughts still further. He said:

"Bubba Red wasn't shod and his feet needed trimming. Now you don't train or run a horse thataway. Use him hard unshod, he can develop split hooves, flat feet, flared feet, what have you. Ruins his action. A racehorse, any horse, for that matter, is only as good as his feet. That's got me to thinking."

No more was said about Bubba Red. It was decided that come morning, no later than daybreak, they would breeze both Rebel and Judge Blair on the prairie near camp.

After supper, Jason joined Dude at his invitation to ride into town and "listen around."

With the coming of darkness, Buffalo Draw had shed its cloak of daytime drowse. Dude thought of an old he-wolf quitting his den when the sun went down and slipping out to howl at the moon. The boxlike Wranglers' Rest was lit up as if for a barn dance, and horses stood in solid ranks at the hitching rails along saloon row, and the constant hum of voices rode the night air. Within the Red Butte a piano was banging to the off-key singing of a woman whose soprano sounded tired and worn. Feminine laughter pealed from the second story of the hotel; the splintery crash of glass followed. A black cat scudded across the street ahead of the riders.

Inside the rackety Red Butte, Jason and Dude elbowed over to the bar, wedged in, and called for whiskey. One brief sip and the big man made a wry face. "Old Scat! I'd know it if somebody spilled one drop in a horse trough."

After a time, Dude, deciding the sunburned cowboy on his right had a friendly face, leaned in and asked, "Where's the war?"

"War?"

"Just wondered. Everybody's packin' so much artillery they look swaybacked."

"Good idea to let your gun hang loose in this town. I'd advise you to do the same, pardner."

"What about the poker games?"

"Don't play unless you aim to lose your money."

"That's good advice."

"Tell you the truth, I wouldn't ride in here if Buffalo Draw wasn't the only town for fifty miles around."

"Guess you heard about the big horse race day after tomorrow?"

"Just did."

"How's it look to you?"

"Daylight all the way. Stick with the favorite, I say. He's never been headed."

"How does Bubba Red shape up?"

A guardedness fell across the young face. "Your outfit the one with the brought-in horse?"

"That's right."

"Can he run?"

"I'll put it this way: He's not the fastest short horse in Texas, but he knows where the finish line is. He can bend the breeze when he wants to." Dude let a confidential tone seep into his voice. "You see, right after we matched Horse Yoder, Sweeney wanted in with Bubba Red. Why I wondered about his horse."

Dude saw an earnest struggle going on behind the young man's eyes. He glanced about, a caution upon him. He seemed about to say something when the bartender, a broken-faced individual, came up and stood there. The cowboy compressed his mouth; he said nothing. The piano player struck up introductory notes, at which the cowboy's eyes left Dude and sought the man at the piano, and the cowboy said, "Sure can tickle the ivories, can't he?"

Dude saw a spangled woman come out onto the nutshell of a stage at the saloon's rear. No longer young, pouches under her eyes, her painted mouth wearing a slack smile, she winked and tilted her head just so and planted both hands on her ample hips and surveyed the crowd, a waiting expression beneath her vivid mask of powder and rouge. A spatter of applause was enough, for she signaled the humped figure at the piano and he ran the keys, and as he cut into the melody she began singing, her weary soprano straining to the words of "What Was Your Name in the States?"

She sang it through once, to the additional accompaniment of betraying guffaws and elbow nudges, and when the crowd stomped and yelled and clapped for more, she sang it again, but no better. After which, bowing, she made her exit, giving a naughty little backward kick as she vanished from the stage.

"I'll buy you a drink on that," Dude said, and turned to the cowboy.

The cowboy was gone. Dude scanned the shifting lake of sweat-glistening faces and didn't see him. He did spy Jason, who had drifted away, meantime, chinning with a bevy of town-dressed patrons. And across the noisy room Horse Yoder was holding court at a table, surrounded by sycophants.

Feeling a tug on his arm, Dude found the ubiquitous Luke. "The mayor wants you to have a drink with him," he said importantly, with a hiss, displaying the gap-toothed grin.

"Tell him thanks. I'll be over."

"The mayor he don't like to be kept waitin' long, you know."

"And I don't like to hurry," Dude said and smiled.

He waited awhile before meandering slowly through the pack over to the table. At Yoder's abrupt motion, the men around him got up and left, and then Yoder, who appeared to be feeling his oats tonight, yelled at the omnipresent Luke to bring whiskey, and the handyman hastened to the bar.

"Hoped you might hearken to a little side bet," Yoder said.

"Already bet the grub money," Dude parried.

"What's another hundred or so?"

"Just what you said — another hundred or so. If I could count the green, I wouldn't be way out here where the hoot owls holler."

Yoder laid his head back in that characteristic scoffing way of his and hummed. "Listen to the man sing hard times," he brayed, and laughed until the jagged line of the scar quivered like a pulse.

Luke, hustling back, set down bottle and glasses and solicitously poured drinks, then stood by, hovering around Yoder like a persistent horsefly.

"I'm just being frank," Dude said.

"Friend Dude, that's why I cotton to you. You don't beat around the bush. You stand right up and talk to a man and say what you think."

"Talk is what makes a horse race, and pride in your horse makes you bet."

"Friend, I just knew you'd come around to it!"

"I might listen to some right favorable odds."

"Odds?" Once more the laid-back head and the discordant humming. "I dasn't do that when

I don't know about your horse."

"And I don't know about Daylight, except I hear he's never lost a race. Hereabouts, anyway. Ever run him in south Texas?"

"Wouldn't run down my horse, would you, friend Dude? But I won't get frothy." Nevertheless, he flushed and his voice rose to an edge. "Just tryin' to give you another chance at me. Most times I'm not that generous."

"You warm my ol' Texas heart. What you have in mind, friend Horse?"

"Daylight money. Four hundred more. says my horse will daylight yours."

"Sweeney's horse as well?"

"Sweeney backed off from me."

"You're mighty confident."

"I've got a good horse."

"I'll bet you this way: you put up that extra four hundred, I'll put up two."

Yoder released that abrasive, humorless laugh. "That's two-to-one odds."

"Your horse is favored."

"How you do take the hide, friend Dude. But no can do."

Dude snapped to his feet. Before he could go, Yoder slapped the table and motioned him down. "Don't hive off," he howled. "I cotton to a man that's not afraid to bet his horse." And he poured the glasses to overflowing.

"All bets payable on the barrelhead right after the race? Agreed?"

"Agreed. I like your style. Case you'd like to

177

settle here after your horse loses, I might even stake you."

Dude sat again. "Afraid Buffalo Draw is too crowded for me. I like the wide-open spaces, where you can see who's comin' across the prairie, and if you don't like his looks you can make far-apart tracks the other way." He let his voice trail off. He winked. "I figure you know what I mean."

Yoder's eyes widened, surprised and suddenly cognizant. "No worry here if a man's on the dodge. Bet a dozen or so perked up a while ago when Maude sang that old song."

"That's a good lay, friend Horse. Now that we savvy each other, I've got a head-on question, if you don't mind."

"Shoot, friend Dude."

"It's about Sweeney's horse."

"What about that horse?"

"Has Bubba Red been raced around here at all?"

"You heard Sweeney say he worked the horse out on the sly. He's always tryin' to slick me. You know as much as I do."

So much for that, Dude thought, unconvinced, and got up.

They were beyond town, on the road for camp, before Dude found his thoughts. "Horse Yoder drawed up like wet rawhide when I asked him about Bubba Red. Claimed he didn't know sic'em about that stud. All I got done was take him up when he offered two-to-one daylight money."

"Funny to me," Jason said thoughtfully, "that nobody would put up a dime on Bubba Red. You can almost always find some prideful money on a local horse. I had the feeling that nobody wanted to talk." He rode on a way. "Dude, that big horse is either a ringer that Sweeney's brought in, or Sweeney's a fool with his money."

"Not him. He's as close as the bark on a black-jack. No gambler."

"In that case, then, he has to figure playing a cinch."

"It's a new wrinkle, Jason, and I'm plumb worried."

CHAPTER 10

On this morning before the race, Dude could hear Uncle Billy, his back to the others, busy whittling and scraping. In the old man's single-mindedness, and between trips to the medicine chest, where he was mixing something, he ignored Dude and Jason smoking and talking about the race, and Coyote Walking, his nose in a book. Dude knew better than to volunteer. If Uncle wanted them about, he'd say so.

After a time, Uncle Billy went behind the wagon where Rebel was tied. There awhile, he scurried back and sat down on the wagon tongue and whittled and scraped some more. Again he hurried around to the horse, an impatience upon him. Again he came back, without a word to the outfit. Again and again. Always particular, Dude thought. This last trip Dude heard him mumbling to himself, an indication that, finally, he was satisfied with his handiwork.

Forthwith, he took a bottle from the chest and stepped behind the wagon. Shortly, Dude heard him leading Rebel off and leading Rebel back. When at last he rounded the wagon and spoke, his eyes had that glint of anticipation. He said,

"We can load up directly. I think we're ready."

Less than an hour remained before post time when the outfit entered Buffalo Draw. A crowd of spitters and whittlers had gathered around the entrance of Sweeney's Horse & Mule Barn. Onward, the crowded street forced the outfit to a walk. Nothing, Dude thought, drew a crowd in Texas like election day, a hot horse race, or a hanging in that order.

He followed the wagon astride Judge Blair, still wearing his sorry state, and led Rebel, groomed like a circus horse today. Blue Grass, bearing Dude's saddle, trailed on a halter rope tied to the tailgate. Jason Carter rode at the head of the wagon.

Precisely in front of the Red Butte Saloon, so close that Dude caught its breath of sour dampness, he turned his head and looked at Rebel. His jaw fell. Shortening rein, he called loudly to Uncle Billy, who was driving the team, "Hold up! Hold up!"

The old man stopped the team and leaned out. "What's wrong back there?"

"It's Rebel. He's limping!"

With a "Thunderation" and a string of cusswords that carried to the Red Butte's swarm of gawking idlers, Uncle Billy tossed the reins to Coyote Walking, scrambled down, and ran back. "Limping, you say?"

"Afraid it's that left foreleg again."

Kneeling, his seraphic features gravely concerned, the old man felt of Rebel's knee, then the cannon bone, then the fetlock joint, then the pastern. He pulled on the fetlock and lifted the foot, looked, and dropped it rather quickly. "Lead him out a way," he told Dude as the idlers crowded closer to watch.

Dude led the gelding forward a short distance. Rebel limped every step. Dude stopped. Uncle Billy examined the knee and the areas of the cannon bone and the fetlock joint, but, Dude noticed, he did not lift the hoof again. Straightening, whiskey chin resting on the knuckles of his left hand, he studied the suffering foreleg, his diagnostic eyes as cheerless as a late spring blizzard.

"What do you think it is?" Dude asked loudly.

Shaking his head: "Could be several things, all serious. The oblique extensor, for one."

"Oh," Dude groaned.

"Or the metacarpal tuberosity."

"Sounds bad."

Pointing farther down along the inside, between knee and fetlock: "Maybe the flexor perforatus."

"I hope not!"

"Or the lateral extensor."

"That *is* serious!"

An ominous pause, the clear blue eyes becoming more and more comfortless. "Or the anterior extensor."

"Lordy," Dude groaned.

Uncle Billy threw up his hands in resignation. "If a horse could only talk and tell you where he hurts. Might as well fetch him on to the track, Dude. Maybe he'll loosen up enough to run, but don't count on it. Good thing we didn't put up any forfeit money." Shaking his head, he slumped to the wagon and climbed aboard and chirruped to the team.

Dude, tugging gently on the lead rope, followed at a careful walk. Rebel continued to favor the foreleg, kindling sympathetic stares as he crippled along.

By this time patrons were lining the race course. Uncle Billy parked the wagon, climbed down, and moved Blue Grass to the side away from the track where Jason was tying his claybank saddler, and Dude tied Judge Blair to the tailgate. There, alone, hipshot, he made a conspicuous sight, which soon evoked expressions of evident pity and neglect from passersby, who, next, glared accusingly at the outfit and back to the sorry-looking horse: head hanging, the worn stock saddle, the tatters of the blanket showing, the cockleburs snarling the unkempt mane and long tail.

Dude, beginning to feel the familiar edginess before a race, took a sweeping look around. The stage was now set, awaiting only the arrival of Yoder and Sweeney with Daylight and Bubba Red to be complete. Dude strolled to the track, surveyed the stretch, and drifted back.

When down the dusty road to town he saw Yoder leading his horse and Sweeney his, he spoke to Uncle Billy, who took Rebel off in a slow, limping circle. Dude followed them with guilty eyes. Poor Rebel! He'd played more roles than a traveling-show troupe.

"Hear you got trouble, friend Dude!" Yoder called, riding up.

"Afraid so, friend Horse. Look at Rebel. Don't see how he can run today."

Yoder watched while Uncle Billy led Rebel limping to the wagon and tied him with Blue Grass and the claybank. "Gonna be a crowd of disappointed folks," Yoder said. "Come from miles around to see a three-horse race."

"Maybe you can match another horse?"

Yoder laughed. "Daylight's headed everything from here to Jacksboro, and then some." He swung around toward Sweeney, coming up. "The race is off, R.V. Their horse turned up lame."

Sweeney showed neither surprise nor disappointment. He had nothing to say.

They had, Dude sensed, reached the critical point of the game. Everything hinged on what he said next, and how he said it. He spoke offhandedly, "You fellows might match up. You're ready to run."

Yoder seemed to mull over the suggestion, seemed to like it more by the moment. Suddenly he said, "Tell you what, R.V, I'll just run you, if you'll slap another four hundred on the line."

"Nothing doing." Sweeney's mouth crimped. "You know I'm no gambling man, Horse. I'll match you as we stand now — for four hundred.

Not a penny more."

"That's no money," Yoder hooted.

"Is to me. I run a barn, not a saloon."

"I won't match my horse for that."

To this, Sweeney made no relpy.

Dude feared that Uncle Billy, who was standing by, would never speak up, like a boy tongue-tied by his one line in the schoolhouse play. Finally, the almost diffident voice, in the drawling vernacular of the locality: "Dude, ain't you forgettin' somethin'?"

"What do you mean?"

"You know what I mean."

"Oh," glancing at Judge Blair, "guess I have. But —"

"We can still run that race. Still keep our word."

"I dunno."

"Well, we can."

"Friend Horse," Dude began, and pulled on his left earlobe, "we'd hate to disappoint so many good folks, friends of yours. If you fellows are agreeable, we'll run that ol' cow pony over there in Rebel's place."

"Him?" Yoder brayed, pointing. "That sorry-looking crowbait?"

"I'll admit Sawdust is not as smooth a horse as Rebel, and he's not as fast. But when he feels good he can stir up the dust a few hundred yards. Has fast days and slow days. It's up to you fellows."

Sweeney's pinched look receded; his long face,

changing, broke through the crust of its niggardly mosaic. Yoder, flashing a predatory smile, whapping his right hand repeatedly against the pommel of his saddle, echoed, "Up to us? Well, come on!"

"One more thing," Dude said, a hedging to his voice. "Since Rebel can't run, could we sorta forget about that daylight money?"

Yoder's face hardened. "A bet's a bet with me, friend Dude. We hold a man to his word around here."

Shrugging in apparent resignation, Dude went to the wagon and uncinched Judge Blair and tossed the stock saddle and ragged blanket inside, while Uncle Billy peeled the flat racing saddle and blanket off Rebel and tethered him to the tailgate for traveling and readied the gear on the Judge, who already had his snaffle-bit bridle on. Meanwhile, Coyote brought the saddled Blue Grass around.

What a sight it was, Dude thought, to see Judge Blair's transformation once that action saddle touched his short back and you cinched him up. He lifted his head now and kept it there, those fox ears flicking, knowing what would be expected of him shortly. Dude could see him begin to tense, his wide nostrils expanding, and to stir and toss his head a little, and his rich brown eyes shone; in that instant, he had the faraway look of an eagle.

Dude felt a rush of pride and affection for him. Good sense. Good manners. An easy keeper. Always giving his honest best, whether on a straightaway bush track in hoot-owl country or on an oval county-fair course. He came from quality folks, no doubt about it; many times Dude had wished he could trace the sire and dam, all apologies to the mythical Buck Shiloh. Now, traveling about, an exile, in a way, because he could no longer be matched under his own true name, the dark bay gelding carried more aliases than a Panhandle outlaw. Whatever, Judge Blair was a runnin' horse.

"All right, Coyote," Uncle Billy instructed when the Comanche was mounted, "job him easy down the track fifty yards and back. Keep his head as low as you can. We don't want to give anything away." The excitement of challenge honed the old horseman's voice to staccato pitch. "I figure we can outrun that short-shouldered Daylight horse. It's Bubba Red that worries me somehow, him and his untrimmed feet. . . . Take the left-hand lane. Looks a little smoother. If they argue, we'll make 'em draw for holes. Don't get between 'em, understand? Dude, you want to stay here for the start or be our finish judge?"

"I'll go down there. Believe we need you here."

"Jason," Uncle Billy said, "remember there's no start till you holler 'Go.' Make 'em stay lapped."

"I know."

Dude mounted Blue Grass. By this time

Yoder was leading his horse toward the starting line after a circling parade for the crowd's benefit. Daylight's jockey was a wizened oldster whose face was as puckered as a prune's, his body as shriveled as a mummy's. If he weighed ninety pounds he'd be hog fat. He carried a bat half as thick as a big man's wrist. That weathered face had sighted down the stretch of countless bush tracks.

Sizing up rider and mount, Dude knew a plunging fear for Coyote and his horse. *Tough. The whole kit and caboodle's a tough lay.*

Yoder waved genially. "You want an outside lane or the middle, friend Dude?"

"Outside on the left, friend Horse," Dude replied, surprised. "Sawdust has the habit of bolting to his left sometimes at the break. We sure don't want any bumping."

"Fair enough. Sweeney says it makes no difference to him. So I'll take the outside right."

Now that was unexpected, Dude puzzled, him so doggoned nice and agreeable. Most horsemen would demand a draw for lanes in a three-horse go.

Farther back, Bubba Red's jock, a brawny young man in his twenties, was having his troubles. The stud kept fighting Sweeney's lead rope and veering from side to side, awkward and powerful. Coyote, on his way down track for the warm-up, reined out to let them pass.

Riding between the crowded flanks of the racing strip, Dude reached the three-hundred-yard finish line, marked by a pole on each side, and tied his horse to a mesquite tree.

Easing through the crowd, he found two men standing at the line. One was Luke, Yoder's handyman. "I'm one of the judges," Dude said.

"Me, too," Luke hissed. "Me an' Mick." Mick nodded. He was the broken-faced bartender at the Red Butte. Dude nodded back, thinking there would be one ding-dong of an argument if the Judge won by a scant nose.

In concern, Dude fixed his attention on the head of the track. The horses were just about ready now, Daylight and Bubba Red free of lead ropes. Jason motioned the jockeys forward and on they came, Judge Blair behaving as usual and in the left outside lane, the stud in the middle, Daylight as composed as the Judge.

Dude's throat caught as Bubba Red, on his starting manners till now, abruptly broke ahead and bucked a couple of times, almost unseating his jockey. A rank horse!

Sweat started to Dude's forehead. If only Daylight had the middle and that stud were on the right!

They were working around for another try, Sweeney's horse under control at the moment, the three of them turning and facing the line, and advancing together at Jason's hand signal. . . . Closer together now; head to head . . . Coyote had his horse where he should be. . . . It looked like an even getaway.

Jason's hand dropped.

The horses jumped, the Judge and the bright bay stud springing ahead of the sorrel Daylight.

It happened at the instant Dude thought his horse, in the swinging start, was going to break out on top. Sweeney's horse barged into Judge Blair, a swift, brutal lunge that looked deliberate.

Shocked, frozen by concern and bursting anger as he suddenly understood everything, Dude saw his horse knocked off his feet — saw him floundering and struggling for traction while Coyote fought to help him bring up his head. Coyote lost a stirrup, and very nearly lost his seat.

Though off balance and disunited, they were coming on. Dude saw Coyote find his stirrup and, simultaneously, the dark bay his feet, his head up. Yet he looked to come out of it in the left lead. Wrong for him, because he ran in the right lead on straightaways, changing to the left only on turns.

It felt like such a painfully long time to Dude, but the entire scene — the break, the collision, the stumbling, the regaining his footing — had passed as flashes. Through hurting eyes, he saw his horse, far back, begin to find himself. So swiftly Dude wasn't certain, Judge Blair seemed to make a flying change of leads back to the right lead, reaching out for ground with that right front foot.

Daylight ran in front, striding smoothly. Sweeney's horse labored one length, now two, behind the sorrel. He would get no closer.

Back there, Judge Blair was coming, oh, how he was coming, and yet so late, running lower, ears flattened as he lengthened his stride, and Coyote was whooping at him.

They caught Bubba Red about halfway. One moment they ran lapped. Another moment and the bright bay stud was eating dust. Dude was shouting, his voice lost in the roar of the crowd. Yoder's horse was three lengths out and striding smoothly, not tiring.

As in a dusty dream, Dude saw his horse coming faster. He ran with fury, eyes bulging, head ever lower, black mane flying. Coyote was an outline of hunched head and shoulders and arms, and clamped thighs and legs, a part of the flying horse.

Dude saw Daylight's jockey, hearing onrushing hoofbeats, whip his head back and crab lower in the saddle and swing the club of a bat. Thrice he slashed the sorrel's hindquarters. Daylight moved faster. No more than one length separated the two charging horses now. And Coyote had Judge Blair still coming.

They caught Daylight just this side of the one-eighth pole. Abreast they ran, stride for stride. Daylight was game.

Come on, Coyote! Bring 'im on!

Coyote's continuous screeching reached a still-higher key of urgency. Judge Blair charged a head out front. Now a neck. Now Daylight's nose bobbed at the Judge's saddle girth. There, something went out of the sorrel. He appeared to check a little, and when he did Dude knew that his horse had the race won.

Judge Blair was opening up daylight when Coyote took him across the finish line. Bubba Red would not finish.

Through the milling confusion, Dude spotted Yoder and Sweeney loping their horses down the track, and behind them, close, Uncle Billy whipping the team, and Jason galloping the saddler beside the wagon.

Luke and Mick didn't move. They looked stunned.

Yoder loped up and stopped, glaring at Luke and Mick, as if they were to blame, and when Luke spread his hands and shrugged, at loss for words, Dude spoke up:

"It was our horse by daylight. Nobody can deny that." He saw faces in the gathering crowd backing him up.

"An' ol' cow pony, huh?" Yoder growled, his face flushed. "I'll pay off at the saloon." He started to ride off.

Dude grabbed the cheek strap of Yoder's horse. "You'll pay off here — on the barrelhead — like we agreed. *A bet's a bet, friend Horse.* Remember!" And for Sweeney: "You, too. You and your put-in horse that can't run a lick! Didn't even finish! Put in to knock our horse down at the break so Daylight could win!"

As he spoke the last wrathy words, Dude felt something prod his back and he heard Luke hissing, "You jes' shut up that kinda talk, friend Dude," even here imitating his bossman. "If you . . ."

Somehow Luke didn't finish, and when Dude swung about, he saw Uncle Billy looking Luke in the eye and holding a handgun on him, a tautness, deadly and alien, on his face that Dude had not seen before.

"Drop it, snaggletooth!" Uncle Billy snarled.

Luke had hardly obeyed when Mick, stepping up from behind, covered Uncle Billy.

Close by, a horse was rushing up. Whirling, Dude glimpsed Jason looming suddenly behind Yoder and Sweeney, and the big man between them, grabbing and hoisting them from their saddles and bearhugging them and clasping their heads together as their startled horses took off.

Momentarily, Mick's attention shifted that way. In that brief span, Dude lurched and grabbed the bartender's gunhand, twisted, and the weapon fell free. As quickly Uncle Billy covered Luke and Mick.

Jason dropped Yoder and Sweeney and when they reeled to their feet, they were looking into the barrel of Jason's six-gun. "Pay up," he ordered. "Drop your gun on the ground, Yoder."

Dude marveled at him. Jason was all business. He meant every word. The mountain had moved at last.

Seeing Yoder balk, Jason nudged the saddler to ride into him. Jason meant that, too. Yoder drew his weapon and dropped it.

"Now the money you owe us."

The saloonman reached for his roll and held it.

"Give it to Mr. McQuinn."

Yoder handed it over and Dude began to count. Finishing, he said, "You held out the daylight money, friend Horse." Glowering, Yoder went to the other pocket.

Once more Dude counted. "It's all here," he told Jason. "Four hundred dollars."

"Now you, Sweeney," Jason said.

Sweeney might have been surrendering his life's blood, so pained did he look. The skin around his mouth was white and his lips were bloodless as he paid.

"It counts up," Dude said, after a moment.

"Walk," Jason ordered, and motioned toward town.

Sweeney left first, Yoder followed, next Luke and Mick. The crowd, which had drawn back at the first sign of gunplay, broke into chattering knots.

Dude's rapid breathing slackened. An enormous tide of ease rolled over him, and he felt quite tired and a longing to be gone. But something was yet wrong. He saw as much in Uncle Billy's fixed eyes.

"Do you see what I see?" the old man said, whipping his trailwise caution at Dude.

Dude turned. Big Whelan, the Texas Ranger, was talking with a cowboy.

"Let's get out of here," Uncle Billy said, low.

Dude regarded him curiously. "What's wrong? We're in the clear. In a way, we're public benefactors. Buffalo Draw can have an honest horse race after this."

"Now is no time to start prying, Dude, boy. Do as I say. Let's ease on and rattle our hocks."

The outfit was rolling down the dusty road, not a cloud in the sky, as Coyote Walking had promised, heading west, ever westward, it seemed to Dude, when Uncle Billy halted the team and got down.

"Forgot all about Rebel back there," he said. There was the print of guilt on his impish face. "Still limping on that little piece of wood I whittled out and fixed on the frog of his foot with some stick-'em potion I mixed up. It sure beats playactors' spirit gum!"

CHAPTER 11

Dude McQuinn rested against his saddle, listening to the steady groan of the windmill's wheel, the slap-slap of the sucker rods, and the musical splash of water in the stock tank. The hobbled horses grazed the filling short grass, their steady cropping sounds emitting a relishing contentment. The mesquite coals of the supper fire still glowed cherry-red, and an evening breeze frisked out of the southwest, its touch on his cheek as gentle as a butterfly's wing.

"Coyote," said Dude, sitting up, "that was the best race you ever rode. Never saw anything like it. You brought the Judge down the stretch like a thunderbolt. Boy, you two were flyin'! Greatest catch-up race I ever saw, bar none. When did you think you could win it?"

"When Daylight we caught. The Judge stand he cannot for another horse out in front of him. Pass, he must."

"Thought I saw the Judge change leads. Did he?"

"I could feel him change, that horse. I knew then he wasn't hurt, though sore he will be for a while. Started riding him I did then, that horse, and my war whoop giving, which very brave makes him, like all Comanches are brave."

Uncle Billy coughed discreetly, the signal for a lecture. "Judge Blair changed leads twice," he said. "If he didn't have that flexibility he'd-a gone done and lost the race after Bubba Red knocked him off stride. What did he do? Why, he switched to the opposite lead, the left, and once he got going he switched back to the right. That's true balance. Not many horses have it, not many racehorses. The inablility to use both leads loses races for many horses when they go into a turn." He paused. "Judge Blair gains ground whenever he changes. How? Because he has to reach farther with a front foot to make the change. Furthermore, when he changes leads he rests the other lead foot and is able to continue that long stride."

"Any idea what his stride measures?" Jason asked.

"We measured it once, soon after Dude and I became pardners. Believe it was twenty-six feet, seven inches. That right, Dude?"

"Right, Uncle. That's when he's movin' on down the track."

"No other leg has to take the punishment the front lead leg does," Uncle Billy continued. "That's why a horse needs sturdy cannon bones to carry his rider's weight through the strain of running and changing and turning, and stopping and cutting on a dime, if he's a using horse. Judge Blair would make a first-rate cutting horse. . . . There's a good deal we don't under-stand about the mechanics of a horse's legwork. Someday these picture-takin' fellas you see in town will find a way to catch a horse's every move."

They talked on, and presently Dude said, "Jason, something has stuck in my mind ever since we left Flat Rock. Maybe you can clear it up for me. It's Colonel Bushrod. Was he really a colonel in Hood's army? And was he really in the Battle of Franklin?"

"I'll tell you what we heard around Flat Rock," Jason chuckled reminiscently. "He never was a colonel. Never was a major, or a captain or a lieutenant or even a sergeant — he was a buck private. Just called himself colonel. But you don't call the richest man in town a liar. Not when you're working for him and his son-in-law . . . Story I heard one night late at the bar was that he was a forager. Day of the battle he was out on a foraging detail. Trying to scare up some chickens and hams. Some fodder for the horses."

"That makes me feel better. At least he wasn't far away, and I guess you could say colonel is a sort of honorary title as he uses it. Foraging was important, too. I just didn't want to show disre-spect to an old soldier from the Lone Star State who'd fought in the War Between the States, maybe alongside Grandpa McQuinn, who was also a buck private, at bloody Franklin."

"You Alamo Texans!" the old man snorted.

"You mean the Great Rebellion. How many times have I had to set you right on that, Dude, boy? Better remember those sneaky sponges of the colonel and son-in-law. And now there's something we all need to augur on. Where'll we mosey to next?"

"No more Buffalo Draws," Dude said emphatically.

"Maybe Jason knows a likely little town where the horsemen are honorable and on the lookout for fresh money, though I have yet to meet one that wouldn't take the advantage, same as I might, myself."

Jason inclined his head in thought, a remembering on his heavy-boned features, a gentleness that served as a balance to his raw strength. It still did not fit to think of him as one who had uprooted two men from their saddles, banged their heads together, and dropped them like empty feed sacks.

He said, "There's a pretty fair little town north of here called Three Springs, and there's another one on north of it called Lone Tree. We might try Three Springs. Used to be the county seat. It's about the size of Flat Rock, maybe a little smaller. The two towns, I understand, have been at odds ever since Lone Tree sorta mavericked the county seat away."

"How'd that happen?"

"They had an election. Three Springs lost by just a few votes. They claimed Lone Tree brought in cowboys from outside the county to vote. Since then, each town has been tryin' to outdo the other one."

"Three Springs, here we come!" Uncle Billy sang, jumping up and cutting a jig. "Another good clean-up, Dude, boy! I'll have enough put away to buy me my hotel where a man —"

"— *can rock on the porch and watch the folks go by,*" Dude stole the words, with a weary mimicking. "If Three Springs turns out to be another tough lay, Uncle, just count this Comanche out. He's headin' back for the reservation."

"It's no Buffalo Draw," Jason averred. "It's a good town. More churches than saloons. School. Bank. Nice stores. A weekly newspaper. Everybody's friendly."

"So was Horse Yoder," Dude said. "How far is it?"

"Three days' ride, about."

"I know what's the matter with Dude," the old man told the others. "He's come to that foolish age where he thinks he wants to step into double harness and settle down. It's a kind of fever." An ominous shaking of the white head. "These sweet-smellin' little cookie pushers may drag short ropes, but they sure can throw a wide loop. Got a rope burn or two, myself."

"Where was that, Uncle?"

"Mind your own business!"

Three Springs shaped ahead about as Jason Carter had described. A thriving, pleasant-looking place below a huddle of greening hills.

200

Dude McQuinn searched for his anticipation, but it wasn't within him. Another town. Another bristly horse race, then the open trail again — somehow they failed to beckon to him as of old. At times he found himself resisting a baffling inertia, hitherto unknown till of late.

He shook off the mood as the outfit trailed into town. A couple of trade horses, a dun and a buckskin purchased along the way, followed behind the wagon with Rebel and Judge Blair, the latter saddled for his role as an ol' cow pony should the need arise.

A well-mounted townsman, heading out, spoke and nodded while he sized up the horses. Onward along the broad street, Dude noticed the air of commerce and stability and well-being. He was impressed and noted the goodly number of citizens going about their business and speaking to neighbors, and long-skirted women strolling in and out of the stores. Which reminded him: he hadn't seen one woman on the main street of Buffalo Draw. Not one. He guessed they hadn't dared.

He took further note of the Citizen's Bank, its stone front and sides suggesting strength and confidence, its shiny windows and polished door inviting entry; and the Texas House, its wide veranda newly painted white; and the Three Springs *Enterprise*, proud, gold letters across the window; and Archer & Dodd, General Merchandise, a striped awning, no less, overhanging the store's entrance; and Turley's Drugstore, a photographer's studio, and a post office. Water barrels here and there in the event of fire. He had to search up and down before he found a saloon. As if self-righteous citizenry had cast it out, the Longhorn occupied a banished sidestreet location.

A school bell was ringing. How long since he'd heard that callow pealing? And, in the distance, the shrill cries of young voices.

He was liking Three Springs more by the minute. His eyes lingered on the old stone courthouse, two stories high, a relic of the buoyant, pioneer past, abandoned now, yet dignified, dressed in robes of judicial-gray stone. A game of horseshoes was going on under the evergreen live oaks.

A man in a brown suit left the bank to cross the street to the general merchandise store, and paused for the outfit to pass. He nodded and waved in welcome. He also observed the trailing horses at length, his interest more than casual.

"Sure is a friendly place," Dude said.

"I told you," Jason said.

The logical place to stop was in the shade near the wagonyard, across from the Three Springs Livery, located as usual toward the end of the street to compensate for shifting winds on hot summer days and the sensitive noses of the squeamish. Uncle Billy and Coyote unharnessed and watered the team, and Jason and Dude led the other horses over to a clanking windmill which lifted water into a long, stone trough.

Afterward, they sat around and waited for the

inevitable local horseman. A short time passed. Dude saw the brown-suited man leave the store and cross the street to the bank, only to reappear after a minute or so and return to the store. Briefly, three men came out and huddled. After an earnest conference, it appeared, and frequent glances in the outfit's direction, the trio started walking this way.

"Company's coming!" Dude called.

"Horsemen?" Uncle Billy called back, his back to the street while he rattled through the medicine chest.

"They don't look like horsemen."

That swung the old man around, intent and curious. "City fellas. All dressed up. Enough to make a man suspicious."

"Maybe they want us to leave town. However, I don't see anybody with a star."

The trio walked up and paused. Their evident friendliness, which brushed apology, dispelled Dude's doubts.

"Good afternoon, gentlemen," said the brown-suited man.

"Howdy," said Dude.

"We . . . ah . . ." Again the apologetic manner. "We saw you coming in and just wondered if you might be carrying a short horse or two?"

"There he is, right there," Dude said, pointing to Rebel.

"Can he run?"

"Can when the sign is right."

"The sign?"

"I mean if he feels right. He seems to do better when there's a full moon."

The other laughing: "Well, there's a full moon right now. Mind if we look him over?"

"Not a-tall."

They marched over to the gelding and scanned him as city-bred men will a horse most times, ostensibly discerning, peering hard, yet missing the telling points. They marched in step to the other side, halted, and scanned once more, their heads moving together, left to right, right to left, up and down. They reciprocated glances and marched back, trying to look knowledgeable about horses. The brown-suited spokesman said, "I'm Solomon Gale, over at the bank," and held out his hand. The other two, he said, were Quincy Archer and Alonzo Dodd. Dude gave his name and the trio shook his hand. They sure seemed friendly, but so had Horse Yoder.

Dude, likewise, introduced the outfit: "Dr. William T. Lockhart, well-known breeder and trainer and veterinarian, late of Bourbon County, Kentucky, and also of the Old Dominion of Virginia. Dr. Lockhart comes pen-in-hand to Texas to observe the fountainhead of short-horse racing blood for various scientific journals back East. . . . To know him is to love him. To us he is plain Uncle Billy. . . . And Mr. Jason Carter, who recently sold his extensive farming and stockrising operations around Flat Rock, and has joined us en route to see about his holdings in California. . . . And Mr. Coyote

Walking, our jockey, who, needless to say, hails from Indian Territory and happens to be the son of the chief of all Comanches."

Everbody shook hands. There was no holding back here, Dude was pleased to see, because Coyote was a Comanche.

Gale was middle-aged, stout and short and of ruddy complexion, a brown beard around his chin like felt, his thoughtful eyes set deep under thick, bushy brows. He showed the understanding face of an affable man forced by profession and circumstances to say *no* more times when he wished to say *yes*.

"We have a horse called Little Ben," Gale said. "He's a sort of common venture, you might say." He paused, apology and hope blending across his face.

Dude looked at Gale without speaking, thinking that of all the approaches leading up to a match race this was the most roundabout and puzzling of his experience.

"You see . . . the three of us own Little Ben," Archer supplied, when Gale said no more. Archer was a stringbean of a man, slightly stooped, his washed-out eyes tired and patient, rather woebegone. He struck Dude as deferential toward Gale, possibly because of Gale's prominence.

And, when Archer did not go on, Dodd said, "We thought . . . perhaps . . . we might match some kind of race with you," and his face, fine-boned and pale, reddened somewhat, and he sent an uncertain hand to his neat, iron-gray beard, fussing with it, as a man might when un-accustomed to the preliminary skirmishing that went with matching races and trading horses and mules. And as Archer deferred to Gale, Dude saw that Dodd deferred to his business partner, Archer.

"Well . . ." said Dude, falling back on the familiar dodge of evasion the first time around, "we've come a long way today. Even so, we could look at your horses."

Gale gave a little hop of pleasure, as a boy might, and Archer swung his arms, and Dodd, the meekest of the three, smiled gratification.

"Hey," said Dude, grinning, "we haven't matched the race yet. We've just agreed to look at your horse."

"Oh, we understand that, Mr. McQuinn," Gale said on a note of apology. "We keep Little Ben in a barn behind my house. It's right down the street. Now, if you gentlemen will be so kind as to accompany us . . ."

Be so kind as to accompany us. Dude shook his head, not knowing how to take such politeness.

Solomon Gale, befitting the leading man in the community, resided in a two-story white house behind which rose the peaked roof of a red barn, and enclosing the front of the barn was a board corral, and within it a windmill and cast-iron water trough.

Gale led forth a seal-brown gelding on halter and gingerly circled him around the corral. A good-looking horse at first glance, Dude judged,

206

until you noticed his thinness through the withers and his pigeon-toed stance and his lack of superior muscular development in the hind-quarters.

"What do you think of him, Mr. McQuinn?" Gale asked. For a man angling to match his horse, he had a decided absence of bluster.

"Little Ben looks like a real track burner to me."

"And you, Dr. Lockhart?"

"A splendid specimen of short-horse breeding, sir. You are to be congratulated. No doubt a product of foundation blood." He nodded sagely, as did Jason and Coyote. "May I inquire as to his breeding, Mr. Gale?"

"Afraid we're a little in the dark about that."

"Too bad. I see certain characteristics traceable to the legendary Steel Dust — the big jaws, the short neck and back, the deep barrel, the wide nostrils, the fox ears."

The trio exchanged looks of obscure meaning. Whatever that import, it held no horsemen's pride; in fact, they acted bewildered. They stood irresolute for another moment, and then Gale said:

"Would you gentlemen consider matching us?" He could not have expressed it more doubtfully and seemed less confident of winning.

"How much do you want to bet?" Dude asked.

The eyes of the three met, uncertainty mirrored in all. "Not very much," Gale said.

"Say, four hundred dollars?"

Again, Gale turned to his partners for guidance, and again Dude saw their hesitation. "That's more than we feel we should wager," Gale said.

"Yes," said Archer.

"Yes, indeed," said Dodd.

"Well," Dude countered, "throw something at me." By now he had the strangest inkling, the reversal that he was making the match for Gale.

"One hundred?"

"Two hundred?" Dude dickered. You couldn't say these Three Springs horsemen were exactly reckless with the coin.

"That's still too much," Gale said. "One fifty?"

"Guess we can saddle up for that."

Instantly, Gale's thanks came through into his face, and Archer and Dodd smiled gratefully, and Gale said, "Thank you for meeting our terms, gentlemen." He turned to his partners, a final motion that said everything was set.

"Hold on," Dude said. "We haven't decided on the distance."

"So we haven't," Gale apologized, flushing an even deeper red. "But we won't run a quarter mile."

"Four hundred yards?"

"Still too far."

Archer tapped Gale on the shoulder, motioned with his head, and the three walked to the barn and stopped, their undertones rising as each began talking at once. Gale said something.

Archer nodded, then Dodd nodded. They marched back and Gale said apologetically, "I was wrong, Mr. McQuinn. We will go the full quarter mile."

Dude was concluding that everything about this match-up was wrong. If the quarter mile wasn't right in the first place, why was it right now? And such talk as "Thank you for meeting our terms." And such an oversight as the distance to be run.

Catching Uncle Billy's glint of warning, he said, "We'll go the quarter with you, but we'll need to rest up a few days before we do."

"Whenever you want to run is fine with us, Mr. McQuinn. We appreciate your consideration."

Appreciate your consideration! Were these Three Springs horseman as naive and fair meat as they seemed, or were they slickering the outfit with some new wrinkle?

"By the way," said Dude, delaying further, "I know your trainer will want to look at Rebel."

"We have no trainer," Gale said. "Just a young jockey. Our trainer went to south Texas long ago."

"And good riddance it was," Archer added, quivering with indignation.

"Yes," Dodd seconded. "Better had he left before that."

Good riddance? Why? What had the trainer done? Dude waited for the particulars.

Nothing came. Instead, the obliging Gale

pointed and said, "There's a nice spring up the street a piece. Plenty of shade and firewood. A nice pasture just beyond. What we call our City Park. You gentlemen are welcome to camp there. Track is a short piece north of town. Just take the main road." And, strangely, after Dude had thanked him and made to go: "Now you gentlemen do have a good horse?"

"Yes, he's a good horse," Dude answered, not wanting to scare him off and surprised that Gale had asked, and further surprised when Gale smiled and said, "Come by the bank when you're ready."

The outfit found the park as Gale had described: a sweet-water spring gushing from the base of a rocky ledge, plenty of live-oak shade and firewood, and a fenced pasture nearby for the horses.

"Never saw such a friendly town." Suspicion dulled Uncle Billy's voice. "Wonder what they've got up their sleeves."

"It's almost like they want our horse to beat their horse," Dude pondered.

Coyote Walking said, "The poet wrote, 'Beware of hasty connections,' although this Comanche thinks he had in mind advice to young ladies. However, it would apply as well to over-friendly horsemen."

Jason laughed softly. "You've been up against so many slick horsemen and traders, you don't know how to take genuine, friendly folks — that's all."

"The test," Uncle Billy reflected, "will come when we see how soon our welcome wears out, and what's behind this nicey-nice talk. Remember friend Horse?"

"And," Coyote Walking contributed, "the colonel and son-in-law, shaking our hands, grabbing us like mean mules?"

Next morning they had scarcely worked Rebel and Judge Blair on the track and cooled them and rubbed them down and fed them, when a mule-drawn light wagon rattled up and the driver called, "Got some feed for you boys."

"Feed?" Dude questioned.

"Compliments of Mr. Solomon Gale. Oats and hay. Where you want it?"

"That's mighty neighborly, I must say."

With Jason and Coyote pitching in, Dude fell to hoisting sacks and bales, and when that was done, the driver, who volunteered that he was Blondy Nosler, owner of the Three Springs Livery, rolled himself a smoke and eyed the horses. He was about fifty or so, his skin too fair for the Texas sun and his beard the color of down. He showed the contemplative set to his blue eyes and broad mouth of a man who spent considerable time judging horses and mules.

"Hear you got a fast horse," he remarked.

"He can ramble a little," Dude said.

"Which one is he?"

"That dark bay on this side."

"What's his best distance?"

"Anything up to five eighths."

"Hmmmmnn. That's what they need, a good quarter-mile horse to run against."

"Why just the quarter mile?"

Nosler scratched his ribs. "Guess you'd have to ask Solomon Gale. See you, boys." He stepped to the wagon and drove off.

"What do you make of that, Uncle?"

"Not normal for strangers to be so generous." Just before noon, a round-faced boy drove up in a buckboard. He roamed appreciative eyes over the horses, drew a piece of paper from his shirt pocket, and read thereon, his mouth laboring. "I'm lookin' for uh . . . Mr. Dude McQuinn and uh . . . Doctor, I reckon it says . . . Dr. William Lockhart."

"I'm McQuinn and there's Dr. Lockhart."

"Got some groceries for you."

"We didn't order anything."

"Know you didn't. It's from Mr. Quincy Archer and Mr. Alonzo Dodd. Said to tell you-all it's with their comp . . ." stumbling, "— compliments." He went to the rear of the buckboard. "Where you want 'em?"

Dude, seeing Jason's I-told-you-so grin, shrugged and said, "Over there by the wagon, young sprout."

Two trips were required to fetch all the boxes and sacks. His mission completed, the boy stuck a thumb inside his belt and took a conversational stance. "I'm Ham Williams, I work around. Some for the store, some for Blondy Nosler. Hear you got a runnin' horse."

"You heard right," Dude said.

212

"He's a good horse, is he?"

"Good enough."

"What's he run the quarter in?"

"Depends if the wind's pushin' against him or pushin' behind him."

"What does that mean?"

"Means fast or faster."

Ham Williams scratched his head, pulling himself aboard, and drove off, whistling.

"There it is again," Dude said. "Do we have a good horse? Gets me."

Jason said, "Maybe he's fishing around to see how to bet."

"Except he asked it the same way Gale did, like he was hoping. Boy, look at this pile of groceries!"

It was past four o'clock, after the school bell had tolled its last for the day, when a solitary figure, black-hatted, black-suited, gaunt, and long-striding, appeared on the road. There was a purposefulness to his step, and when he turned in at the camp, a dour smile relieved his austere face, and he said, "Good afternoon, gentlemen. I am Professor Obadiah Huff, the local school superintendent and president of the Three Springs Mutual Improvement Society." His manner of speaking was distinct, lending the effect that each word had been ground and fitted and weighed for import before deemed worthy of utterance. "Needless to say, we of Three Springs are pleased to have you pause in our community. In that connection, and speaking for the society, I take this occasion to invite each and all of you to our monthly literary meeting tonight at the schoolhouse. The program commences at seven o'clock."

Whereupon he began seizing and shaking hands, first Uncle Billy's, then Jason's, then Dude's, and asking each his name, the handshaking the mean-mule-grabbing variety, and Dude saw Coyote Walking's instant shrinking back, helpless, as his hand was pumped and his name asked and given.

"Our meeting," Professor Huff continued distinctly, "commences, as I said, at seven o'clock, neither before nor after — at seven sharp. Patrons of our school will be in attendance. There will be readings and declamations, dialogues and songs, and a spelling bee. If someone can be found who plays the banjo or fiddle or guitar, there will be music. Unfortunately, our last musician was the loser over the disputed ownership of a cow pony which turned up bearing his blanket and saddle. So he will not be with us again. A likable fellow he was, too." The dour smile materialized again, behind it an assessing of sorts. "I am also chairman of the program committee." (Now, Dude figured, we are coming to the nub of this-here visit.) "The committee is in dire need of some noteworthy gentleman, as all of you are, I'm sure, to render a reading tonight . . . inasmuch as Mr. Grady Brown, one of our staunchest patrons, had the misfortune yesterday to fall from his wagon in front of

Archer & Dodd, General Merchandise, and break his leg." He leveled forceful eyes on Uncle Billy.

"Now what was that again?" the old man asked, head cocked, hand to ear, shoulders hunched, his voice way higher than normal.

A perceptible wave of irritation washed over the severely academic features. "I said that we need some gentleman like yourself to render a reading tonight . . . since Mr. Grady Brown, one of our patrons, fell off his wagon and broke his leg in front of Archer & Dodd, General Merchandise."

"Shady who?" Uncle Billy shrilled, leaning farther in. "Didn't quite get all that, mister."

"He don't hear so good," Jason came to the rescue.

"Then may I invite you, Mr. Carter, to assist with our program? You have a compelling voice."

Jason was clamping a hand to his middle, his face hurting, before Huff could finish. "Been feelin' poorly all day. Chills and fever, seems like. Had 'em ever since I was a kid about this time of year."

A certain desperation was evident next: "It would indeed be a feather in our collective caps, Mr. Coyote, if you, a civilized aborigine, a product of America's untamed wilderness . . . its sweeping prairies, its forested hills and mountains, its lush meadowlands . . . would consent to appear on the program."

"Me no tamed." A series of rapid and rejecting

215

signs. "Me Comanche. White man's talk no speakum much. And white man's talking paper me no savvy nothin'."

Beaten, Professor Huff turned in supplication to Dude. "Talent, like gold, is where you find it. You impress me as a man of scholarly tastes and literary leanings. Surely you will help us promote the cultural growth of Three Springs?"

"Afraid that's out of my line, Professor."

"I know he can read," Jason guyed him.

"Some of our patrons can neither read nor write," Huff said. "Every time we meet I have to comb the town and countryside for performers."

Dude, glaring at Jason: "Thanks, Professor. But I'll have to pull out of this go." Still, while refusing, he could feel within himself the bent to help when asked, and, also, to be around families again, to hear the voices of women and children again. And hadn't the professor mentioned scholarly tastes and literary leanings?

CHAPTER 12

During supper, Dude could not erase the meeting from his thoughts. Supplicating voices and faces kept tugging at him. On impulse, he changed into fresh shirt and trousers, slicked down his dusty boots clean, pulled on his town coat, blew the dust off his hat, crimped it precisely, and announced, "Believe I'll drift over to the schoolhouse for a little look-see."

"What did I tell you?" Uncle Billy roared to the others. "He's got the fever for certain!"

When Dude arrived, late patrons and children were hurrying inside. Vehicles and saddle horses filled the schoolyard. Dude removed his hat and entered the amber glow of lanterns lighting a room narrow and cramped. Seeing the benches full and people standing, he stood hatless at the rear near the doorway. Across the small stage of rough lumber hung curtains of brown sacking on rings.

A settling hush of anticipation. Now, faintly audible, the whisper of instructive voices backstage, and suddenly the curtains parted as on another world and jerked to the wings of the stage, revealing a background of blue waterfall and brown rocks and green trees crudely painted on a wagon sheet.

Professor Huff made a dignified appearance, nodding left and right, and received courteous, if not warm, applause. He raised his hand for quiet, as he might in the schoolroom, and said, "Good evening, patrons and children. The Three Springs Mutual Improvement Society welcomes you and thank you for your attendance and participation . . . And before we commence, I should like to take this occasion to express our thanks to Miss Bridget Pettibone" — instant applause at mention of her name — "who has worked unceasingly with our youngsters on their drills and recitation. . . . The Reverend John Isaacs will now lead us in prayer."

A forbidding figure, unsmiling and inflexible, with a face like retribution, rose and said, "Let us bow our heads," and began praying in a strong, funereal voice. He prayed so long that the children started to squirm and fidget and the elders to yawn; when it seemed that he would go on forever, he spoke a sonorous "Amen!" and sat, and Professor Huff took over:

"Our first reading of the evening will be by little Johnny Armstrong, who will recite 'Spartacus to the Gladiators.' "

Little Johnny fairly ran to the stage and on, bowed stiffly and swiftly, got set, and disgorged himself of his lines at breakneck speed, bowed, and fairly ran off the stage to hearty applause.

There followed "The Face on the Barroom Floor," and "The Lips That Touch Liquor Shall Never Touch Mine," and "The Barefoot Boy," and "How We Tried to Lick the Teacher." Each young reader received long applause.

It was evident, thought Dude, that in the tradition of *McGuffey's Readers* most of the readings, even when humorous, sought to teach a moral or lesson. Now and then, when a child stumbled over a word or forgot a line, a young woman's mellifluous voice offstage would convey the needed prompting.

As the evening advanced, a freckled girl of nine or ten, dressed in blue and white calico, and a blue ribbon adorning her pretty auburn hair, advanced shyly to the stage to recite "Old Ironsides." She began well enough:

"Ay, tear her tattered ensign down!
    Long has it waved on high,
And many an eye has danced to see
    That banner . . . [faltering] . . . in the sky

[the sweet voice prompted and the child repeated]

Beneath it rung . . . [faltering, repeating]
    . . . beneath it rung —"

Even as the helping voice whispered, "the battle shout," the frightened child, weeping tears of humiliation, fled the stage into the arms of her parents to the most thunderous applause of the night.

When the confusion ceased, Professor Huff took the stage. "Susie's a mighty fine little girl," he said, "and we're all proud of her. You bet we are." Another storm of applause. Then: "Due to the unfortunate accident of our good patron Mr. Grady Brown, who slipped and fell from his wagon this morning, breaking his left leg, we should like to ask for a volunteer from the audience to read Edgar Allan Poe's immortal poem, 'The Raven.' . . . Will some kind gentleman please step up and render this reading for us?" He gazed hopefully over the audience.

Not a man rose. An uncomfortable silence took hold, broken only by the shuffling of boots and the squeak of benches and chairs as patrons stirred self-consciously, and the whimpering of a tired and sleepy young one.

Without warning, Dude felt himself propelled forward from behind. He gave a startled sound. Instantly, Professor Huff called out, "Yes — back there!" Pointing: "Thank you, sir! Please come forward!"

Heads craned to see and Dude discovered himself the focus of all eyes. His backward glance exposed Uncle Billy, Jason, and Coyote as the cat-grinning culprits who had pushed him forward.

"Talent, like gold, is where you find it," the tenacious Huff went on, raising his distinct voice still higher. "I do believe it is my new and good friend, Mr. McQuinn — Mr. Dude McQuinn, the well-known horseman, who has so generously volunteered. Let's all give him a great big hand, folks!"

Red of face, helpless and furious, hat in hand, Dude started down the aisle, not without fright. He would, he knew, look even more ridiculous if he backed out now. Everything seemed unreal. It could not be, but here he was stumbling up the steps and onto the stage, and Professor Huff, his smile satanic, was handing him an open book.

Like the small boy, Dude bowed, planted his feet, and began mumbling:

"Once upon a midnight dreary, while I
   pondered weak and weary,
Over many a quaint and curious volume
   of forgotten lore —"

Jarringly, a voice bellowed from the rear of the packed room, "We can't hear you back here!" A familiar voice. "Louder!"

Dude froze and stared, speechless. The voice, he saw, belonged to one Jason Carter, standing shoulder to shoulder with one William T. Lockhart and one Coyote Walking. Just wait till he got back to camp! He coughed and cleared his voice and continued hesitantly:

"While I nodded, nearly napping, suddenly
   there came a tapping,

221

As of someone gently rapping, at my
  chamber door.
'Tis some visitor,' I muttered, 'tapping at
  my —' "

"Louder! Louder!" three voices shouted together. Freezing, Dude saw Uncle Billy and
Coyote and Jason, hands cupped to mouths. Just
wait! he fumed.

Professor Huff snapped up out of his chair and
marched at threatening step down the aisle, and
the noisy threesome vanished through the doorway. Turning back, Huff motioned Dude to
continue.

Clearing his throat, Dude worked out of his
hesitant mumblings. His voice deepened as his
confidence grew and he forgot his audience,
absorbed in the poet's sorrow for "the lost
Lenore," and the "ghastly grim and ancient Raven wandering from the Nightly shore" filling
his mind. He began to thrill to the sound of his
delivery, despite balking over *seraphim* and *ne-
penthe,* and he gestured dramatically at each
crucial "nevermore," his voice rising and falling
as his hand lifted and fell.

"And my soul from out that shadow that
  lies floating on the floor
Shall be lifted — nevermore!"

He had finished, though he could not believe
that he had, for he could have gone on and on. In

222

his ears beat the heady applause of patrons and children, too. He bowed graciously, a sweeping bow, smiling as he did so, and slowly left the stage. As he came down the steps, Professor Huff, in pride, motioned him to a chair and he seated himself, still in his fantasy world, still hearing the vibrancy of his own voice.

"Thank you, Mr. McQuinn," the professor said, warmly shaking Dude's hand. "That was well done." And facing the audience, Huff announced, "There will now be a brief recess, folks. Then we shall have a debate."

In moments the room was half emptied as the children scrambled outside. The professor hastened away to speak to a patron. It was time to leave. Rising, Dude heard quick, light steps descending the stairs amid a flutter of skirts, and next the prompter's voice that he had heard offstage, speaking behind him, a somewhat breathless voice, "Oh, Mr. McQuinn. May I speak to you?"

He turned.

She was tall, quite tall for a woman, nearly up to his shoulder, and her face was plain but well formed and her eyes, gray and luminous, matched the eloquence of her voice, and her mouth was full and smiling, yet with a certain stiff decorum.

She said, in that unforgettable voice, "I wish to thank you for helping us tonight, for volunteering. You read quite well, even with interruptions."

"My friends," he said, frowning.

"I am Bridget Pettibone. I teach here."

"Please to meet you, Miss Pettibone." Her plain dark dress, high-necked and severely prim, could not, however, conceal the pleasing lines of a full-bodied Miss Pettibone, and of which she seemed totally unaware. She was, he gathered, a most proper young lady.

Dude hung his head. "He was stretchin' the blanket on that. I'm just an ol' country boy."

She possessed a fetching way of wrinkling her nose. "I do believe you are modest, Mr. McQuinn, a rather uncommon virtue. What do you deal in . . . saddle horses?"

"Not 'specially. I have a short horse."

"You mean a racehorse?"

"That's right," he answered, seeing the first sign of her disapproval. "Our outfit travels around. We match races, and we do some trading."

"I see. You must excuse me, Mr. McQuinn. I must hurry the debaters along. I hope you can stay."

He hadn't meant to stay, but he did, and when the room filled, Professor Huff announced the subject for tonight's debate: "Resolved, that the right of suffrage should be extended to women."

For the next half hour or more the debate raged, only one speaker for each side, a high-school girl taking the affirmative, a high-school boy the negative. They fired their arguments in flights of rhetoric, interspersed with numerous belittling references to "my honorable opponent."

Dude smiled at the foregone two-to-one deci-sion for the negative, two of the judges being townsmen, the other Miss Pettibone.

Professor Huff spoke brief words of apprecia-tion, and the Reverend Isaacs spoke many, on and on, until the young ones' restlessness reached a ferment of squirming and shuffling.

"Amen!"

An immediate rising and departing.

Dude stood but did not leave, a brash excite-ment upon him. When Miss Pettibone came down the stairs, he was waiting. He hung his head and slanted a look at her. "May I see you home?"

She was startled. For an instant only she seemed to lose her composure and he feared she was going to refuse. "Thank you, Mr. McQuinn. I live nearby, at the Quincy Archer residence. That would be troubling you unnecessarily."

"Not one little bit," he said gallantly, bowing from the waist. "I'd be honored."

"Very well, Mr. McQuinn."

As they left the schoolhouse, the evening was starlit and the pungent breeze off the prairie felt lightly cool. Taking her arm protectively when they crossed the dusty street, he drew in the de-lightful scent of her hair. Lilac? Verbena? Lily of the valley? He could guess no further. Whatever it was, he liked it. Once across, he felt her move away from his touch. Proper, indeed!

"Wasn't hard to figure out who cast the affir-mative vote back there," he teased her.

"It was the same when we debated whether barbed wire has had a civilizing effect on Texas. I still believe it has."

"I take it you're not a native of the Lone Star State, Miss Pettibone?"

"Boston. Here to impart knowledge and manners to the children of our brave pioneers. I like Three Springs very much."

"I got the impression that Three Springs likes you."

"It is generous of you to say that. I do hope so."

"Never been in a town where everybody was so friendly and generous to a total stranger. Mr. Gale sent over a load of horse feed, and Mr. Archer and Mr. Dodd sent groceries."

She slowed her step and faced him, the soft light picking up the even molding of her features and the wide, deep eyes. "Three Springs has a mania for horse racing."

"Most Texas towns do. It's entertainment, a way to show local pride."

"Pride will have a fall, Mr. McQuinn, for pride goeth before and shame cometh after. Both have come to Three Springs."

"Just how do you mean?"

"Then you don't know what happened here about a year ago? It made an indelible impression on me, a newcomer, because of the town's almost total involvement and the dire consequences it had. It was truly a blow."

"A blow?"

"I can't believe that no one has mentioned *that horse race* to you."

"All I know is that we've matched Little Ben."

"You don't know about the bitter rivalry between Three Springs and Lone Tree?" she said, maintaining the same tone of disbelief.

"I heard about the courthouse election steal, sure."

"It wasn't that, although it was a contributing factor." Her voice transmitted genuine reluctance. "I see that I shall have to tell you. . . . You see, Little Ben was matched against a Lone Tree horse called Hondo. Hondo beat Little Ben. A great deal of money was wagered — and lost that day — and any is too much. I believe that is known as losing one's shirt. People suffered. Businessmen lost heavily. . . . That happened just when we were trying to raise funds through public subscription for a new schoolhouse, which is sorely needed. You saw something of our needs tonight — that little building, inadequate for the needs of a growing community. As you might guess, our schoolhouse project failed."

"So you blame horse racing?"

"Not horse racing per se. I adore horses. No creature is more beautiful. But I wholeheartedly oppose gambling on races. I was brought up to think of racehorses as gamblers' horses and gambling as a sin."

Gently, he said, "Fast horses were put here on earth to run, Miss Pettibone."

"But not for money, Mr. McQuinn."

"If people didn't bet, there'd be no races. Think of all the fun and excitement they'd miss. And I wish you'd call me Dude."

Her laughter spilled, clear and musical. "You are a worthy opponent, Mr. McQuinn." *So it was still "Mr. McQuinn" and likely would continue so,* Dude thought. "You make a firm point, then follow it with blandishments to feed the vanity, thus weakening the other side's stand. I shall counter with another thrust: Racing horses is cruel. They are put to undue stress and injury. What is your reply to that, honorable opponent McQuinn?"

"Got'cha, ma'am. Compared to a workhorse or cow pony, a runnin' horse lives on the fat of the land. Gets his feet trimmed and shod regular, gets his oats and hay regular, and after he's breezed or races, he gets cooled and rubbed down, a nice blanket on his back. If he comes down sick, he gets doctored. When he's not travelin' around seein' the country, he loafs in his own stall and own private pasture. Generally, he lives to a ripe old age, and when people pass by they look at him with respect and affection and say, 'Boy, could he fly!' "

Her pleasing laugh, and, "You almost make me concede, Mr. McQuinn, but I cannot forget that schoolhouse we need."

"I can understand that. How much did Hondo beat Little Ben?"

"I didn't see the race. I believe I heard Mr. Archer tell Sadie — that's his wife — that Hondo daylighted Little Ben. Would that be the proper term?"

"You are catching on, Miss Bridget."

They strolled on in silence. Dude was thinking hard, adding and rejecting thoughts as fast as they formed. Why, a matter-of-fact voice kept asking, should he concern himself with any of this? Wouldn't he soon be gone?

Her voice brought him up sharply. "Here's where I live. Thank you for seeing me home, Mr. McQuinn."

"Been a real pleasure, Miss Bridget." He walked her to the steps of the wide porch. A light burned in the parlor. "May I call on you again?"

She hesitated. "If you like."

"Say, Wednesday evening?"

"That would be nice, Mr. McQuinn. We can go to prayer meeting. That is, if you don't mind?"

"Nothing I enjoy more than prayer meetings."

"How redeeming. You, a gambler's horseman, going to church."

"In all honesty, Bridget, I'm going because of you."

"No matter — you are going." Her voice acquired a fresh earnestness. "Other horsemen like yourself have come here since Hondo beat Little Ben and they've all failed. I wish you luck. Good night, Dude."

She went up the steps, leaving him lost in puzzlement. Failed at what? There was only one thing a horseman could fail at and that was winning a race. And why would she wish him luck against the local favorite? More important, she had called him Dude. He lingered, the pleasing scent of her still about him.

His steps were airy as he turned toward camp.

Solomon Gale's office was much like the stone bank building itself, simple, austere, formidable, unadorned save for a framed likeness of Sam Houston, an elkhorn hat rack, one shiny brass spittoon, and a plain oak desk behind which he sat hunched over a thick ledger. He rose and shook hands. "You ready to run, McQuinn?"

"How about three o'clock tomorrow afternoon?"

"Fine with me. I'm sure it is with Archer and Dodd."

"Sure much obliged to you for all the horse feed. Appreciate it."

"You're welcome," Gale said, giving an aside wave. "We can flip now for the starter, a local man or yours."

"All right," Dude said, surprised and suspicious as always at ready cooperation. Was this another Horse Yoder come-on?

"Flip if you like, McQuinn."

Dude found a coin, said, "You call it," and flipped. Gale called heads, and when the coin came down showing tails, the townsman showed one of his amiable smiles. "Just so we get a fair start."

"It will be. Jason Carter will see to that." Dude settled back in his chair. "Understand you had quite a little horse race here about a year ago?"

Gale's friendly features clouded. "We did. Lone Tree hung it on us with Hondo. It was more than a horse race, it was a community disaster. You might compare it to a total crop failure or a late spring die-up when a blizzard hits. We're coming out of it, though."

"How much did Hondo beat Little Ben?"

"Three lengths," Gale said, and groaned, shaking his head over the painful memory.

"I know how you feel," Dude said sympathetically.

"That Lone Tree bunch just laughed at us. You heard, maybe, how they stole the county seat? Brought in cowboys from outside the county to vote? We couldn't prove they did, but we know they did."

"I heard that, too. Was the race on the up-and-up?"

"So far as we know. Their horse just flat outran ours." His eyes were questioning. "Just how good is your horse, McQuinn? Really?"

Again! thought Dude, and an old caution tapped him, cool and reminding. "Rebel's a good horse," he evaded. "How good, we'll see tomorrow. You can't always tell about a horse, Mr. Gale." Talking this way, Dude felt a stab of conscience. Judge Blair could take Little Ben, so his experienced judgment told him after seeing the other horse. To make matters worse, Dude was beginning to like this Solomon Gale, which was dangerous, because if you turned soft-hearted before a match race, you might let the advantage slip away; and generosity had never bought horse feed or grub or whiskey. Dude's further judgment was that Gale and his two friends didn't know beans about racehorses; if he was wrong, they were the slickest glad-handers he had ever encountered.

"Tell you what," said Dude, envisioning an above-board race, "there's a sure-enough scorpion down in south Texas you might bring in to run at this Hondo."

Gale perked up. "Who's that?"

"None other than Judge Blair."

It warmed Dude's heart to see Gale's face light up like a small boy's. "Nothing I'd like better," Gale said. "But Judge Blair is too well known. And I don't think the Lone Tree bunch would match us unless they got heavy odds, when we're the ones who need the odds to recoup."

"I've heard tell of instances," Dude drawled, "where a top horse like Judge Blair was brought in and run under another name."

"First place, somebody would recognize Judge Blair. That blaze face, those white feet. Believe me, that Lone Tree bunch has been around — they'd know! Second place, word would get out here in Three Springs what we were up to. The boys at the Longhorn would know in five minutes. You can't cover up something like that in a small town." He looked at Dude. "And why Judge Blair?"

"Happens I know the man who owns him.

Last I heard he was still in south Texas. On top of that, I've seen Judge Blair run — that's enough for me."

"There you are. Too many people know about Judge Blair." Solomon Gale sank back and folded his arms. From time to time he rubbed his chin. A disturbing realization seemed to grab him, and he half rose from his chair. "Mr. McQuinn, I hope you're not advising the citizens of Three Springs to bring in a ringer to run against Hondo?"

Dude smiled disarmingly. He lifted one shoulder and let it fall. "Just thinking how you might get back at that slick Lone Tree bunch after what they did."

"There's the matter of ethics involved."

"Ethics? Ethics didn't win the county seat election for Lone Tree." Standing, he thought how unschooled Gale and the others were about matching races, and that sometimes the innocent had to be protected from themselves. "I'll run along," he said. "See you at the track."

"Say," Gale called, looking sheepish, "we forgot the judges. How about Dr. Lockhart, Blondy Nosler, and Cal Turley?"

Dude nodded.

Mounted on Blue Grass, Dude led Judge Blair, his blaze face and white feet dyed dark bay like the rest of him, down the track and past the crowd and back, trailing Little Ben. Jason waited at the starting line, Uncle Billy at the finish line.

"I think we can take this horse," Dude said, dropping back to speak to Coyote. "Beat him less than three lengths in all we need."

"Less than three lengths?" Coyote was puzzled.

"Yes. Pull up if you have to, but don't make it noticeable."

"Grandfather won't like that."

"I'll explain later. Uncle Billy will understand."

"You are very sure of winning, white father."

"I'm never that sure."

When the horses turned to face the starting line, Dude had his first misgiving of the day. Little Ben, behaving calmly with a lightweight boy aboard, looked fast and eager. You could say a horse lacked this or that; some horsemen went so far as to claim that color was a factor, such as the misjudgment that a golden-hided palomino was too pretty to run. What they overlooked was the measureless heart and honesty of a good horse.

This time Dude rode down the track a way to watch.

The horses walked toward the line, almost head to head. Coyote turned Judge Blair. At that split second Jason dropped his hand and shouted.

The Judge took the break by half a jump. They swept past Dude and ran on down there like that, no veering, no bumping. This Little Ben had heart!

At about the one-eighth pole Dude saw his

horse begin to roll. Daylight opened between the horses. The boy tapped Little Ben, and the seal-brown gelding made his move. He closed to Judge Blair's hindquarters and there he battled, refusing to throw up his tail and quit. Somewhere past three hundred yards Judge Blair widened the gap, for he was flying now.

Suddenly it was over by daylight.

Dude rode to the finish line and caught Uncle Billy's all's-well wave.

"McQuinn!"

It was Gale, flanked by Archer and Dodd, waving him over. It occurred to him that the trio seemed out of place here, and it wasn't their business suits and white shirts. No, not that. It was their greenhorn manner. They just didn't belong in the horse crowd of oldsters and idlers and the Longhorn's sportin' gentry.

"Your horse won by a length and a half," Gale told him, his tone congratulatory. So Coyote held the Judge up, Dude thought. "Come with us down to the bank. We'll pay off there."

Dude rubbed hard at his forehead, nodding, almost hating to take their money, because they had been taken so easily.

The three climbed into a buggy and Dude followed. At the bank Gale led off upstairs to a door, which he unlocked and which opened on a room overlooking the street. Gale closed the door behind them and went to a wooden cabinet and, surreptitiously, took out a bottle and glasses. The place had the snug look of a retreat.

Soft-looking chairs and sofa. On the wall, heads of buffalo and deer, on the floor a bear rug. Poker chips and cards in the center of the round table. Beside each chair an obsequious cuspidor.

"Let's begin by paying Mr. McQuinn," said Gale, "and having a drink." To Dude: "It's wiser to talk here. Tongues would wag if we were seen going to the Longhorn. Three Springs is a very straitlaced town."

First they paid cheerfully. Now they treated the winner. It was odd. Feeling he must give something in return, Dude said, "Your Little Ben is a good horse. Rebel got the break and that was the difference between them the first furlong. Believe you'd do best not to match him much longer. That looks like his best lick. Up to two fifty. Believe he'll make you some money over the shorter routes."

Gale poured Dude a glass of whiskey and handed the bottle to Archer. "Thank you, McQuinn. Wish we had you as our trainer. The last one misrepresented certain facts to us before we matched Hondo."

"Mind telling me what?"

"He led us to believe that Little Ben could outrun Hondo at the quarter mile."

"Why?"

"Simple. He was working for that Lone Tree bunch all the time."

"So he took you."

"By three full lengths, you might say. He faded out right after the race. We were hoping today that your horse would beat Little Ben by that much or more. In which case we'd have had an unknown challenger to match against Hondo at good odds."

Dude sipped. He had another sip. "You are a good judge of good whiskey, Mr. Gale."

"And a poor judge of poor horseflesh."

"All of us," lamented Dodd. "We got cleaned."

"Believe me, we've all been taken at times," Dude said. "However, I have some good news for you. . . . You have your challenger at hand — if you want him."

"You mean Rebel?" Archer plopped down his glass.

"I mean Rebel."

"I don't understand. He didn't beat Little Ben as much as Hondo did."

"He could have, and more. I told our jockey to pull him up if he got a good lead."

"Why?" Gale demanded, thunderstruck.

"So you can get those great big odds you need to recoup with a fast, unknown horse. Had Rebel won by three lengths or more, the Lone Tree bunch might shy off. Or howl for even money or odds. Maybe they wouldn't even run at you. Meanwhile, this way, the boys at the Longhorn will pass the word for you . . . sorta set it up."

Gale shook his head. "How did you know Rebel would win?"

"You can never be absolutely certain what a horse will do on a given day. But Rebel's a consistent runner and always gives his honest best. Loves to run."

The trio's eyes locked.

"I'll admit it was a wild notion," Dude said. "I like the town and I heard what Lone Tree pulled. Guess I wanted to help. Don't feel you have to do it. Horse racing is always chancy. You could lose again."

"Boys," Gale said suddenly, raising his glass, "I think we've found our horse at last!" They downed their drinks, after which Gale, in that apolegetic wont of his, said, "McQuinn, now we can tell you something. Rebel has passed the test, so to speak. We've matched horse after horse of outfits traveling through, hoping some-day we'd find a real speed demon." He rubbed his hands gleefully. "For a while there I was afraid we'd have to bring in a ringer. Now we can do it fair and square. We must think of public opinion and the moral aspects."

"Frankly," said Archer, "I don't give one tin-ker's damn about public opinion or morals, just so we get even. My wife's been on the warpath ever since that schoolhouse subscription drive failed. Miss Pettibone rooms and boards with us, you know."

"I want blood," Dodd swore, his mild face stiffening. "Let's challenge 'em again."

"One thing bothers me," Dude said. "Why didn't you ask for a speed trial with Rebel? I'd've gone along with you."

"We wanted to see your horse in actual competition, running for real money." Gale was glowing. "We can send a delegation over first thing after tomorrow. Let's give news of Rebel's victory a day to reach Lone Tree and Shag Fallon. We'd like you to go along, McQuinn, you and Dr. Lockhart."

"Glad to. And you might as well start calling me Dude. Uncle Billy and I will want a close look-see at this Hondo horse."

"You'll see him," Gale promised grimly.

The outfit was resting around the wagon and Judge Blair, wearing cooling blanket, had his nose in a *morral* of oats when Dude returned. "Coyote," he called, with a smile and a wave for them all, "better start doing some dry-weather dances, 'cause Three Springs is gonna run Rebel . . . I mean the Judge . . . at that Lone Tree scorpion, Hondo." Eagerly, he told them what had been agreed on at the bank, and awaited their approval. No one spoke. "What's wrong?" he asked.

"You tell him, Coyote," said Uncle Billy, disgusted.

"Only one thing is wrong, white father," Coyote said, his dark eyes pained. "The Judge had to run as hard and brave as he could, that horse. This Comanche dare he did not pull him up."

CHAPTER 13

The Three Springs challenge delegation reached Lone Tree as the whiskey mills were opening for the 10 A.M. trade. The town presented a cocky mien from the boldness of saloon row, which occupied one side of Main, to the courthouse, still showing the recency of its stone face.

"They built that three years ago, right after the election," a glaring Solomon Gale muttered to Dude, riding alongside the two-seated buggy. "That stone front is no more than a false face. Behind it is nothing but an old frame building. Everything we do they try to go us one better. Last summer, for instance, we advertised a Fourth of July rodeo. They immediately announced theirs with bigger prize money. Naturally, the top contestants went there. I'm thinking of staging a potato-sack race to see how they'll beat that," he said bitterly. "But you know, Dude, there is one thing they'll never outdo us on, and that's our school system. All we need is that new schoolhouse to make it the most modern in this part of Texas. We've got to build it somehow."

"You bet," said Dude, thinking of Miss Pettibone.

Gale drew rein in front of the Fair Play Saloon, and he and Archer and Dodd stepped down. Dude and Uncle Billy dismounted and tied up. Today the old gentleman favored frock coat, white shirt, string tie, and flat-topped hat. His air was that of a visiting dignitary as he surveyed the motley surroundings.

"We're going to see Shag Fallon," Gale told Dude. "He owns Hondo and most of the town."

"Don't go in there with blood in your eye," Dude advised, "or he's liable to back off. Let Uncle Billy and me do most of the palaverin' about the horses, after you open the ball."

Just as the delegation stepped up on the boardwalk, voices clashed inside the Fair Play and a man crashed headlong out the batwing doors and sprawled, heaved there by an aproned bartender, who shouted, "Don't come in here again!"

The man yelled back, "Your whiskey's still watered down!" and picked himself up, dusted his trousers, and sauntered away.

After a short wait, Gale led the delegation inside and over to the bar. "We're here to see Mr. Shag Fallon," Gale informed the bartender, who hooked a thumb rearward.

The office door was closed. Gale rapped three times, and when a voice bellowed, "What the hell you want?" Gale opened the door and said cheerfully, "Good morning, Mr. Fallon. We're here from Three Springs to talk match race."

Shag Fallon, some forty or upward, was an

over-fleshed man, bull-necked and square-jawed, who obviously hadn't slept well. The wells of his eyes flung up a murky red and he did not rise, just sat at the rolltop desk, toadlike, his ropy lips working on an unlit cigar, one hand playing with a gold watchchain linking his open vest over a hummock belly. He grunted around the cigar:

"What d'you mean — match race? Why, Little Ben got beat. I heard all about it — length and a half. Figured you'd had enough of Hondo. Here you aim to run at him again."

"Not with Little Ben," Gale said. "The horse that beat Little Ben, a horse called Rebel, owned by this gentleman — Mr. Dude McQuinn. And this is Dr. William T. Lockhart, a horseman friend of Mr. McQuinn's from back East."

Dude nodded civilly. Uncle Billy said, "How do you do, sir," quite formal about it. Fallon grunted.

"You understand," Dude put in, "I'd have to see your horse before I agreed to anything?"

Fallon burst out laughing. His body shaking, he rose and patted his middle. "Some people never learn." Within him rose a quaking amusement, quickening by the moment, until he was shaking all over with laughter and his eyes watered. "I can still see Hondo daylighting Little Ben those three lengths — and the shock on your faces. Next thing you know, Gale, there won't be a board left in Three Springs. Everything will be moved up here — lock, stock, and barrel." For all his blow, Dude judged, Fallon was a sharp adversary, accustomed to recognizing the advantage and seizing it. Fallon's eyes cut from Gale to Dude and Uncle Billy and settled there, not without speculation. "I'm just about in the mood to retire Hondo to full-time stud. He's outrun everything."

"It's not like you to turn down a challenge," Gale came back.

"Challenge, eh? Well, I don't have to match every Tom, Dick, and Harry that comes by."

Dude took a step toward the door. "Maybe we're wasting Mr. Fallon's time as much as ours. Dr. Lockhart needs to get on. He hasn't finished his look-see of Texas for the eastern scientific journals. As a matter of fact, I'm just showing him around and matching a race now and then as we go. However, I did want him to see Hondo — reputed to be an outstanding example of short- horse breeding and speed."

"Reputed?" Fallon bristled. "And just who is this Dr. What's-His-Name?"

"The name," said Uncle Billy, abruptly distinct, and stepping to the center of the office, "is William Tecumseh Lockhart, sir. On special assignment to report the growth and development of short-horse breeding and racing in the great Lone Star State. Perhaps you've read my treatise on *Equus caballus* in Cadwallader's widely circulated scientific journal, *The Herbivorous Mammal?*"

"Can't say I have."

"Or my *History of the American Turf*, published by the Kentucky Academy of Science?"

"Seems I've heard of it," Fallon weakened, to save face.

"Or my *Horse Breeders' Guide*, publication of the Old Dominion Jockey Club of Virginia?"

"Come to think of it, believe I have." Fallon's voice was growing defensive. "Saw it in Fort Worth one time."

"Well, I am flattered and delighted, Mr. Fallon. Be that as it may, if you don't have time to show us Hondo, I understand, sir, you a busy breeder and devotee of the turf, and Lone Tree's leading entrepreneur." He turned ever so slowly, an obvious movement of disappointment, murmuring, "I was hoping I could include a description of Hondo in my report, along with an account of his owner."

"Hold on, Doc," Fallon broke. He snapped his fingers. "I'll just take the time. Day's yet young." He reached for his hat.

In less than half an hour, Shag Fallon was pointing dramatically to a big dapple-gray stallion being led from the barn. "There he is, Doc — Hondo — fastest horse in all of Texas. Stands sixteen hands, weighs fourteen hundred pounds. Sometimes he takes off so sudden the ground breaks right out from under him. Tried out half a dozen jockeys before I could find one that could stick on 'im at the break."

Memorandum and pencil in hand, Uncle Billy stepped briskly closer and began making rapid notes, his face keen and appreciative, while Fallon talked on: "He was never headed when he turned for home. Hondo's out of the great Arizona sprint queen, Never Miss. A hard-luck gal. She was injured early in her three-year-old year and wasn't raced much after that. Despite that little time on the track, she cleaned out everything from Nogales to Flagstaff and the state of Sonora. No wonder! She comes straight down the line from Steel Dust on her mammy's side and Shiloh on the other."

Dude almost gagged on his grin. Boy, how this Fallon could lay it on! Not just that mossy Steel Dust claim, but Shiloh to boot!

"What's his best distance?" Uncle Billy inquired, pencil poised.

"Any distance up to seven eighths. He can go that, too, if he has to. Even the mile. Runs the quarter mile in twenty-two and change. That half mile in forty-seven flat."

"Is forty-seven flat faster than forty-seven?" Uncle Billy asked innocently.

"In a way it is — means none over," said Fallon, hardly pausing. "Hondo's won thirty-three straight match races. Only time he ever lost was on a muddy track at Fort Worth, when he broke so fast and hard that he fell down. As it was, his nose was at the other horse's throatlatch when they crossed the finish line. . . . Reckon I'll have to retire him before long. Last time I campaigned him was up in southern Colorado, and after just two outings I couldn't match him anymore. Everybody shied off, even when I offered odds."

"Speaking of odds, Mr. Fallon," Dude stuck in, "and in view of Hondo's great record, I feel we'd have to have three-to-one money."

Fallon glared at him. "Three to one?"

"Hondo daylighted Little Ben three lengths. My Rebel horse only did by a length and a half."

"So what makes you think you can win?"

"Rebel's just getting over bucked shins. He still hurts some. I know he can do better. A gamble, I'll admit. You never know what a horse will do on a given day. Any way you look at it, Hondo has a wide edge."

Somewhat mollified, Fallon said, "That's still mighty big odds," and turned away in rejection.

All this time Uncle Billy was observing Hondo and making notes. He circled the stallion slowly, and again, and paused, frowning.

"Something wrong, Doc?" Fallon shot out.

"Nothing much. He's a splendid animal. Excellent bone. Outstanding in the gaskin and stifle areas. Flawless pedigree. About as good a horse as I've ever seen . . . except for one little drawback."

"Drawback? What do you mean?"

"I shouldn't even mention it, and I hope you won't take offense."

"Out with it, Doc. I want to know." Fallon was getting red in the face.

"Well . . . he's just a trifle short in the shoulder, is all."

246

"Short in the shoulder?" Fallon looked for himself; disbelieving, he hurled his resentment at the old man.

"Don't take it personal, Mr. Fallon," Uncle Billy said. "I just said he's a trifle short through the shoulder. And, too, he carries his head a mite high, and he's just a shade thin-peaked through the withers, and he stands higher in front than he does behind. Not that you can always pick a winner by the way he meets the eye."

"Meets the eye!" Fallon's full face turned burning red. "Tell you what," he roared, his indignation meant for the entire Three Springs delegation, "our delegation will be in your town tomorrow and we'll just see about this!"

He stormed to the gate. There was a rattle as he fumbled the chain. Hondo snorted and rolled his eyes. Then the hired hand was leading the stud back to the barn.

In silence, the delegation took the road back to Three Springs. Uncle Billy rode some distance without speaking, more reflective than Dude remembered in a long time.

"There is nothing wrong with Hondo's conformation," Uncle Billy said. "He's a well-built horse, as good as the Judge."

"You baited Fallon pretty hard," Dude said.

"If you want to make a man mad — and impulsive — just kick his dog around or run down his horse. What I can't figure out are those three lengths, when the Judge couldn't do it."

"Maybe it wasn't the Judge's best day."

"He looked good to me."

"Maybe Little Ben was fixed. That trainer, you know . . ."

"Else we've tied into a real bolt of lightning. I'm a little uneasy, Dude, boy. If we match this one, I think we'd better ask Jason to make a little sashay up to Lone Tree. Meantime, I'll get the Judge ready for inspection."

Lone Tree's delegation, two buggyfuls strong, arrived at two o'clock the next afternoon. Dude, watching the north road, saw them drive on to the bank and Shag Fallon descend and go charging inside.

At Dude's "Get ready — they're here," Uncle Billy led Judge Blair to the tailgate and tied him, then donned the frock coat and flat-topped hat. Coyote and Jason busied themselves around camp. Shortly, when the buggies drew up, Gale and Archer and Dodd striding alongside, Uncle Billy was writing studiously at a camp table. He glanced up and went on writing.

Fallon, the first down, marched straight over to Dude. "Where's your horse?" he asked, and looked toward the pasture where the other horses grazed.

"Right here." (If you're gonna sell a horse, Dude, boy, give him center stage all by his lonesome.)

"Him? That's the horse that daylighted Little Ben?"

"That's him."

Carrying the battered stock saddle and tattered blanket, Judge Blair stood hipshot, tail-switching flies while he dozed. Burrs again clotted his black mane and tail. His coat was dull and peroxide streaked his shoulders and sides and hindquarters. Bandages covered his front cannons. Possibly it was the afternoon heat, the way he hung his head so low.

"You work him in harness, too?"

"He was broke to plow. Those old harness marks still show, don't they? Bought him off a Red River Valley farmer to help pull the wagon. One day found out he could run a little. Not a bad saddler either."

Other members of the delegation stood around, wearing amused grins. Not Fallon. Eyes keen and skeptical, he circled the gelding. Dude feared that they had overdone it, what with the bandages, and thought that instead they should be showing Rebel, except that he looked too smooth. Just as that thought worried through his mind, Fallon said, "Maybe pulling a plow was where he got those stout hindquarters?"

"Guess so."

"How'd he get the burrs?"

"This morning in the pasture."

"Why the stock saddle?"

"Was getting ready to ride him down to the blacksmith shop."

Moments passed before Fallon spoke, the ghost of hidden laughter behind his eyes. "I wouldn't give three-to-one odds matched against a Shetland pony, but I might talk some two-to-one money."

"Well . . ."

When Dude did not go on, Fallon swung his shoulders impatiently. "How much you want to bet at two to one?"

"Three hundred."

"We feed that to the crows around Lone Tree."

"Five hundred," Dude replied, coming on stronger. "Mr. Gale and the other gentlemen may want to put up some money, too."

The trio nodded.

"Like last time, boys?" Fallon rubbed it in.

"We paid off, didn't we?" Gale flared. "We'll expect you to do the same." Their eyes clashed.

Fallon put his glance on Judge Blair for a space, and turned to Dude. "I'll match you that five hundred, give you two to one, and run you a quarter mile."

The advantage: Fallon thought he had it over a sorry-looking, sore-shinned horse at that distance. Let him think so. Dude rubbed the underside of his nose. "Hadn't figured on quite that far."

"It's a quarter mile or else. None of these little-bitty bush sprints for Hondo."

"You're matched."

"We'll run at Lone Tree."

"We'll flip to see," Dude retorted, and reached for a coin. "You call it." Shrugging, Fallon called tails and Dude caught the coin in his open palm. Heads it was. "We'll run it in Three Springs," Dude said.

"Rather beat you here, anyway. I'll even let you pick the day."

Fallon's arrogance was almost too much to take, but Dude forced calm into his thinking. Time was important. Time, so that Jason could ride to Lone Tree and put his ear to the ground. Time to prepare a horse, steadfast and true, for the most important race of his wayfaring life.

"Week from Saturday," Dude said, "if that's jake with Three Springs."

Gale and company nodded, and suddenly the Three Springs delegation crowded forward. Gale waved his arms. "We can have the finish line on Main Street, between the bank and the store. We can start the race south of town. That's a nice, straight stretch. We'll even grade it."

"We can decorate the town," Archer bubbled. "Banners and flags and such."

"We can," Dodd echoed.

"We need a starter," Dude interrupted them. "I know you can suggest a good man, Mr. Gale."

"Blondy Nosler is the best around."

"Nobody I'd rather have," Fallon condescended. "Started the first race, didn't he?"

"He's fair — that's all that matters. We can confer later about the three judges."

Fallon, sporting that overbearing expression of secret amusement, left them still palavering. As the Lone Tree delegation drove away, a troubling reminder raked Dude: those three lengths. Had he overmatched his horse for the

251

first time? Fallon was so confident that he'd even forgotten to demand forfeit money.

Gale was hopping up and down. "We can put up a judge's stand."

"Drape it red, white, and blue," Archer expanded.

"We will," Dodd followed.

Gale stopped in mid-hop, one knee lifted. "We need a name for the event. What'll we call it?"

"I know!" Archer burst forth. "The Great Horse Race. We'll have posters printed and nailed on every fence post from here to Jacksboro." His washed-out eyes snapped. His normally subdued voice crackled.

"Perfect," Dodd appended.

"Good for business, too," Archer swept on, imbued. "Lord knows we need it. Alonzo, maybe we'd better rush a wagon to Fort Worth for extra knickknacks and souvenirs, flags and bunting. Straw hats. Cardboard fans like the funeral parlor gives to the bereaved, only we'll sell ours. Get a barrel of horehound candy."

"Peppermint," Dodd differed, shaking his head.

"Well, peppermint, damn it. And add some crates of lemons. Be hot that day. Folks'll drink lemonade by the barrel."

"Ideal," Dodd said, and made a note.

They were like that, the three of them, heads together, swapping ideas, speaking in bursts of enthusiasm, when Dude saw the women coming. Not just a few, but a crowd of militant marchers. Heads up, advancing shoulder to shoulder, arms swinging. In the first rank a comely young face stood out: Miss Pettibone's.

Archer discovered them a moment later. He stiffened. Gale and Dodd froze, their excitement waning. Like a column of infantry, the women marched up and halted.

"Now, Sadie," Archer appeased, addressing the foremost marcher, his hands raised, fending off, "we're just talking a little horse race."

"There will be no horse race, Quincy. You can put that in your pipe and smoke it. You, too, Alonzo and Solomon."

Whereas her husband was thin and somewhat stooped, Sadie Archer was robust and aggressively erect, her hatchet-sharp expression boding ill for those who crossed her; and whereas he was the obliging storekeeper, she was as grim as stone.

"You don't understand," her husband said. "Mr. McQuinn, here, has the horse that can beat Hondo."

"There will be no such race, Quincy."

"Shag Fallon is giving us two-to-one odds. We can make back what we lost the first time and more."

Dude sensed that something was happening: Archer was standing up to her, maybe for the first time.

"I said there will be no horse race, Quincy," she clipped, and folded her formidable arms.

"We have taken a vote, the women of Three Springs. No schoolhouse, no horse race — that is final." She looked to her cohorts, whose heads upped and downed as one. "Furthermore," she said, "if you persist in this, there will not be one home meal cooked in Three Springs. Not one dirty shirt or pair of socks or underwear washed and ironed. Not one bed made. Not one floor swept."

"Now, Sadie."

"Furthermore, you, Quincy Archer, will have to sleep in the corn crib."

A titter among the women, hushed when Sadie Archer, wheeling, eyed them to silence.

"You know, Mrs. Archer," Dude said, speaking almost before he realized it, "I have to go along with you — the schoolhouse comes first." He didn't know he was going to say it. He ought to stay out of this and let the race expire unmourned. Instead, he had blurted it out and they were all staring at him, the women with pleased surprised, the trio with expressions of shocked betrayal. And he was saying: "It's just a thought, but why not ask every Three Springs man to pledge a percentage of his winnings to the schoolhouse fund?" There it was, out of him, and he was dragging the outfit in deeper and deeper.

"Why, that's an excellent idea," said Gale, quick to follow up. "This way we can get the whole town behind the race. Public opinion! We'll get right to work on that, Mrs. Archer.

You can depend on us. Yes, ma'am! Don't you think ten per cent would be about right?"

She glared, her bristling silence reply enough.

"Now, Sadie," her husband said, "you're being unreasonable."

"Ten per cent is unacceptable."

"Twenty?" Gale purred.

"You're not even close."

Gale swallowed. "Thirty?"

She folded those stout arms. "It's fifty per cent or no race. Take your choice, gentlemen. We shall expect every man in town who bets to make that pledge, including those loafers who hang out at the Longhorn. Believe me, we'll know who doesn't play fair!"

The trio's eyes met. For a stalemated moment none responded. Then Gale nodded, and Archer, and Dodd. "You ladies win," Gale conceded.

Sadie Archer said, "You can forget about the corn crib, Quincy," and blushed. Like a mother hen, she collected her brood and they marched away. Gale and company followed shortly afterward, chattering like schoolboys.

Dude's guilt came upon him. *Me and my big mouth.* Had sight of Miss Pettibone caused him to lose his judgment? What had begun as just another bush-track race, and the outfit soon moving on to another town, had suddenly outgrown its intent. An entire community's hopes and future hung on the outcome now. And what if Judge Blair should lose? He shuddered coldly. Just then he heard Uncle Billy say:

255

"Jason, would you mind sashaying up to Lone Tree and making yourself generous and earful at the Fair Play? We need to find out all we can about Hondo and what happened in the first race."

CHAPTER 14

That evening Dude called on Miss Pettibone. Mrs. Archer, trying her best to smile despite her characteristic grimness, met him at the door. "Come in, Mr. McQuinn. I'll tell Bridget you're here." She opened the screen door for him. "Thank you for championing our cause this afternoon."

"You need no champion, Mrs. Archer. You bargained sharper than any horse trader."

"You flatter me. I was speaking for all the women patrons of the Three Springs school."

She showed him to the dimly lit parlor, where he waited nervously amid the musty-smelling surroundings of horsehair-stuffed sofa and chairs resting on a rose-patterned carpet, and lace curtains, and volumes of Dickens and Scott and Hawthorne ensconced behind glassed bookcases. All mighty proper, he thought, running a finger around his damp collar.

He turned at the sound of someone coming lightly down the hallway stairs. In a moment Bridget Pettibone entered the parlor. She wore another high-necked dress, but not so sober this time, one of light blue, and her dark hair was parted in the middle and knotted on the back of her neck. Although her face was devoid of rouge or powder, he decided she required no artifice, for there was an inner uniqueness about her that came through in the open and hopeful look of the wideset hazel eyes.

"You look mighty nice, Miss Bridget," he said, bowing.

"Thank you, Mr. McQuinn; however, I fear you are being overgenerous." So we're still on the "Mister" basis, Dude thought. "Please make yourself comfortable."

She seated herself across from him and folded her slim hands on her lap, the epitome of parlor propriety.

"Guess I'm a little early," he apologized.

"I was ready."

"Been a nice day."

"It has."

"How've you been?"

"Very well, thank you. And you?"

"Never better."

He kept shifting his boots. Where was his never-failing gift of gab? For the life of him, he couldn't dredge up one thing to say, and she was little help. He would look at her until aware that he was staring like a moonstruck country yokel, then look away, then back, irresistibly drawn to her face, which he had first thought of as plain, and which, instead, he knew now, was lovely and mysterious. He loosened his collar again, too tongue-tied even to comment further on the weather.

"Would you like to sit in the front-porch swing?" she asked, to his gratified deliverance. "There's so little breeze this evening."

He stood at her words. They came out into the hallway so suddenly that they almost bumped Mrs. Archer, listening by the parlor doorway; hands fluttering, she pretended to search for something around the hall tree.

Bridget carefully occupied one side of the swing and he the other; for all that formality, the swing was small and they still sat quite close together. He breathed the scent of her hair. His senses swam. Boy, did she smell sweet! Yet the coolness of the porch evoked no more conversation than had the stuffy parlor, and, presently, thinking he heard Mrs. Archer cat-footing near the door, Dude said, "Would you like to take a stroll before we go to church?"

When they were beyond earshot of the house, she whispered, "Mrs. Archer eavesdrops, though she means well, good soul."

"Means to listen, you mean."

She took his arm as they strolled. The evening was like gossamer. When a church bell tolled, they slowly changed course in that direction. It was nearly dark.

"Thank you for speaking up this afternoon, Mr. McQuinn," she said.

"When are you going to drop the *mister?*"

Ignoring him: "Sharing the winnings for the schoolhouse will help compensate for the race's immorality."

"We haven't run yet." He stopped abruptly. "Hate to admit it, but I'm afraid I've made a mistake."

"Why? You only tried to help us."

"There's too much at stake. The whole town's future. Racing is a sport, not a do-or-die thing. Everything's gone too far. I should've stayed out of it."

"This isn't like you. You've always sounded so confident."

"I know. That's my nature. I talk a lot — too much. Shag Fallon is a tough man to beat, and I keep remembering that Hondo beat Little Ben three lengths, which is considerable. Little Ben is a good horse."

"But Mr. Archer says your jockey held Rebel in."

"Any horse race is a gamble. There are always unknown factors."

"But you have a good horse."

"Yes, he's a good horse. Always give his best."

"Then what are you worried about?" In her concern, she leaned toward him and instinctively he bent his head to kiss her. But just before his lips could touch hers, she turned her head and strolled on, murmuring, "You're very sudden, Mr. McQuinn."

"Too sudden, I guess. Like talking the whole town into betting on my horse." She had hesitated for another reason, he suspected, and he said dryly, "Lips That Touch Liquor Shall Never Touch Mine. Is that it?"

"I'd hoped that you didn't drink."

"Come to think of it," he said, once more his old, offhanded self, "I did have a toddy at the Longhorn. Just a little one," he said, and held up measuring forefinger and thumb.

"I wonder if I shall ever get used to Western ways. The horror of drink appalls me. Wine is a mocker, the Bible tells us."

"Oh, it can be, I know," he said, sounding righteous. "The Bible also says give drink unto him that is about to perish, and wine unto those that are heavy of heart."

"Why, that's from Proverbs! Very good, Mr. McQuinn."

"All except the *mister* part. I recollect the Bible also says let a man drink and remember his misery no more."

"True. But a warning goes with it in Proverbs as well: 'At the last it biteth like a serpent, and stingeth like an adder.' "

"Don't recollect that. I figure the whole question on liquor hangs on whether it's taken for medicinal purposes. As a matter of fact, Bridget, I've been under considerable strain lately, jousting with this Shag Fallon and gettin' my horse ready." He realized that he was losing ground fast. By now he sounded like a kid caught with his hand in the cookie jar.

She was thoughtful for a long moment. "Early in the Song of Solomon, it says: 'Let him kiss me with the kisses of his mouth: for thy love is better than wine.' "

He threw up his hands in mock surrender, laughing. "Miss Bridget, you've got me hog-tied and branded. You win first money."

She touched his arm. "They've started. I can hear the Reverend Isaacs praying."

The Reverend Isaacs was still praying, his retributive voice rolling on and on, when they peeked inside the church door. Minutes more he continued. Heads turned and Bridget drew quick smiles when, at last, they slipped into a rear pew. Dude saw the Archers, the Gales, the Dodds, and on their faces, for him, he read the expectation of the race and what the odds would bring. He smiled them a reassurance he by no means felt.

Bridget Pettibone sang a pleasant soprano, to which Dude joined his passable bass, and as they held the song book together, heads close, he felt now and then the slightest brush of her hair against his cheek. His senses spun. Gallantry surged through him, the powerful desire to protect her.

To please her, he sang lustily and strived manfully to listen to the reverend's mournful words. Sitting there, seeing the crowded pews, he thought: The lives of everyone here, especially the children, will be changed for better or worse a week from Saturday when Judge Blair goes against the mighty Hondo.

It was too much. But the match was made and there was no turning back, thanks to the big mouth of one Dude McQuinn. He groaned to himself.

When the prayer meeting let out, they strolled to Turley's Drugstore for ice cream sodas and small talk. Then: It seemed that such a short time had gone by since they had sat in the swing, yet now they stood at the steps of the Archer house, dark save for the dimness in the parlor, ready to say good night.

"It's been such a nice evening," she said. "Thank you, Mr. McQuinn."

"You're still saying *mister.*"

"You must forgive me. It's the way I was brought up."

"You were well brought up, I know that. A little straitlaced, maybe, but that's all right." He paused and went on solemnly, with effort. "Bridget, you're the finest young lady I've ever known or expect to know. But please, don't try to reform me. Don't short-rein me. Don't try to save me from anything. I couldn't change if my life depended on it."

"Why, Dude," she said, touched, and suddenly, impulsively, she lifted her face and kissed him fully on the mouth, a quick but wonderfully warm kiss, and fled up the steps and into the house.

He was too stunned to move for several seconds. Whipping about, he stomped out a cowboy jig, let go a curdling whoop that Coyote Walking would have approved, and broke on top for the Longhorn.

Jason Carter did not come back the next day

or the next. Just when Dude and Uncle Billy were preparing to go after him, he rode into camp, sleepy-eyed and spent.

"It's not so much what I found out, but what I didn't find out," he told them. "I've listened till both ears are flapping, I've bought enough drinks at the Fair Play to flood the Brazos, I've had about as much sleep as a hoot owl at midnight."

He unsaddled and watered and fed his horse, helped himself to coffee from the pot on the fire, and slouched down to rest.

"First off," he said, "that's no brag about Hondo's record. Since losing that match race at Fort Worth three years back, he's won thirty-three straight, in Texas, Colorado, and western Kansas . . . so they say. He's made Fallon a rich man."

"As a matter of curiosity," Uncle Billy asked, "what about his breeding?"

"That was all bull. Fallon bought him off a south Texas trader who was on hard times. Bought him for a song. Guess he knows a track burner when he sees one."

"No by Montezuma, champion of all Mexico, no out of Never Miss — straight down the line from Steel Dust and Shiloh?" The old horseman was waxing sarcastic.

"Those horses exist or did . . . so they say . . . but Fallon just made up the connection. Like somebody claiming kin to Sam Houston."

"It's performance that counts, anyway. Did

you see Hondo work?"

"See him? You can't get within a mile of that horse. Fallon's got him guarded around the clock. Double guards after sundown. They say he plans to haul Hondo over here the morning of the race in a hooded freight wagon, escorted by shotgun guards. Aims to put up a tent and rope corral. Won't let the public eyeball his horse till he comes out to run for the money."

"Now that gets me," Dude chimed in. "A hard-boiled *hombre* like Fallon afraid somebody might slip in and fix his horse. We're the ones that'd better be on guard. Pick up any particulars about the first race?"

"Both horses broke well. Head to head for about three hundred yards, till Hondo's jockey tapped him a couple of times. At that point he just seemed to run off and leave Little Ben."

"So Little Ben hung even with Hondo longer than he did with the Judge. Our horse opened daylight at one eighth."

"Boys at the Fair Play said it was something the way Hondo grabbed those three lengths. Seemed to take off. Ran like he was scared. Ears flat back. Wall-eyed."

"Was Little Ben fixed?"

"Didn't hear that. Fallon's close-mouthed, even to the Lone Tree bunch."

"How's the betting up there?"

"Sky's the limit. They're gonna bet the town."

Dude flinched inwardly. Things were sure getting out of hand, and Three Springs would meet every wager out of civic pride and confidence in Rebel — er, the Judge. He asked no more, assailed by doubts, by fears, concerned afresh that something might happen to his horse.

That night the outfit took turns guarding the Judge and thereafter worked him early every other day. During daylight he assumed the anonymity of the pasture among the trade and saddle stock, while Rebel played understudy in camp.

Two days after Jason's Lone Tree reconnaissance, a man rode into camp. He tied his horse to a live oak and paced over to the wagon, his step deliberate. The first feature Dude noticed about him was his eyes, ice-blue and protuberant. He gave the effect of finding it impossible to smile. His hands were large and well kept. Gray hair hung long below his hat. He wore a star and a six-gun.

"Dude McQuinn around?" he asked softly.

Dude smiled. "You're lookin' right at him. Who are you?"

"Wolf Garrity . . . marshal at Lone Tree. Come to see your horse." He didn't offer his hand.

"There he is," Dude obliged, pointing to Rebel tied to the tailgate, and wished Uncle Billy were here. He had gone with Jason to town for veterinary supplies.

Garrity's eyebrows flew up. "Fallon said he was a sorry-looking horse."

"Was, till we slicked him up for all the company he's having. Pulled the burrs out of his mane and tail."

Garrity circled Rebel twice. "Smooth," he said, and drew a long, bone-handled knife, opened it with ostentation, which did not escape Dude's notice, and commenced shaving hairs off the back of his left hand.

"What else can we do you, Marshal?"

"Just wanted to make certain you're on the fair and square over here."

"That we are . . . as open as a country church. We want the public to see our horse. Happens we're just ready to take him out to the track. Like to go along? It's in walking distance."

"Now? Work a horse in the heat of the day?"

"Oddly enough, he seems to do better when it's hot. Funny, him just gettin' over the colic, too."

"Colic?"

"It's no secret. Everybody in town knows it. He had a spell of it yesterday."

"Well, I'll be damned. Sure, I'd like to see him work."

Coyote Walking, who had been reading in the shade of the wagon, put down his book and saddled Rebel and they set forth to the track. While fussing with the cinch, Dude gave Coyote instructions in a loud voice. "Bear down on him. Blow him out good."

Coyote hung back. "Mebbe so him still got devil in belly."

"Best way I know to find out."

Coyote walked Rebel a way, and trotted him a way, and when Dude signaled, he broke Rebel down the straightaway. They ran for an eighth or more, somewhere between slow and so-so, and circled back.

"Him no run like wind," Coyote yelled, "but him no got devil in belly. No like yesterday."

"He's feeling better, all right," Dude said. "Careful how you cool him down." And for the watchful Garrity: "He's a funny horse. Seldom looks good when you work him. I think it's the crowds. He cottons to crowds."

Garrity bared the threat of a grin. "I'd say he got over the colic mighty quick."

"I hope so. But I know he couldn't beat Hondo today."

Uncle Billy and Jason were waiting at the wagon. The old man nailed Garrity a questioning look. He stared intently, hollered, "Wolf Garrity — you old son of a gun!" and ran over and slapped Garrity on the shoulder and they shook hands.

"Billy," Garrity marveled, equally surprised, "by hell's foundation — it's you! Fallon said there was a Dr. Lockhart with this outfit, but I didn't tie it to you. Not you."

"Been a heap of water under the bridge, Wolf. Most of it muddy. You know how that goes sometimes?"

"Well, I should smile."

"If you've ever smiled."

"Don't ruffle my fur, Billy," he said, managing

268

an officious grin, and pointed to his star.

"So it's come to that?"

Dude saw that it was time to set the day straight. "Mr. Garrity's the Lone Tree marshal. I was showing him Rebel. Looks like that colic cure you mixed up this morning did the work."

"Oh . . . that. Sure."

"Same old Billy, mixing up potions," Garrity said. The icy eyes lost their semblance of funning, if they had ever been funning, and turned doubtful. "Since when did you get to be a doctor?"

"A wink's as good as a nod to a blind mule."

"Now what the hell does that mean? I remember when —"

"That calls for a drink," Uncle Billy cut him off. "Get your horse." Seizing Garrity's arm, the old man virtually propelled him in the direction of town.

Sometime late in the long night Dude heard a singing floating down the street from town. He sat up. The thick voice was not familiar and the blurred words didn't make sense. Now and then, as the singing neared, he caught a word or two about the Chisholm Trail. Suddenly everything connected. He crawled from under the wagon and stood, arms folded, waiting, and when a figure stumbled out of the darkness, Dude growled:

"What's the big idea of treating the enemy with drinks? You know Fallon sent Garrity over here to spy on us. That's why I made up that story about the colic."

The vague, weaving shape became Uncle Billy, plopping down on the wash bench and pleading, childlike, "Hep me off with m' boots, Dude, boy."

"You didn't answer me. And who is this Wolf Garrity?" Dude straddled one boot leg and pulled on the heel, while Uncle Billy pushed on Dude's buttocks with his other foot.

"Ah . . . tha's good. Ye're like a son to me in m'sundown years. Now th' other 'un, Dude, boy."

"Answer me! Who is this Wolf Garrity? Where'd you know him? You two looked pretty chummy to me. If I ever eyeballed a hardcase, he fills the bill. Got eyes like ice." Dude yanked and the second boot suddenly came loose in his hands, throwing him sprawling flat on his face. He pushed up and sat a moment in disgust, rose, and turned to the wagon, summoning more questions.

But Uncle Billy wasn't on the bench. As Dude glimmed the darkness under the wagon, the old man's whistle-shrill snoring reached him. Dude gave up for the night.

CHAPTER 15

A day did not pass without a new rumor surfacing through the smoke and foam of the Longhorn Saloon and sweeping Three Springs:

Hondo had just breezed the quarter mile in twenty-one flat under a tight hold.

Hondo was breaking so fast that his old jockey couldn't stay aboard, so at great expense Shag Fallon was importing the top reinsman in Illinois, one Bud Clegg, for the big race.

Lone Tree bettors were offering three-to-one money.

Racing fans were coming from as far as Fort Worth and Dodge City, where Hondo was known.

The Texas House was booked to the rafters and there wasn't a spare bed in town.

"Believe I'll dab me a little salt on that twenty-one flat-bear story," Uncle Billy snorted. "However, I have heard of Bud Clegg. He's a top-money rider. . . . Those three lengths still puzzle me, though. Can't see that much difference, after the way Little Ben ran at the Judge, unless Little Ben was fixed the first time . . . or this Hondo is the fastest thing since the telegraph."

Dude worried in silence, thinking of all that rode on the outcome.

"I know Hondo's a good horse," the old man said, his eyes bright, "except he's a mite too long in the back, and come to think of it, I don't like his forearm."

"You didn't say that before."

"That's hindsight, Dude, boy, and plain prejudice."

At dawn the day of the race, Uncle Billy and Dude gave Judge Blair his final touch-up to match Rebel's dark bay coat, and later, having rented Blondy Nosler's livery to stable their racehorse, they led the Judge to the red barn on Main Street and bunched Rebel with their trade and saddle stock in a holding corral behind the barn.

"If you don't mind," Dude had explained to Nosler, "we'd like to pen the rest of our stock nearby, in case Rebel gets nervous, starts pacing his stall, and we need to walk him back there away from the noise of the crowd. He likes to be with his friends. Some horsemen, you know, keep an old billy goat around for mascot to quiet a high-strung horse. Rebel just likes his four-footed friends."

"Go right ahead," Nosler obliged. "I'll clear my stock out for the day. That kid, Ham Williams, will be around if you need him."

Over the barn's entrance Dude and Coyote and Jason stretched a banner: REBEL, PRIDE OF THREE SPRINGS.

At this time and place you made a show of keeping the curious away from your horse. . . . Oh, all right, sonny. Maybe just one peek from the stable runway. Now run along. . . . As Dude turned back an eager looker now and then, the crowd grew along the street, roped off on both sides and festooned like the Fourth of July. Banners and flags. The bedecked judges' platform. Cold-drink stands at close intervals. People tramping back and forth, raising a veil of dust. Sunbonnets and big hats. Kids frisking like yearlings.

Ham Williams sidled over, an obliging smile on his plump face. "Anything I can do, Mr. McQuinn?"

"Nothing. Thanks, Ham."

"Just give me a holler if Rebel needs anything. I'll be around. Found me some two-to-one odds and bet my little wad on him. All right if I look at him?"

"Sure. But don't stay long. Might make him nervous."

Coyote came in off the street, head down. "This Comanche worried is he, white father."

"What's wrong?"

"Rain, maybe. Sign is bad."

"Sign? What sign? There's not a cloud in the sky."

"I can't explain it. Something Comanches feel. Old-time thing. Way off, now." He walked away.

Around ten o'clock Dude heard a rising murmur as of wind and saw the crowd shifting to gaze north. A procession was approaching. A man on a fine bay saddler leading it. Shag Fallon wore a broad white hat, checkered shirt, tan riding trousers, and concho belt that flashed sunlight. Somebody jeered. Fallon, grinning with relish as if he expected it, made a throat-slitting gesture, and the jeers multiplied.

Trailing Fallon, three matched teams, black, strawberry roan, and chestnut, pulled a hooded freight wagon. Inside it Dude caught the hoof clatter of a nervous horse. Armed men escorted the wagon. Behind it followed a wagon fetching water barrel, loose hay, and sacked oats. Behind it trailed a retinue of noisy Lone Tree citizens. They began to trade jibes with the local residents.

Dude watched Fallon lead his outfit through town and on to the starting line, marked by stakes and a white flag. Beyond the line he turned off and the wagons parked in a circle. Smart, Dude thought. Away from the crowd where he can keep his horse quiet.

Jason, also watching said, "I'm going out there," and saddled his horse.

"Before you go, mind looking for some three-to-one odds for us?"

"Will do."

About half an hour filed by.

"Mr. McQuinn. I mean Dude."

It was Solomon Gale, and Archer and Dodd, as usual, siding him like appendages. Gale, flushing excitement, said, "That Lone Tree bunch came loaded for bear. Are they cocky! Some are flashing three-to-one money. Two to one's easy to find."

"We just bet our entire stock of goods against Ballard & Crawford," Archer announced, a reckless tilt to his thin shoulders. "We'll show those Lone Tree merchants."

"You bet all that!" Dude couldn't hold back his shock.

"We did," partner Dodd confirmed.

"That's not all," Gale said. "Cal Turley just bet his drugstore."

"Oh, no!"

"We're not afraid," Gale said. "You said your jockey held Rebel up."

Guilt smiting him, Dude said, "You gentlemen excuse me. I have to see about my horse," and went heavily to the rear of the stable where Uncle Billy and Coyote sat on bales of hay by Judge Blair's stall. A handgun shaped inside the old man's waistband.

"How does he look?" Dude asked hopefully.

"Standing there like an ol' saddle horse," Uncle Billy said, swelling with pride. "I gave him a light feed at daybreak. Don't want much, if anything, inside him when he runs at two-thirty. We'll leave off his water at noon. Just a sip or two. Anything wrong?"

Dude told them about the Three Springs merchants wagering their stores.

"You can't stop a man from betting on a horse

275

once he gets the fever."

"Only I encouraged 'em. Guess it was the schoolhouse."

"And Miss Pettibone?"

Dude posted himself again by the runway. The crowd was growing impatient at this early hour, just waiting, no doubt feeling some of the tension he did.

Without warning, he was looking into ice-blue eyes, and the inscrutable face under the big hat was asking, "Where's Billy?"

"Back there with the horse. What do you want, Garrity?" Dude let his dislike and distrust sound.

"Want to make certain everybody's in his proper place."

"Now just what does that mean?"

"That your outfit sticks to its own camp."

"Well now, that happens to work both ways. Nobody from Fallon's camp gets inside this barn. That includes you."

"You wouldn't talk that nasty at Lone Tree." Garrity sent a brushing hand to his star.

"Nastier," Dude said, "if somebody tried to fix my horse."

Shrugging: "You got the wrong slant, my friend. Tell Billy I said howdy." Garrity started on, then half turned. "Thought I'd tell you that Bud Clegg got in."

"Who's Clegg?" Dude taunted him.

"Best jock in the Middle West — that's who."

"We supposed to scare? Well, you tell Fallon

that a wild Comanche rides for us and he's never lost a race. Best in the West!"

Garrity went on without speaking.

Noon.

The dusty air redolent of food smells as the crowd swarmed the few eating places or snacked from picnic baskets and jammed the cold-drink stands. Lone Tree partisans, waving fistfuls of greenbacks, swaggered from group to group. Ham Williams brought sandwiches and cold lemonade for the outfit, "compliments of Mr. Gale and Mr. Archer and Mr. Dodd."

At twelve-thirty, Archer, trailed by Dodd, came outside the store and smiled at the milling crowd. Dodd smiled, too. The damn fools! Dude swore silently. Risking everything.

Coyote Walking moved to the barn's entrance and eyed the southwestern sky, as if drawn there by some primitive sense. Looking, Dude noticed dark clouds for the first time, and the air had changed from the fresh brightness of the morning to an oppressive sultriness. The Comanche shook his head and turned back.

About one o'clock Jason Carter saddled through the restless throng, went into the barn, and stepped down fast. "Got something you'd all better hear," he told Dude, and looked as grim as Coyote had. As Uncle Billy and Coyote listened: "Think I've figured out those three lengths. See . . . Fallon's gunhawks don't like to get their hands dirty, so I volunteered to help put up that big tent where they've got Hondo out of

277

sight. . . . Here it is: They've been *conditioning* Hondo with a chain before he runs."

"It fits," Uncle Billy cried. "Remember when Fallon showed us Hondo that day and how jumpy that stud got when Fallon happened to rattle the gate chain?"

"I remember," Dude said, and nodded.

"Sure, first work him over in his stall. When the jock rattles a few links of chain down the stretch that horse gets wings on his feet. Haven't seen this in a long time."

"Where was that, Uncle?" Dude asked, not meaning to pry.

"Here and there, Dude, boy," cutting Dude his rebuke. "This means we have to get the break, Coyote. Swing your horse into it."

"Sky sign bad it is, too, grandfather." Coyote made a chopping gesture. "Just like white man. Big race, big rain. Not so if Comanches my Texas had. Their ghosts crying they are today crying."

They dispersed, the Comanche to gauge the sky again, Jason back to Fallon's camp, Dude to his stand at the barn entrance, feeling the day turning hot and humid. While he watched, the moving clouds grew darker and hid the brassy Texas sun. Coyote went back to the stall.

Garrity passed slowly by in the throng, his face turned to the barn.

It was after one-thirty when Bridget Pettibone, all dressed in pink, paid a call. Dude showed so much pleasure that she blushed.

"I came to wish you luck," she said.

"That's very nice." He drew her inside the runway. "Just pray the rain holds off till we run this race."

"Wouldn't rain hurt Hondo's chances as well?"

"Hondo's a mudder. Rebel's not." He felt he had to say that, yet he detested lying to her.

"Oh. So much hangs on the race, so much more than the new schoolhouse."

"Then you know that Archer & Dodd bet their stock of goods, and Cal Turley his drugstore?"

"Mrs. Archer told me. She's frightened. They'll be ruined if Rebel loses. So will the Dodds and the Turleys."

"Bridget, I want you to know I wasn't for this win-or-ruin betting. This started out as a simple match race. I just wanted to help get the school-house. Now everything's out of hand. People have lost their heads."

"But don't you understand, Dude? They believe in you and your horse. You're an honorable man. You're trying to make possible a vital public need. It's their big chance. They believe in you, and, well . . . so do I."

He had to avoid her honest eyes.

"Good luck," she said, and squeezed his arm and became lost in the crowd. As he watched her go, Garrity passed before his eyes.

Young Ham Williams popped up, this time coming from the rear of the barn. "Need anything?" he asked, and went out when Dude shook his head.

Garrity stopped in front of the barn, looked in, and walked on. Dude threw him a hard look of distrust and worriedly considered the sky, darkening and more threatening by the minute. Time dragged.

A stranger rushed up, out of breath. "You Dude McQuinn?"

"Yeah. What about it?"

"Young lady's been hurt down the street. She fell. She's calling for you. Said you'd be here."

Dude's instant reaction was concern, tempered, after a moment, by suspicion. "A young lady? What's her name?"

"Don't know," the man faltered.

"What does she look like?"

"Tall, pretty . . . and she's all dressed in pink."

Dude tensed, cold with fear. "How bad is it?"

"Mighty bad — looks like. Come on!" He whirled away.

Dude ran after him, shoving and elbowing a path through the shifting crowd. He kept looking for a telltale knot of people, and saw none. Searching, he slammed into a man coming out of Turley's Drugstore and was roundly cursed. Now he saw the messenger look back for him and wave and turn off Main onto a sidestreet. It was, Dude saw, the street that led to the Longhorn. There was an alley ahead.

The messenger halted and pointed. Dude ran

there and turned to look, dreading what he would find.

At that moment he discovered two men waiting for him. A violent gleam smeared their bearded faces. Too late he drew back. Before he could duck away, something smashed his head from behind. He was falling, the littered earth of the alley rushing up to meet him. He struck and lurched sideways, saw the sky spinning darkly. Dimly, he heard footsteps close about him, and grunting voices and the footsteps hurrying away. The sky turned black, and he heard no more.

When he opened his eyes he was lying in the alley and no one was about. His head was bursting and his heart pounded like mad against the drum of his chest. He became conscious of a distant and puzzling murmur or drone. What was it? Comprehension crashed through — the crowd, the race-day crowd. He staggered to his feet, fell, gathered himself, and horsed himself up again, feeling the belated sounding of alarm. How long had he lain there? He felt for his pocketwatch; oddly, he still had it and his wallet. He glanced at the watch. It was two twenty-five. He'd been out some minutes.

He started running and felt something spatter his hands. Raindrops. Tearing to Main, he found the street cleared and the crowd lined up, faces turned away from the wind-whipped dust and rain.

Miss Bridget stood in front of Turley's Drugstore, hands clenched, anxiously scanning the faces and looking up and down the street. When he touched her arm, she gasped, "I've been looking all over for you. Something's happened! And your face! What in the world . . . ?"

"Never mind. What is it?"

"Something's dreadfully wrong, Dude. There was a big street fight outside the barn. Your Uncle Billy and Coyote Walking rushed out to watch. While they watched, a man with a star led Rebel out the back way to the corral and brought in a horse that looked just like Rebel."

"Who said this?"

"Blondy Nosler's stableboy — Ham Williams. I heard him tell Mr. Gale right here only half a minute ago. Meantime, everybody wondered what had happened to you."

He clamped a hand to his bursting head. "Where's Uncle Billy?"

"At the starting line, of course." Her eyes were enormous and bewildered. "The race is about to start. What's this all about, Dude?"

Outslicked! Garrity had switched the slow horse for the fast horse. Now Rebel was running in place of Judge Blair. Stunned, Dude saw how it had happened, step by step. First, himself suckered away and knocked out. Then the faked street fight, while Garrity made the switch. How had Garrity known? Had Uncle Billy told him? They'd been mighty friendly that day, even got drunk together. The accusation sickened Dude, yet as much as he wanted to he could not silence it.

"Dude, you look pale. What's wrong?"

"Maybe," he said dismally, "we'd better pray for rain."

"I don't understand."

"Right now, Bridget, all I can say is I hope Rebel's got more than one good race in him."

She looked at him in bewilderment. "What do you mean?"

For reply, he took her hand and turned to watch the foregone conclusion of the race that he was powerless to stop.

A figure arrested his eye. A man, a big man, sat his horse behind the crowd massed on the other side of the street, while he methodically played his gaze back and forth. Dude wouldn't have noticed were not this man of extraordinary size and manner: the shoulders of a bull, the mouth of a mastiff.

Dude's recognition burst. Big Whelan had just ridden into town, and he was looking for a man. Could a third time be mere coincidence? Or finally — and Dude's breath came short at the thought — was it Uncle Billy he wanted?

Bridget's "Look! They're ready to start!" yanked him back to the race. The horses were approaching Blondy Nosler, who waited, hand upraised. A light rain was falling steadily now. Poor Rebel! He couldn't run fast on a smooth track, let alone in mud. This was going to be terrible. Dude had to look away.

As he did, a roar soared up from the crowd and a man shouted, "Rebel took the break!"

Son of a gun. Miracle of miracles. So Rebel had. They were off and running and Coyote had his horse out in front by a length. But, Dude knew, poor Rebel would start fading, like always. Dude prepared for the inevitable.

He stiffened, unable to believe his own eyes. Rebel still held the lead at one hundred yards. And he continued to hold it. Never had Rebel run like this.

Now Dude saw Clegg's right arm whip up and down. The chain! Instantly, the dapple-gray Hondo surged faster. He seemed to fly to Rebel's girth all at once. Rebel had run his race, now he was going to fade.

In contradiction, Dude caught Coyote's high-pitched Comanche yell. And when Rebel, glory be, opened daylight again, Clegg laid on the short chain. This time Hondo, as if running for his life, flew to Rebel's neck. Poor Rebel! He couldn't possibly stave off the stud's driving finish.

It happened as Clegg used the chain again and Hondo began to move up to Rebel's head, as they pounded stride for stride to the end of Main. Coyote whooped twice — lengthy, curdling, primitive screeches that shrilled above the wind, chilling to the ear.

Rebel flattened out and picked up momentum. Daylight broke between the horses.

They flashed past the judges' platform like that, two greenish phantoms sprinting through the slanting film of rain.

And chasing them, coming like the storm itself, rode Uncle Billy on Blue Grass, and behind him, Fallon.

Dude couldn't believe it. Yelling, he looked at Bridget for confirmation. She looked at him, all decorous barriers down. "Dude — we won! We won! The school! The school!" They kissed and hugged, and kissed and hugged again. Around them Three Springs danced in the street, heedless of the rain, and fired shots into the air.

Searching down the street, Dude saw only the dejected Clegg turning Hondo about. Coyote Walking and Rebel and Uncle Billy and Blue Grass had vanished. Now that was quick. Dude thought nothing of it, still in his euphoric state over Rebel's amazing run.

Hearing angry voices, he saw Garrity and Fallon complaining to the three judges and gesturing. The group moved out of the rain to the porch of Archer & Dodd's General Merchandise. One of the judges gave a we'll-see nod; with Garrity and Fallon leading, they marched for the barn.

Dude's face quivered. What now? Telling Bridget to wait, he quickened step to follow.

A man swung in behind him from out of the crowd, moving as quickly. Glancing back, Dude saw Big Whelan and kept on walking.

Inside the barn, Garrity tore to the rear stall where Coyote and Uncle Billy had a cooling blanket on Rebel, as wet as a beaver, and were rubbing him down. The Comanche watered

Rebel from a bucket. Blue Grass stood nearby, reins down.

"This horse is a ringer," Garrity howled at the judges while pointing at Rebel. "He's been dyed. He's not Rebel, he's another horse."

"Prove it," Uncle Billy bit back.

"I will," Garrity swore. Flushing certainty, he rubbed Rebel's wet forehead. He peered at his hand. It was clean. He jerked up the water bucket and dashed water on Rebel's face, and rubbed again, vigorously. Still, his hand showed clean. Garrity began to look foolish.

"There's another horse," he shouted. "Just like this all-dark bay. He's out in the corral behind the barn."

Without hesitation, Uncle Billy stepped to the door and swung it wide. Through the sheet of driving rain the outfit's other horses were visible, rumps to the slashing storm.

"Take a good look," the old man invited. "There's our sorrel team. Couple of trade horses — that dun, that buckskin." He was speaking distinctly. "And there's that ol' blaze-faced cow pony we call Shorty. Sure don't see an all-dark bay."

It was Fallon, not Garrity, who exploded. "Wolf, dang you, you said —"

"That's enough," Dude broke in. "Get out, Garrity. You too, Fallon — after you pay off."

"Did I hear you say Garrity — Wolf Garrity?" Big Whelan, moving swiftly for so large a man, emptied Garrity's holster and towered over him.

"You look just like your picture at the post office. Only uglier. I have a state warrant for your arrest . . . that bank robbery last year at Two Sands. I'd heard you might make contact with a horse outfit working up from east Texas. I was wrong, but this one did lead me to the right man after all." In a blink he handcuffed Garrity. "Come on."

Bitter, Garrity turned, pleading, "Billy —"

"All's fair in love and war and horse racin'."

Finally, Dude could feel some ease, because a year ago Uncle Billy was with him. Seeing Fallon about to sneak off, Dude grabbed him. "Oh no you don't. Pay up!"

Fallon was slow and, oh, how it pained him. But it was all there when Dude counted.

Big Whelan started walking his prisoner away, behind Fallon and the judges. As if on second thought, the Ranger turned. "Whatever happened to that bolt of lightning you beat Pepper Boy with at Cottonwood? That ol' harness horse?"

"You mean Red River Dan," Dude said. "We traded him off."

"A horse that fast?"

"Well, this trader offered us plenty. He was headed for Arkansas, on the lookout for fresh money. Hated to let the ol' horse go. But money talks!"

So it was over. The barn fell quiet save for the music of the rain and Rebel munching hay. Dude shook his head. "How did you do it?" he asked Uncle Billy in a tired voice. "Ham Williams saw Garrity take the Judge out the rear of the barn and bring in Rebel during the street brawl."

A humoring smile. "You mean Garrity *thought* Judge Blair was in the barn. It was Rebel. You see, I got worried about the Judge, in case somebody slipped in here and tried to fix him. So I took him back to the corral with the other horses and stabled Rebel in here."

"Why didn't you tell me?"

"Why, you'd just've worried yourself some more. Besides, you and Miss Pettibone seemed mighty occupied at the time. That street fight was just a diversion that Garrity planned. Old stuff to draw a man away from his horse. Had moss all over it. I knew what was up. So Coyote and I went outside and pretended to watch the fight, while Garrity, unknowing to him, switched Rebel for the Judge. I was gonna give you the high sign, but didn't see you. Coyote and I had to go ahead."

"No wonder. Garrity had me lured away, knocked out in an alley. But tell me — how did Garrity know all this and how did you?" Dude demanded, his old suspicions reviving.

The old man put on his saintly face. "You see, I used to know Garrity years ago. We worked the ringer switch right smartly, till I caught him holdin' out on me." The clear blue eyes mirrored an appealing innocence. "Of course, the other horsemen tried to outslick us, too."

"Of course," Dude mimicked him, all sarcasm. "Where was this, Uncle?"

"Never interrupt your elders, Dude, boy. Let me finish. . . . Now Garrity figured I'd already switched the fast horse for the slow horse the way we used to — just one switch a few hours before the race. He didn't know I'd pull a double switch on him. And, after the race, switch the horses again!"

CHAPTER 16

Returning to camp near noon the next day, after meeting with jubilant town fathers and members of the Three Springs School Board, Dude was surprised to find the outfit packing. A strange horse, a dark bay, was tied to the tailgate.

"What's this all about?" he asked.

"We're drifting," Uncle Billy said.

Dude was shaken. "What about your hotel? You on the front porch, watchin' folks go by? Wintertime, you in your rocker and your place by the f'ar? You've got enough money now."

"I'd get just like a rocker, I'd be creaks. We're all gonna be pardners. Jason our front man . . . like you used to be." He sounded old and forsaken and turned his face away. "Gonna drift up into Kansas and Colorado and match us some races."

Dude looked down, aware that he was going to miss them all very much. "What about horses?"

"Was comin' to that."

"I'm going to retire Rebel. I promised."

"Promised who?"

"Myself. After all he's been through."

"I understand. Kinda figured that. It's time."

Some of his downcast mood lessened, and when he spoke again it was in his familiar lecturing tone. "It's not good for a horse's character to lose all the time. You see, it's a matter of memory, which is his strongest mental endowment. All he remembers is defeat. All he can see is that other horse ahead of him as he crossed the finish line. Could lead to a nervous breakdown." He kicked at a clod. "I was hoping, Dude, boy, you might let us campaign the Judge for a season."

"What will you do for a slow horse of like conformation?"

"Was comin' to that, too. Fella brought a smooth three-year-old gelding by while you's gone. Dark bay. We tried him out. Even Rebel outran him. . . . Bought him for thirty-five dollars. He's right over there. The spittin' image of the Judge. Even four white socks."

"I see. Yes, he is. Well, sure you can take the Judge. And you'll need a wagon and team, Uncle."

After they had finished packing and harnessed the sorrels, they shook Dude's hand in silence, Coyote Walking and Jason Carter and, last, Uncle Billy Lockhart, and then Coyote and the old man climbed to the wagon seat and Jason mounted his claybank saddler.

"Dude," Uncle Billy called as Coyote took the reins, "remember that rainbow I told you about long time ago when we first met?"

"I remember."

"Well, you've found it."

Coyote chirruped to the team and they drove off, faces straight ahead.

Watching, Dude felt a sharp wrench of loneliness and something seemed to get in his eyes. As the shapes dimmed, a worn question crossed his mind. Was Uncle Billy's name really Lockhart? Could he be the all-knowing Professor Gleason? Dude decided that he would never know, and that it didn't matter. For what was a name, anyway? It was the man you remembered.

The employees of G.K. Hall hope you have enjoyed this Large Print book. All our Large Print titles are designed for easy reading, and all our books are made to last. Other G.K. Hall books are available at your library, through selected bookstores, or directly from us.

For information about titles, please call:

(800) 223-1244
   or
(800) 223-6121

To share your comments, please write:

Publisher
G.K. Hall & Co.
P.O. Box 159
Thorndike, ME 04986

LARGE PRINT
Grove, Fred.
    The great horse race

		DATE DUE	

10/00